Acc

Caiti,
Thank you for
your support! ♡
LD

Chapter One

I was already plastered when Kyle walked into the bar. He was the last person I expected to see in this small bar less than a mile from my home. He was the last person I wanted to see. I couldn't even be an alcoholic in peace.

Kyle was my boss, and a dick.

He looked around, as if he wasn't sure if he really wanted to be in this hole in a wall. I crossed my fingers, hoping he'd turn and leave, and he almost did. I almost breathed a sigh of relief, but then he looked right at me.

Darn.

For a moment I thought he was going to turn and leave without acknowledging me, and my feelings would not have been hurt, but to my disappointment he started walking in my direction.

Oh crap, I thought. God, give me the strength not to break a barstool over his stupid head.

"Emmy," he said, sitting himself down in the stool next to me.

"Kyle." I surreptitiously took in his dark brown hair and chocolate brown eyes while he called the barmaid over. Once upon a time, I thought he was kind of hot, but then he opened his mouth.

"I'll have whatever she's having," he told the bartender.

"I'm having double shots of Hennessey."

"Hennessey it is," he shrugged.

"What are you doing here?" I asked in an accusatory tone.

"What are you doing here?" He looked at me.

"I live here."

He smirked. "Here in this bar?"

"I mean I live nearby. Less than a mile."

He nodded and stared at the drink the bartender put before him. "I was passing through," he said quietly.

"Passing through where? Where were you coming from?" I asked.

"You ask a lot of questions. In fact, I think this is the most I've ever heard you talk at once, unless it's regarding work."

"Maybe you're just not listening to my eyes and my facial expressions, because I talk a lot with those."

"Really." He smirked in amusement.

"Yeah. You should pay attention." I let my eyes lazily look around the rest of the bar. I didn't want the dick to think that I was putting too much effort in socializing with him.

"What do you say with your eyes and facial expressions?" he asked, leaning towards me.

"Depends on what you said to me with that hole you call a mouth." Another shot was put before me and I took it like a trooper. "Are you going to drink that or are you going to make love to it?" I asked, gesturing to his drink.

He gave me a full blown smile now. I had never seen anything like it on his face before and was a little taken aback.

"You're drunk," he stated the obvious.

"Yeah, and my intoxication makes you only a little less of a dick," I snorted.

He looked at me, and I looked at him. I had no mute button tonight. He had pushed me to the edge earlier in the day, barking more orders at me than I could keep up with, and then barking some more when I didn't complete them in a timely manner, and then barked some more, just to hear himself be a man yelling at a woman. Dick.

"I guess I can't argue with you. I can't deny it." His smile faded and for a moment he looked sad and I felt bad, but only for a moment. He swallowed his Hennessey and his expression changed.

"I guess you're not a drinker," I said, watching his face contort from the burn.

"Beer is my beverage of choice," he said, trying to smooth his facial features. "Bartender, can you keep them coming? For both of us."

Great. I was going to need every drink I got if Kyle was planning on hanging out for a while. I looked over at him as he downed another drink.

"You better eat some nuts or something, or you're going to puke for sure," I warned.

With a cocky confidence that had me tempted to shove him off of his stool, he said "I'm not going to puke."

Two hours later I was mopping puke off of my jeans in the parking lot. At least it wasn't chunky, and I said as much.

"I'm so sorry," Kyle slurred. He was looking a little on the purple side.

"You can't hold your liquor!" I slurred back. I threw the bar mop in a nearby trash can. I seriously doubted that Lilly, the perturbed bartender, wanted the towel back. "I told you to eat some nuts!"

"Then I'd just be throwing up nuts."

"That sounds funny," I snickered.

"It sounds funny when you say nuts, too."

He dug his keys out of his pocket and the movement had him stumbling.

"You can't drive, Kyle. You'll kill someone, maybe yourself." Even drunk beyond all that was reasonable, I knew that driving while intoxicated was not a good idea. I had something like a phobia of getting a D.U.I. or hurting someone else because of my own stupidity.

"If you hate me so much, why does it matter to you what I do?" He tried to look at me with a serious expression, but couldn't get his eyes to focus.

With a small smile, I took the keys from his hand.

"I don't hate you…much. But you can't drive."

"Well, how did you get here?"

"I walked. Just come to my house for a little while until you are sober enough to drive."

He thought about it for a moment, and then agreed.

Walking while intoxicated, I found, can be almost as dangerous as driving while intoxicated. Twice Kyle stepped into the street without looking, almost getting hit by angry drivers (in New Jersey, all drivers are angry). He fell in my driveway, and when I tried to help him up, I fell down with him. I wanted to be angry, but I found myself rolling on the gravel, laughing with him at nothing in particular. It took us a long time to get up and make it the rest of the way to the house.

We stumbled through the foyer, down a hall, and into the family room. I didn't turn on the light, because I was too messed up to think of something as brilliant as that, and both of us tripped over the coffee table and ran into the couch before collapsing onto it, giggling like little school girls.

After the giggles died down, Kyle rested his head on my shoulder. His hair smelled edible, and I wondered what shampoo he used. In sober times, I would have never allowed any physical contact from a tool like Kyle.

"You're such a tool," I said more to myself, than to him, but he heard me anyway.

"I know," he sighed deeply. "But I've been okay tonight, right?" I could feel his eyes looking up at me, searching for approval.

"Yeah, you've been okay. Almost normal."

"I don't mean to be. I mean I guess obviously I mean to be a dick sometimes, but sometimes I just can't help it. Life has just molded me that way," he said quietly.

I was a little unnerved by his quiet admission, but then I remembered how much of a dick he was to me earlier in the day and it put me back in a bit of a pissy mood.

"That's a load of crap Kyle Sterling. You make choices in life. You can choose to be a dick, or not to be a dick."

He was quiet. I didn't know if he passed out or if he was thinking about what I said. After a few minutes he said "You never talk this much at work."

"I told you, I say a lot with my eyes and my facial expressions."

"You know what I mean."

"You keep me too busy for conversation," I said dryly.

"I would have never thought I would hear you call me a dick. You're so different at work."

"Work is work. Outside of work is outside of work. I know how to be professional." At that moment, I remembered that I was wearing puke pants. I jumped up and started to undo my jeans.

"What are you doing?" Kyle asked. Even though there weren't any lights on in the family room, light from the foyer gave the living room an eerie glow, and we could see each other a little bit.

"I'm wearing puke pants!" I stripped out of the jeans and turned the light on. I wanted to make sure I didn't get any puke on my Mom's couch. She would kill me and bury me inside of the thing.

After thoroughly searching the couch for traces of puke, I looked at Kyle, who was looking at my underwear with a stupid smile on his face.

"Who lives in a pineapple under your jeans?" He sang softly. "SpongeBob booty pants!" He ended his little song with a soft slap to my rear.

I stared down at him, a hand on my hip.

"You're a pig."

"I thought I was a dick."

"You're a pig dick."

"Now we're going into new and crazy territory." He laughed and I couldn't help but to laugh with him.

I sat down beside him again. Why, I don't know, when I could have sat on the loveseat, or in the big chair, or on the floor, or on the moon or anywhere else besides right next to an attractive drunk man when I was drunk and half naked myself. I wasn't seated for more than a few seconds when he leaned over, grabbed the back of my head and kissed me. I kissed him back for a moment before remembering who and what he was. My boss, the dick. I pulled away, and when he tried to pull me back, I put a hand on his chest.

"No, Kyle," I was saying no, but his kiss was awesome. My lips were getting all pissy with me because I stopped. "It's the alcohol that's making you like this. You'll regret it in a few hours."

"Give me more to regret then." He pushed me back on the couch and his mouth found mine. I should have stopped him again. I didn't think he was going to make me do anything I didn't want to do, but I didn't stop him. I kissed back and didn't stop his hands from roaming wherever they wanted to.

"You're still a dick," I whispered into his ear, and then he proved to me what a dick he really was and I hoped my mom would never find out what we did on her couch that night.

<u>Chapter <u>Two</u></u>

At six a.m. the alarm on my cell phone startled both of us awake.

"What time is it?" Kyle blinked at me. He looked way more sober now, and I guess I did, too.

"It's six. I have to get up." I found my shirt and put it on, backward.

"Why do you get up so early? You don't have to be at work until nine." He scratched at the shadow of a beard that had appeared on his jaw.

I was a little irritated at his question and statement, but I tried my best to mask it. "You go in at nine. I go in at seven, seven thirty at the latest."

"Why? You're not scheduled until nine." His brow furrowed with confusion.

"I haven't come in at nine in a year. I try to get a head start on the day, and it takes some time to get everything ready for you."

He thought about this, probably for the first time since I started working for him almost a year and a half ago.

"You have to get up. You need to get home and get yourself presentable. You have a meeting at 9:15, and the rest of your day is pretty packed. I'm going to go put on some jeans that don't have puke on them and drive you to your car."

I walked out of the room before he could get up. I didn't want to see him naked, even if I had felt him naked. Seeing him naked in this sober state would be something entirely different, even though he saw me naked. Crap.

When I returned to the first floor, he was ready and waiting at the front door. He looked serious again, not the fall down drunken guy that he was a few hours before. I'm sure I looked all business again, too, even with my shirt on backward.

On the quick drive to his car, I gave him a rundown of his schedule for the day and reminded him of the phone calls he had to make before his first meeting.

"But don't worry," I said out my window as he stood by his car. "As usual, I will have everything written down for you on your desk when you get in."

He nodded. I put my window up and drove away without looking back.

At quarter to nine, Kyle and an entourage walked past my desk. He didn't even glance at me, which was typical, and I was okay with typical. I followed a moment later, coffee in hand, just the way he likes it. I put the mug on a coaster on his desk while he sort of yelled at the entourage. He raised his voice, but not nearly as loud as usual, and every few seconds he'd rub his head. Hangovers can be a bitch.

I tapped my watch on the way out as a silent reminder that he needed to make a few phone calls and would have to finish yelling later. On his way to the board room for a meeting a few minutes later, he stopped at my desk.

"Reschedule my second meeting, Emmy." He rubbed his head again. "Maybe reschedule all of them after this one."

"I can clear your schedule up until one. That's the best I can do," I said without looking at the schedule.

"How do you know that without looking?" He frowned.

"I know every aspect of your schedule up until Wednesday of next week, where it gets a little murky. I know which meetings are more important than others, who can wait, who can't wait, who will be irate, and who will be more irate."

He frowned some more. Typical. "Just clear my schedule as far as you can," he snapped and walked away, rubbing his stupid head.

When he returned a little more than an hour later, he didn't look any better.

"Did you clear my schedule?"

"Yes, sir," I said, following him into his office. He collapsed into his chair and held his head. I put a blue Gatorade on the coaster and three Tylenol next to it. He looked at the Gatorade, confused, but before he could ask me any questions I walked out of the room. I returned a moment later with a baked potato that I ordered from a diner down the street while he was out of his office.

"What the hell is this?" he snapped.

"Eat the potato, drink the Gatorade and take the Tylenol. Eat and drink slowly so you don't make yourself sick," I spoke briskly, professionally, as I lowered the blinds. "Rest for a little while. I'll hold all of your calls and keep anyone from coming in. You should feel better just in time for your 1:00 meeting."

Before I closed the door, I saw him staring at the three items I left for him as if they were alien. Typical.

Kyle's lack of enthusiasm for work didn't make my work load any lighter. I threw myself into it head first, completely emerged myself in it. The more I worked, the less I thought of the night before. It was only a one night thing. It didn't change the fact that he was still my boss, and obviously it made him no less of a dick. Reminiscing about it would only be a stupid distraction from important things. Besides, it was a mistake, an accident even.

Forget the fact that he was the first person I had slept with in almost a year or that even though I was drunk I remembered it clearly (and it was effin fantastic!). Forget the fact that I had a hickey for the first time since high school on my neck under the scarf I was wearing, tied fashionably around my dumb neck.

A little before one, before anyone arrived for the meeting, Kyle came out of his office, looking well rested, and less hung over. I didn't ask him if he was feeling better, I barely took my eyes off of the computer screen.

"Emmy, email Diedrick with the financial reports I told you to do yesterday. Did you do the reports?"

"Yes." I wrote down the note about Diedrick, while he continued on, giving me extra work to do on top of the heavy work load I already had.

"Did you order my tux for the gala?"

"Yes, I did that last week."

"Emmy, I didn't even know about that gala until Monday." His tone was accusatory, as if I was lying to him.

"I have known about the gala since they first announced it two months ago, Mr. Sterling."

"I need a copy of that guest list, who's who."

"It's already on your desk."

He barked a few more orders at me before going back into his office. Once the door shut, Eliza the receptionist said just loud enough for the few of us in the office to hear: "What a dick."

By six, almost everyone in our part of the building had cleared out. It was snowing, and I sometimes found myself staring out of the window. I loved to watch the snow fall onto the city, but I had a lot of work to do if I didn't want to have to work long hours over the weekend. Kyle came out of his office, jacket slung over his shoulder, sleeves rolled up, as if he had been in his office doing physical labor. I almost snorted at the idea.

"Did you need anything else before you leave?" I asked him, not taking my eyes off of the monitor as I typed.

"I don't mean to do it," he said quietly. I looked up, surprised at his demeanor.

"You don't mean to do what?"

"Be a dick."

I looked away. He sat down in the chair next to my desk, but I kept my eyes on my work. In the near two years that I've worked for him, he'd never once sat in that chair. Most women would feel flattered, but I felt a little uneasy.

"I know you said I have a choice, but I almost feel like I can't help it."

"You have a seven o'clock dinner date with Miss Venner," I said softly, continuing to work. "If you're not careful, you'll be late, especially with the snow."

He was quiet for a moment, probably feeling put off by the way I changed the topic.

"I forgot about that," he finally said and stood up. "You shouldn't work too late, the weather is supposed to get worse. You don't usually work so late on Fridays, do you?"

"No," I sighed, not wanting to say what I was going to say next. I really wanted to leave the events of the night before in the past and get over it. "I usually stay up late Thursday nights and get ahead, but I lost a night of work. So…"

"Oh."

"You should go. I will see you Monday. Enjoy your weekend, Mr. Sterling."

"Thanks." Before the elevator doors closed, he said "Don't stay too late."

When I heard the doors slide shut, I breathed a sigh of relief. That was awkward. I think I liked it better when he was just being mean and bossy.

An hour later when I was getting ready to leave, I noticed a piece of paper in the chair Kyle had sat in. I hoped it wasn't one of his little notes regarding an appointment or something. I picked it up, turned it over, and my face flushed. I covered my smile as if there was anyone left to see it on my face. He hadn't left it behind by mistake. It was a SpongeBob sticker.

<u>Chapter</u> <u>Three</u>

The phone was ringing when I walked in the door. I already knew it was my mom. She called every Friday to see if I was engaged or married yet, and that was usually followed by a string of insults veiled as concern. I loved my mother, but I really didn't like her, and often thought of creative ways of shutting her up.

I am the youngest of five kids and the black sheep of the family. My two brothers and two sisters were everything I wasn't - perfect, married to equally perfect mates, with perfect children and perfect careers. At thirty, I was nowhere close to being married, let alone having children, and according to my nut job mother, my choice of employment was voluntary slavery.

When I finished college, my parents retired to the main family home in Louisiana. My siblings settled in nearby while I stayed in New Jersey in the home I grew up in. I was fine with the arrangement, not really feeling any kind of real attachment to my siblings, but my mom hated it. She couldn't meddle with my life and offer me her unsolicited and ridiculous opinions. So, every Friday I allowed her a moment of my time, because if I ignored her entirely, she would be on the next flight to Jersey. Couldn't have that.

"Hi, Mom," I said, catching the call before it went to voicemail.

"Esmeralda." My mother's southern drawl was just as strong as it was when she first left Louisiana in her late teens. "I called you twice before already. Where have you been?"

"I was working, Mom." I kicked off my shoes, soaked from the snow. The bottoms of my pants were wet as well, so right there in the kitchen, I stripped off my pants.

"I wish you would go back to school. It's not too late to be a doctor or a lawyer. Better yet, marry yourself a doctor or lawyer and you can stay at home and have babies."

"Mom, this isn't the 1800's and my job is fine."

"You never even have time to meet anyone because of that damn job!" She lowered her voice for what she said next. "How do you get your...needs met without a steady beau?"

What! Beau?

"Mother!" I was irritated that she went there - again, but I had a secret satisfaction knowing I had my "needs met" on her couch last night, by my boss no less.

"I'm just asking, Esmeralda. You can't just go giving it up to random men."

"I'm not giving it up to - you know what? I want to speak to a rational human being. Let me speak to my dad."

"She don't want to talk to me, her mother," I heard her say as she gave the phone to my dad.

"Dad, why did you marry a crazy woman?" I asked after the usual pleasantries.

"I didn't know she was crazy before I married her. By the time I found out, she was already knocked up and it was too late."

I talked to my parents for another fifteen minutes before they had to go meet my sisters Charlotte and Lucille and their families for a late dinner around a bonfire.

Even though I enjoyed the winters while my parents were gone, sometimes I felt very lonely in the big house. No one really came to visit, even most of my friends got married and moved away or were too busy with their families to pay attention to poor, single Emmy. My two brothers Fred Jr. and Emmet lived in Florida, not far over the Louisiana border. Sometimes I had the nagging feeling my parents only kept their partial residence here out of concern over what would happen to me if they closed up shop and left.

Even though I was fine with our living arrangements, I sometimes felt a little low after the phone calls from the south. I sometimes wished that I had a closer relationship with my siblings. I never quite felt like I was really part of the family, even when I was a kid.

After the phone call, I went into the formal living room and made myself two drinks at the bar. I turned the radio on in the kitchen and took out the chicken I left in the fridge to defrost. Cooking, drinking, dancing, and singing in my skivvies was perking me up a bit, but in the back of my mind, I knew it would be hard to get through the weekend with those alone. It's not that I was incapable of finding a man to spend a weekend with. My dark brown hair and greenish brown eyes and flattering figure were easy on the eyes and I was fairly intelligent, but even pretty and smart girls have a hard time finding a decent guy.

Several times I found myself looking at the SpongeBob sticker. While on the phone to my parents, I had used a magnet to secure it to the fridge. I was wearing SpongeBob panties again, but in a different color. What did he mean by leaving the sticker? Was he trying to be funny? Was he flirting or was he making fun of me?

I was drunk before dinner could finish in the oven. I carried the tequila bottle with me. It was snowing like mad outside, but the heat was on in the house and the alcohol kept me pretty toasty, too. I was about to take the chicken out of the oven when the doorbell rang.

Who the hell?

I crept to the foyer and carefully peeked through the curtain. Forgetting how I was dressed (I had put on a tee shirt, but I was still missing pants), I threw open the door. Snow blew in onto my bare legs and arms. Kyle stared at me a moment, looked at the bottle in my hand, and offered a hesitant smile.

Chapter Four

"I can't find my wallet anywhere," Kyle said after I let him in. "I checked the bar and it wasn't there. I'm hoping it's here somewhere."

"You can go check. Maybe it got kicked under the couch. I have to go take something out of the oven."

I put the bottle down long enough to take my chicken parmesan out of the oven. The music was still playing so I didn't hear Kyle enter the room. I turned around and jumped when I saw him standing in the doorway, watching me.

"Found it." He held up his wallet. "It was under the coffee table."

"That's good. I bet Miss Venner wasn't too happy to have to pay for dinner," I said, taking another swig of tequila.

"Once I realized my wallet was lost, I canceled the date." He looked at me with...I don't know...he looked at me funny. "Aren't you cold?"

I looked down and then closed my eyes for a moment. I knew my face was turning bright red, I could feel it.

"Excuse me," I whispered. I put the bottle on the counter and with my head hanging low, I slipped past Kyle to go change.

I was so embarrassed, that it sobered me up some. This was the second time in twenty-four hours that I willingly appeared in my SpongeBob booty pants in front of my boss.

I went downstairs, in pants, and immediately said "I'm sorry. I am usually here alone. My parents spend the winters in the south. No one really comes over, so I never have to really worry about answering the door, drunk, and undressed. This isn't typical behavior, to find myself undressed in front of men."

"I have seen you in less," he said quietly.

"Are you hungry, Mr. S?" I asked, ignoring his comment because it made my neck hot and my palms sweaty.

"Call me Kyle, and sure, I could eat."

"Calling you Kyle is a little strange for me."

"You called me Kyle last night. In fact, you screamed it at least...how many times?"

I threw an oven mitt at him. "You're being a dick, Kyle."

He chuckled and I realized that I liked the sound of it. "I'm sorry."

I sighed and couldn't help but to smile a little. "You never smile," I said quietly as I set the table. "You're always scowling and growling. It's almost as if you hate your job, you hate being there."

"That's not far from the truth." He looked at me seriously, leaning against the kitchen counter, arms crossed.

"Then you should find another career, because you're not being fair to your employees and you're certainly not being fair to yourself."

"I'm doing what is expected of me."

"If I were doing what's expected of me, I would be married, popping out a kid every couple of years."

"You don't want a family?"

"Of course, but look at me. I'm the poster child for Alcoholics Anonymous. I don't think I'm quite ready to raise any children." I took another swig of tequila to prove my point. "My mom thinks I'm throwing my life away, that my best years are behind me."

"It's like they have no confidence that you can be anything else other than what they've set you up to be." He was speaking from experience. Kyle's dad was always nice to me, but he had extremely high expectations for Kyle.

We sat down for dinner, but I traded the tequila for iced tea. We sat at the table for a long time after the food was gone, talking and laughing. I was amazed at how easy he was to talk to when he wasn't being a complete penis. Kyle was also attentive when I spoke. He listened and asked real questions to show he was listening. I was shocked at this. I never ever before got the impression that he gave a crap about anyone enough to engage in real conversation, including his girlfriend.

"Your Mr. Hyde is really good," I said sometime later. He was helping me clean up the kitchen after dinner. He washed and I dried.

"What?" The confused expression on his face was comical.

"At work, you're Dr. Jekyll. Now you're Mr. Hyde."

He thought about this a moment, his eyes on the dishes he was washing.

"I'm sorry," he said softly.

An apology! Who is this guy?

"It's kind of scary, because I don't know which one is the real you," I said. "Are you more like Kyle the dick or Kyle the good guy?"

"I'm not going to lie..." he started slowly. "I am a well-meaning person, but I can be a jerk sometimes. I was raised that way, to have a hard exterior."

When I remained silent, he turned off the sink and looked at me.

"I haven't been nice to you and I'm sorry. You're brilliant, always five steps ahead of me, and you work really hard. I would fall flat on my face without you. I have to be tough, though. Everyone there, including you, knows that I only have this job because my family owns the business. No one respects me because of that. So, to keep order...I have to be a dick."

"That's stupid."

He blinked at me. "What?"

"That's stupid. You're right, everyone pretty much believes you're a spoiled brat who never had to work for anything in your life."

"Thanks. You're making me feel so much better." He frowned and I almost laughed because it looked so boyish.

"Kyle, you could have just chosen to be a good guy. You alone made the decision to be mean and nasty. Because you are who you are, there would have been order. But that's all you have is order. No one is happy working for you. If only you knew how detrimental that is to your job."

I turned the faucet back on. We finished the dishes in silence, but every now and again, our eyes would meet. He looked like he was thinking, but I was still trying to get over the fact that he was the same man that I wanted to kill yesterday morning.

"Do you want coffee?" I asked when we finished. Admittedly, I wasn't quite ready for him to leave, this new Kyle Sterling.

He was staring at nothing, deep in thought. I was beginning to feel like a dick myself. He was being something like a normal human being and I was beating him down. It must have been hard for him to open up to me like he did.

"My mom tells me all of the time that I talk too much, say all of the wrong things," I said softly, not adding that I get that from her.

He finally looked at me. "You're a little harsh, but..." He ran a hand through his dark hair. "You're not wrong."

"I didn't have to be so blunt," I said, biting my lower lip.

"I like that you're blunt, but it's such a drastic change from how you are at the office." He gave a small smile.

"If I start talking to you however I want, everyone else will think they can, too. Then it would be a mess."

He nodded. "I understand."

We were standing very close. The way he was looking at me made me feel a little funny. There was an unexpected fuzziness in my belly. As a distraction, I went to the back door and pushed the curtain aside to check out the weather.

"Holy snow!"

Kyle came over and looked out. "Damn."

The snow was falling fast and heavy. Visibility was very low and there were several inches on the ground. We looked at each other and without a word rushed to the foyer and opened the door. If Kyle left then, he would have to dig himself out first, and dig a path out to the street, which had yet to be touched by a plow.

The temperature had dropped significantly. I shivered in the open door, but Kyle pulled me back a few steps and closed the door. He rubbed my arms to take away the chill. I was extremely aware of how strong his hands felt and how my skin felt under his touch.

"How much snow are we supposed to get?" Kyle asked. He looked reluctant to stop touching me, but backed up and let his hands drop.

"I don't know," I shrugged. "I haven't watched the news."

He looked out of the window again. "It's going to be a crazy ride home,"

"Are you crazy? You can't drive home in that! Thank goodness it's a weekend and you don't have to work. You have a few appointments, but they're lunch dates and such. Personal things." I went on about his schedule, telling him who to call, who to email. He was looking at me funny, so I stopped talking. We just stood there staring at one another.

"Hey," I said to break the freaky silent staring contest. "Let's go watch a movie. How about *Transformers*? I love *Transformers*. You know the third one will be out this summer."

"I've never seen *Transformers*."

I was walking to the family room, but when he said that, I stopped so suddenly he ran into me. I whirled around to face him.

"I'm sorry. Did you say - what did you say?"

"I've never seen *Transformers*."

"Do you live under a rock!"

"Jess isn't really into those kinds of movies," he said, but immediately looked away from me.

"Well, Jess isn't here. So allow me to introduce you to one of the best movies in the entire universe."

In the family room, I ordered him to sit down on "our" couch while I got the movie started on our enormous flat screen. I sat down on the opposite side of the couch. I didn't want to give the impression that I wanted to cuddle and be all cute.

At first Kyle seemed unfazed by the awesomeness of the movie, but by the time it ended he was grinning and leaning forward excitedly.

"Do you have the second one?" he asked as the credits began to roll. His face was lit up like a light bulb.

"It's like one in the morning," I yawned.

"You don't have to work tomorrow, and even if you did, you're snowed in." He stood up and stretched.

"I do so have to work," I scoffed. "My boss gives me a tremendous amount of work. I would literally drown in my work if I didn't work outside of the office, too."

"Your boss is a dick."

"Tell me about it." I yawned again.

"Really. You don't have any work to do," he said with an air of dismissal.

"Really. I do." I stood up to stretch, too.

"I don't believe you."

Annoyed at his attitude, I said "Do you not realize the amount of effort it takes to run your office?"

He shrugged. "Well, I know it takes some."

"Some?" I stared at him. "Oh, no." I shook my head and walked down the hall. Kyle hesitated and then followed me.

I went into my dad's office where I set up my own work station. On the large Mahogany desk were stacks of files, my laptop, a thick appointment book, post it notes stuck in various places with various notes scribbled on them, and a photo album. There was also the usual office stuff - pens, staplers, and paper clips, etc.

"What's all of this?" Kyle asked, his brown eyes big.

"This is mainly where I do your schedule, research, and a few other things." I picked up the photo album and opened it. "This has all of the guests for the gala. With everyone's picture there is a brief profile - or biography. Even the guests who are of little use or importance are in here. Some guests, of course, require a little more information, like this one. This guy has a whole page to himself."

Kyle looked through the album in awe.

"Last year you didn't like not knowing who people were. This year, I am going with you to aid you, through text message, little notes, or a discreet whisper. I won't hang around you, but I will be watching you and be there if needed."

He looked at me, mouth hanging open.

"How do you get this information? How will you remember all of these people? There must be two hundred people in here."

I smiled. "Two-hundred and six, and the list is rapidly growing. I don't mean to sound conceited, but I'm good at what I do. You only see the surface of what I do in the office - if you really see it." My smile faded, because we both knew he didn't care to pay attention before. I put my hand on a stack of files. "These are various upcoming events, meetings, dates, and other things you have to be present for or acknowledge. Most of it you don't know about yet."

He put the album down and looked at the desk in amazement.

"You're amazing." He looked at me. "I had no idea you worked so hard. I feel like such a douche bag."

"You're worse than a douche bag. You're a douche puddle, the excrement of a douching."

"Fine. I'm a douche puddle, you're right. No wonder you think I'm a dick."

"Yeah." I nodded.

"As your boss, I'm giving you the weekend off," he said with a firm nod.

"I don't know...it still needs to be done." I looked at the desk with longing. Okay, maybe I had a work addiction.

"I will hire someone else to help you," Kyle insisted.

"Yeah, right," I rolled my eyes. Convincing him to hire Eliza the receptionist was like pulling teeth.

"I mean it. You can't spend your life planning mine."

"That's why I get paid the big bucks." I shrugged.

"Emmy, seriously," he said softly. "Just leave it for a day. It will be okay. Take a break."

"I don't know. I don't want you to fall behind..."

"I won't. I will be fine." He put his hand on my waist and pulled me away from the desk, toward the door. I looked back at the desk, actually feeling a nervous pang about leaving it.

We stood outside the office, looking in. Kyle closed the door because I wouldn't walk away.

I looked up at him and opened my mouth to speak, but before I could speak, he leaned over and kissed me, hard. I started to back away, but he pulled me into him and held me so tight, I thought he was going to break a rib. I gave in and kissed him back.

He pressed me up against the wall, moved his hand down to my thighs, my ass, and then slowly back up my body. He stopped just under my breasts, just enough to tease me. When he finally took his lips off of mine, I couldn't even catch my breath before he simultaneously started to kiss my neck and flicked his thumb across a nipple. I gasped and my knees betrayed me.

Kyle didn't let me fall, but he lowered me to the floor. Right outside of the office where I spent countless hours working for my boss, he gave me a bonus I'd never forget.

<u>Chapter Five</u>

When I woke up around ten, Kyle was still asleep in bed next to me. I watched him for a moment before I remembered what that usually implied in a book or movie when a woman did that. While I had an amazing night with Kyle, I was not all doe eyed and dreamy about him.

I got out of bed, slipped into my robe and went to a window. It was still snowing. There must have been two feet of snow out there. After our romp in the hallway, Kyle and I checked the weather report. We were getting hit with a Nor'easter, four whopping feet of snow. I don't remember ever seeing that much snow in Jersey, and now I was snowed in with my boss.

Kyle was going to stay for the duration of the storm, and maybe a day or so more until the roads were somewhat drivable. Most women I know would be downright giddy about being in my situation. After three times (once more after the weather and milk and cookies) in two days, I guess I could say we were officially sleeping together. If I were normal, I would have been thrilled to be stuck with him, having someone to cuddle with on the couch, having someone to keep me warm as winter pressed against the windows, but I never claimed to be normal.

I looked at Kyle again, but not with lust. I wondered how either of us was really going to hold up over this weekend. A sensation of being trapped suddenly came over me. Trapped in a box with a guy who just two days ago I thought was a huge tool.

As quietly as I could, I gathered what I needed from my room and crept out. I showered in my parents' bathroom so I wouldn't disturb Kyle. I made a cup of coffee with my Keurig, slapped some butter and grape jelly on toast and went into the office. I never actually promised not to work. Besides, it made me feel like I was putting necessary space between us. By the time Kyle came into the office, I was in full work mode. I barely glanced at him when he sat down opposite of me.

"I thought you weren't going to work," he said, rubbing the sleep out of his eyes.

"I never made any promises," I murmured, trying to concentrate on a cluster flip of an upcoming week in March.

He sat quietly for a moment. When I made no attempts to communicate, he abruptly left the room, slamming the door behind him.

I saved what I was working on, but didn't immediately get up. I didn't know what he wanted from me. We were just having sex, and just barely. I wasn't going to be all over him or anything, and I didn't exactly feel like having sex again. I didn't understand his attitude.

With a sigh, I got up and went to find Kyle. He was in the kitchen, making eggs. He didn't look at me, but said "I'm sorry."

"No big deal." I shrugged and put my coffee mug in the dishwasher. But it kind of was a big deal. I had never heard the man apologize before he found me at the bar, and now he offered his apologies freely.

"Do you want some eggs?"

"No, I'm good. I see my brother's clothes fit well." I had given him some of Emmet's clothes he had left behind on his last visit. His brown hair was still wet from the shower.

"Yeah, they're great. Thank you." He flashed me a heart-stopping smile.

And did he just say thank you?

"Come here." He motioned with his finger.

I hesitated, but slowly approached. When I was close enough, he leaned over and kissed my forehead, which made my heart skip a beat, which made me mad at my stupid heart for being so stupid.

Involuntarily, I smiled. Stupid mouth.

After Kyle ate, he helped me do my Saturday cleaning. I dusted, he vacuumed. I cleaned two bathrooms and he did the powder room on the first floor. He helped me change the sheets on my bed and then we tackled the kitchen and put in a load of laundry. I panicked when I realized how domestic we were being, how well we worked... together. The cresting moment was when I really thought about the fact that his boxers and my SpongeBob panties were washing in the same confined space, possibly grinding up against each other in their efforts to get clean.

I excused myself abruptly and locked myself in my personal bathroom, the only one we didn't clean. I sat on the edge of the tub for a long time, thinking.

I didn't want to feel so comfortable with Kyle. This wasn't something that was going to go beyond this house. I didn't want to feel...let down when it was over. I wanted to feel relieved, to say a good riddance.

"Are you okay?" he asked softly through the door.

I opened the door to step out but he was standing there, looking concerned. I didn't want him to look concerned. It made my heart flutter.

Cripes.

"I'm fine," I tried to smile, but failed. I couldn't meet his eyes.

"Em," he sighed my name and I almost died because it sounded similar to when he sighed my name while we were getting it on.

"This feels a little weird," I admitted. "I hated you two days ago and now my panties are tangled up with your boxers in the wash."

"That sounds sexy," he grinned.

I slapped his arm. "I'm serious!"

"Why don't we just go watch the second *Transformers* and chill? I will sit in the man-chair and you can sit on the couch."

He tapped my nose, smiled and walked out of the room. I blinked in his direction for a moment before following him to the family room. He took my dad's chair and I stretched out on the couch. When the movie was over, I got the clothes from the dryer and folded them at the kitchen table while Kyle started dinner. He was making us BLTs.

"This is starting to feel a little weird again," I sighed, folding his boxers.

"I know," he said softly. "But what else should we expect? We're literally trapped here together, and alone. Things have to get done, right? I think it just feels more domesticated because it's just us."

"And we slept together," I said a little too loudly.

"Yeah," he glanced wearily at me. "If it wasn't for that..."

I was about to say more, but my cell buzzed in my pocket. "Ick," I said when I saw who was calling. I did not feel like having a conversation with my mother.

"Emmy! Are you okay?" It was my dad, thankfully, but I could hear my mom's twang in the background.

"Yeah, dad. What's up?"

"We tried calling the house countless times. It just rings, and you weren't answering your cell."

"Hold on. Let me check the phone, dad. I've been here all night and day." Kyle handed me the house phone off of the counter. When I turned it on, I only heard static and no dial tone. "The land line is dead."

It took me a minute longer to explain to him that I wasn't ignoring their calls to my cell. I had found it between two cushions on the couch while watching the movie. I did not mention that I really didn't feel the need to return their call since I knew my mom would just whine and my dad would give a speech about me being in a snow storm alone without a husband. Then he asked me how much snow I had, how I was holding up, and expressed deep regret that I was alone in such a bad storm. He went on about it so long (with my mom in the background yelling about how I wouldn't have this problem if I was married) that I was tempted to tell him Kyle was here. Killing two birds with one stone, I could have also told my mom that I got laid and pacify her as well.

"Dad, I'm thirty years old. I have traveled the world by myself. I can handle a snow storm. Seriously." I rolled my eyes and looked at Kyle with an exasperated sigh.

My dad, unlike my mom, did not enjoy pestering me. With a sigh, he told me to be careful and stay prepared for an emergency. My mom got on the phone, and I thunked my head against the fridge.

"This is ridiculous," she said. "You need a husband."

"I don't need a husband."

"Maybe it's your hair. Men don't like ugly hair styles."

Let the string of insults commence.

"My hair isn't ugly," I sighed.

"Maybe it's the way you dress. Maybe you need to show some cleavage."

"Trust me, mom, I'm not going to find a decent guy by showing my cleavage."

Kyle grinned and looked at my chest. I punched him.

"Listen, I'm hanging up now," I said.

"You never want to talk to me!"

"Because I don't like you very much."

"You're a horrible child."

"Yep. The bad seed. Bye, Mom."

I ended the call and sighed in relief.

"You've got a great relationship with your mom." Kyle laughed.

"When I'm in the same room with her, I want to cause her physical harm," I admitted bitterly.

He nodded appreciatively. His mom was a trip, too, but for different reasons. My mom talked too much and said whatever she thought, good or bad. Kyle's mom was cold and calculating. She was always polite to me, but stand-offish. I thought maybe she thought she was somehow better than me, but I saw that she treated Kyle the same way.

"My mom..." Kyle started, staring down at his plate. "My mom was awesome when I was really young. She was fun, funny, and so loving, so full of life." He picked at his lettuce. "Overnight, it felt like, she changed. She's bipolar."

"Oh," I said quietly. What I thought was coldness and indifference was really just numbness. The kind of numbness a person can get from some anti-depressants and anti-psychotic meds.

"She was doing really well, but sometimes it gets bad."

"I'm really sorry," I said, and actually put my hand on his. He flipped his hand and laced his fingers through mine.

I stared at our hands. He stared at me. I wanted to let go, but couldn't make myself do it.

"Emmy," he said my name in a way that made my stomach flip, but before he could continue, his cell rang.

It wasn't the first time it rang during the weekend, but he only answered maybe half of the time, and they were always business calls. But this one was different. He looked from the phone to me, me to the phone, and back to me. He let go of my hand and raced out of the room to take the call.

I heard bits and pieces of the conversation. It was Jess Venner, the elephant in the room, Kyle's girlfriend.

<u>Chapter Six</u>

Jessyca Venner was the elephant in my head, too. Every time I would come close to thinking about her, my mind conveniently walked around her, as if she wasn't there. Except for the one mention of her the previous night, we always managed to skip around her. Discussing your current girlfriend while lying in bed with your employee just didn't seem like much fun. Now that the focus was on her, I felt really strange, and I didn't like it.

When Kyle was finished with his phone call I carefully told him I wanted to get a little more work done in the office. It didn't take much convincing because he seemed like he needed the space, too.

I never claimed to be a saint, but that doesn't excuse my behavior. Jessyca was a world class stuck up bitch, but that didn't make it okay for me to sleep with her boyfriend. Furthermore, sleeping with my boss wasn't going to make our jobs any easier. It was going to be awkward for a while.

It was three hours later when Kyle came to get me. He told me he had found and prepared everything we would need to dig us out in the morning. He had even shoveled the front steps and part of the walkway. I was relieved to have him here to do all of that man stuff for me and said as much, but I would never admit that to my parents.

"We should get to sleep," he said softly and the words hung in the air. Naturally, when we were having sex we slept in the same bed. Now either of us knew what to do without the sex.

"I will be up in a few minutes," I said, trying to appear busy.

He stood in the doorway for a long, silent moment and I could feel his eyes on me. When I didn't look up, he went away.

I waited almost a half hour before going upstairs. I was leaving the decision up to him. Since he went upstairs ahead of me, he surely would make the decision of where to sleep. If he chose to sleep in another room, I would be okay with that, but if he chose to sleep in my bed, I couldn't even think about what that implied.

The lights were off in my room when I walked in, but I could vaguely see Kyle's form in my bed. My emotions ranged from relief to nervousness. Instead of questioning it any more, I pulled back the blankets and slid into bed and into his open and waiting arms.

We were silent for a long time. My head rested on his chest and I listened to his racing heart.

"Why is your heart beating so fast?" I whispered.

"I don't know. I guess it's because of you."

I could have left it at that, but I didn't.

"Kyle," I said a few minutes later.

"Hmm."

"I had a good weekend but..." I patted his arm. "When you go home tomorrow, it's over."

He took so long to respond, I thought he had fallen asleep.

"I know," he sighed. "But I don't want it to be."

We didn't need to say anymore. We both knew why it couldn't continue. He was my boss and he had a serious girlfriend. I didn't let my mind wander to the what-ifs, but I was feeling a little woozy thinking about how we got to this point. A little more than seventy-two hours ago I strongly disliked him, and thought he was truly an asshole who needed a beat down. So quickly my perspective changed, I wondered if I was just a big sucker, but it didn't matter. What's done is done and it was just a weekend fling. We were both obviously lonely and bored and nothing more.

That thought was actually comforting, and I fell asleep easily.

<u>Chapter Seven</u>

We woke up before the sun came up, showered (separately) and ate a quick breakfast of eggs, toast, and coffee. Kyle dressed in some warm clothes of my brother's again and I had found a pair of boots that fit him.

"I don't think I've ever seen so much snow in my whole life," I said when we stepped outside for the first time.

"Probably not," Kyle sighed and handed me a shovel.

It took us longer than expected to finish outside. I thought having the snow blower made things faster, but really all it did was save Kyle from killing his back shoveling. After we got inside and got out of our wet clothes, I made us some hot chocolate to take some of the chill out of our bones.

"I haven't had hot chocolate in years," Kyle smiled at the mug I gave him. He happily poked at the large marshmallow I added.

"You've been deprived."

"I have. Thank you." He grinned at me. "The chili smells awesome." He glanced toward the counter where the crock pot was. I had started it as soon as I woke up.

Kyle cocked his head and looked at me kind of funny.

"What?" I tugged on my shirt, trying to cover my legs a little. We had literally stripped out of our wet pants, socks, and footwear in the foyer. We were standing in the kitchen in just our shirts and underwear.

"Nothing." He looked away, and before I could press him further, he started talking about work. We ended up in the office for over an hour.

Even though we were on a different level of understanding now, office talk seemed to turn Kyle into a dick again. I knew he didn't necessarily mean it, but it was hard for him to stop. I didn't comment on it. Why should I? I knew that he knew that I knew he was a dick when it came to work.

We ate chili in the middle of the afternoon and while Kyle got ready to go, I packed him some chili to take home. He stood in the foyer, hesitant to go, talking about anything and everything. I finally had to cut him off.

"You should go. We still don't know how bad the roads are and it would be better for you to go in daylight."

Hesitantly, he nodded in agreement.

"I will see you at work tomorrow," I said, opening the door for him.

"Sure." He walked out of the door and didn't look back.

Chapter Eight

Three weeks slipped by. The first couple of days back to work were more awkward than I think either of us expected. On that first day while I was standing next to him at the copy machine, he whispered that I smelled really good. I had whispered a thank you, but whispering in a corner with him made me feel funny and I walked away before all of my copies were even finished.

Since I was always last to leave, I found myself alone with him at the end of the night more than once. In the past, neither of us felt the need to fill the silence with useless conversation, but those first couple of nights we both did it. It stopped being awkward when one night as we were filling the silence, Jess stepped off of the elevator. Although we were already a few feet apart, we both backed up and quickly went our separate ways.

It was another Monday morning, and Kyle was being a dick. He was so wound up, he snapped at anyone and everyone, including me. His bad attitude was putting the entire office on edge, starting a chain reaction of short tempers, making everyone's work suffer. Most of the time I was able to calm the staff, lighten up the mood with rewarding comments about their work, or by offering some kind of incentive for good work done despite their asshole boss.

This day, however, nothing I said worked. People rolled their eyes or huffed out irritated sighs when I tried to smooth things over. I suppose I couldn't blame them, even with my new insight into the man he was outside of work, my own patience was wearing thin.

I sat at my desk, staring at his office door and thinking. I had to do something before the whole damn work week went to hell. I was absent mindedly playing with a few strands of my hair when a memory flashed in my mind. During our last romp, Kyle kept burying his face in my hair.

"Your hair always smells so good," he had whispered.

Later, I asked him "Are you in the habit of smelling my hair when I'm not paying attention?" I had asked as a joke, not prepared for his response.

He smiled sheepishly. "Maybe I am..."

I couldn't respond, didn't know what to say to that. I was maybe a little freaked out by such a stalker-like thing, but at the same time, my heart sped up with pleasure.

"Ah-ha," I said at my desk. I jumped up and walked over to Kyle's office door, running my fingers through my hair as I went. As an afterthought, I rushed back to my desk and grabbed a file.

"What!" he barked when I knocked.

I let myself in and walked over to his desk. I almost always stood on the opposite side of his desk when I talked to him, but this time, as if I did it all of the time, I stood next to him. I put the folder on his desk and opened it.

"What is this?" he grumbled.

"You have to sign these," I snapped, trying to match his tone.

"Now? Don't you realize how busy I am!"

"We're all busy!" I leaned over him and started rifling through the papers. I flipped my hair so that it hung over my shoulder a few inches from his face. I took a painstaking amount of time to search through the paper work, cursing under my breath.

Kyle was always tight on time, and bumbling about wasting his sacred time was never acceptable, and wasn't something I was accustomed to doing. However, I took my time pretending to look through the paperwork that didn't even really need to be signed. After a half of a minute of this, I started to worry that my dumb blonde plan (and I'm a total brunette) wasn't going to work, but I suddenly realized how quiet he was. After another moment, I felt his fingers raking through my hair. I pretended this was okay, didn't even acknowledge it, and magically found the paperwork he needed to sign.

"Here. Sign these, please, Mr. Sterling." I handed him a pen and stood up straight.

He stared up at me for a few seconds before he started signing. He looked a little calmer, but I couldn't be sure until he opened his mouth.

"Feel better?" I asked when he stood up and handed me the folder.

He reached out and entwined his fingers in a few wavy locks, leaned in close to me and inhaled.

"Yes," he said simply. His hand slowly slid down the length of my hair and the back of his hand lightly brushed my neck before he let go.

The skin on my neck felt like it was on fire, and I actually stood there with my dumb mouth hanging open for several seconds before I was able to collect myself and leave the room.

When Kyle came out of his office a short time later, his demeanor was pretty relaxed. He made sure to find a reason to visit several areas of the office so that his new mood would hopefully rub off on everyone else. I was shocked by this, and thought maybe he had been paying attention after all that night at my house. Of course, my awesome scented hair was a big contributor.

As he passed by my desk, he smiled and winked before disappearing into his office. I smiled, despite myself, and then got mad at my smiling mouth and bit hard on my bottom lip as punishment.

Dumb mouth.

***

Every now and then, I went with Kyle on business lunches, depending on the clientele. While I understood much about the business, I wasn't there to participate. I was there as eye candy. Kyle told me this directly early in our professional relationship. I was slightly offended, and was tempted to beat his face in, but I knew appearances meant a lot to many of our clients. It was absolutely ridonkulous, but I understood that fact. If Jess wasn't available, and she often was not, I would go. The Wednesday after the hair smelling thing was one of those occasions.

My hair was pinned up that day, but in the back of the company car on the way to the restaurant Kyle insisted that I let my hair down. He helped me unpin it, and didn't hesitate to take a whiff when I was finished fixing it.

"Do you have earrings in your purse? Put them on."

"I feel like an upscale whore," I grumbled, digging out a pair of small gold hoops.

"But I pay you so well," he smiled and took the earrings from me. It was true, I did get paid extra every time I did this. He put the earrings in my ears, letting his fingers linger a little too long on my skin. It took everything inside of me not to gasp.

Much attention was paid to me by the two clients at the beginning of the meeting. I played along, flirting lightly and smiling too much, until they finally got down to business.

Even though Kyle had the tendency to be a dick, I liked watching him talk when he was negotiating. He spoke passionately, expressively, and with a conviction not even the hardest ass business man could ignore. As usual, I watched him as he spoke, watched him flash his million dollar smile, and watched his muscles move under his dress shirt.

Oh shit. When did I start paying attention to that? I also watched his lips, and would find myself daydreaming about the places his lips had been on my body. I tried really hard to redirect my attention elsewhere, but it was a long meeting. At some point, I gave up, and let myself go a little wild in the head, remembering how his fingers felt on me, and in me. I looked at his hair, recalling how it felt to run my hands through it. When he looked over at me, my own face must have given me away, because I immediately saw something like lust form in his eyes before he reluctantly looked away.

A few minutes later, while one client was on a telephone call and his partner was speaking to the waitress, I jumped when I felt Kyle's hand on my upper thigh. He didn't look at me, and his other hand was out in the open on the table. He traced small circles on my thigh, slowly moving down my leg until he hit my stocking clad knee. He paused for a few seconds before moving his hand to the inside of my leg and traced circles up, under my skirt as far as his hand could go without making noticeable adjustments.

I froze, shocked and incredibly turned on. I didn't know if I should move away, move his hand, pinch him, or shove his hand further up my skirt. Before I could figure out what to do, he pinched me, kind of hard, and I started in my seat. The motion somehow closed the distance between us, and his fingers were on my garter straps, following them up my thigh until he reached pay dirt.

I cleared my throat to cover the moan that started to escape my lips. The meeting was coming to a close, and Kyle reluctantly removed his hand. When he shook hands with the men, he used his clean hand. When they departed, I slumped in my seat and noisily exhaled. I took the straw out of my girly drink and downed the thing in one swallow. I then reached over and drank the rest of Kyle's drink, too. He watched me with amusement.

"It's not funny," I growled.

"Why are you so mad?" he asked, draping an arm around me.

I sputtered some incoherent words before growling in frustration.

"What?" he asked in a low, velvety voice. "You mad at me? Did I violate you?"

He was making a joke of it, which set my head on fire. Our booth was in a back corner and no one sat close by. He felt free to put his hand back up my skirt.

"Do you want me to stop?" he whispered in my ear.

I couldn't answer, because I was in the middle of an intense (very quiet) orgasm. I allowed myself two more, before I shoved him away.

"We agreed not to go there again," I said, breathlessly.

"You started it."

"I did not!"

"Oh no?" His eyebrows went up.

"No!"

"So, you didn't purposely lean over me on Monday? Exposing your cleavage and perfuming the air with the scent of your hair I love so much?"

I stared at him. "I didn't mean to show you cleavage."

"Ah," he smiled. "But you meant for me to smell your hair."

I looked away, my face burning. "You needed to get a grip and calm down. Your attitude sucked and was fucking up the morale of the entire office."

"But you did start it..."

I looked at him with what I hoped was a hard expression. "Now I'm ending it. Again. Now move so I can go to the bathroom."

***

It was snowing again, this time on an early Monday morning, weeks after Kyle violated me in the restaurant. By the time I got into the building, I looked like the abominable snow woman. On the elevator, Luke from legal also looked like a snow beast.

"You're melting," he pointed to the puddle growing at my feet.

"I feel like the Wicked Witch of the West."

He did an impressive impression of the witch during her watery demise, making me laugh.

"Do witches eat?" Luke asked me after we reached his floor. He held the elevator doors open, surely pissing off anyone on the ground floor waiting for it to return.

"What?" His question caught me off guard.

"Do you want to have lunch with me today?"

It wasn't the first time he's asked me to lunch and I have only gone a couple of times. I didn't have anything against Luke. He was a nice guy and we had a similar sense of humor, but I was usually too busy to have lunch anywhere but my desk. My mom was right, although I would never tell her. My job kept me from a lot of things. Not that I had considered rolling around in bed with Luke or even dating him, but I haven't even opened myself to any possibilities. Luke had not asked me for any kind of date, lunch or otherwise, in months. This could be my last chance. Besides, I had to get Kyle completely out of my system instead of revisiting those memories throughout any quiet moments of my day. What happened with him was ridiculous behavior not to be repeated, and we were supposed to be moving on. Therefore...

"Lunch would be great," I said, surprising Luke. "How's 12:30?"

"Perfect." He smiled widely. "Meet you at your desk? I will bring something."

"Sure. Now get out so I can get to work." I gave him a small shove and the doors closed.

"So, I guess I should have asked you this before," Luke said on our lunch date.

"Asked me what?" I said, through a mouth full of salad. I knew it wasn't lady like to talk with my mouth full, but I never claimed to be a proper lady.

"If you were seeing anyone. I ask you every now and then and most of the time you say no." He watched me with anticipation.

"Oh." I swallowed my food before speaking again. "The answer is still no."

"Cool."

"I mean..."

"Yes?" He looked at me warily.

"I'm not seeing anyone. I..." I hesitated. Luke was a very good listener and good at keeping secrets, something I learned a long time ago, soon after meeting him. I was having some family issues and during one of our very first lunches together, I unloaded on him; but I didn't know if I could tell him about Kyle. At least not directly.

"I had a fling...thing...with someone not that long ago," I admitted.

"And you want more than a fling," he guessed with a frown that nearly broke my heart.

"No, no. I mean, maybe if circumstances were different, but..." I sighed. "He's had a steady girlfriend for a long time. It should have never happened."

"Wow."

"Yeah, I'm a horrible person." I stared at my salad, my face red with shame.

"No," he sat up straight. "I didn't say that, and I don't think that at all. I'm just...surprised."

"Well, it's over."

"Do you...have feelings for this guy?"

"Not really," I lied. "It doesn't matter anyway. He's not mine to have and even though I hate his girlfriend, I'll never feel right about screwing her over. I don't like the guilt I feel."

"Hey, we all make mistakes," he said softly, giving my hand a quick squeeze. "But are you sure it's over?"

"For me it is."

"What about him?" Just as he asked that, Kyle walked in. His eyes immediately fell on Luke's hand resting on mine. He boldly stared at me as he passed by.

"I hope so," I whispered.

Luke looked at Kyle's back with a thoughtful expression. If it connected in his head, he didn't let on. He turned back to me.

"I had a motive when I asked if you were seeing anyone," he said, with a sly smile.

"Oh?" I cocked an eyebrow.

"Would you like to go out on a real date with me?"

Luke was gorgeous, super smart, and he made me laugh, and he was very single, unlike Kyle. It would be nice to get out instead of working in my office or shuffling around the house alone.

"I would love to," I smiled warmly at him.

Later that night while I was reading in bed, my phone rang. I knew who it was before I looked. Kyle had been calling or stopping by a few nights a week just to shoot the breeze. I liked talking to him like this. He was only half as obnoxious as he was at work, and the conversation came easily. It was a compromise of sorts. We could carry on this friendship, but it had to stay out of the office, and it had to stay platonic, and the last part was the hardest part.

"What was up with the hand holding?" Kyle asked after I answered the phone.

"It was a friendly gesture," I answered in a bored tone.

"You two looked really cozy."

"Yeah. I suppose we were."

"Are you sleeping with him?"

"Wow. Not that it's any of your business, but no. I'm not. What if I were?"

"There are rules against that kind of relationship at Sterling Corp," he said smugly.

"There's no rule against me sleeping with Luke."

"Yes, there is."

"No, there's not," I rolled my eyes. "He's not my boss, but I guess you should fire me, because I did sleep with him."

"He doesn't count."

"Neither does Luke. Is that the only reason why you called me? To question me about Luke?"

"Maybe. I was curious, but I feel better knowing you're not dating him."

"I said I'm not sleeping with him. I didn't say I wasn't dating him," I said.

"You're dating him?" The question mark in his voice nearly jumped through the phone line.

"Kind of. He's taking me out Saturday."

"I don't like it," he said darkly.

"I'm not asking you to, and I don't really care," I lied. "You're stepping over that platonic line again."

"Sorry." He didn't sound sorry at all.

"Yeah. Do you have anything else to talk about?"

"What are you wearing?"

"Goodnight, Kyle."

I clicked the phone off before he could object.

Chapter Nine

"Wow, you look hot." Luke was standing at my front door checking me out with a big shit eating grin on his face.

I was wearing short shorts and a tee shirt so riddled with holes it looked as if I had been shot. A lot. The shorts and shirt had matching bleach stains and perpetually smelled like Lysol no matter how many times I washed them. My hair was in the messiest of buns and I was sporting a pair of pink rubber gloves that went almost up to my elbows.

"What are you doing here?" I asked, completely flustered to find him at my door.

"Don't tell me you've changed your mind."

"About what?"

"Our date?"

I shook my head. "Our date isn't until tonight. Nine o' clock."

"Let's face it, Emmy. We're both getting a little too old for late night dates."

"You meant nine in the morning?" I asked dumbly.

"Well, it's nine, and it's morning, and I'm here, so..."

I suddenly felt extremely stupid. Now it all made sense - the pancakes he wanted to treat me to, the trip to Atlantic City, and something about having me home before it got too late.

"I'm sorry," I said, waving him in. "I'm such an idiot."

"Yeah, but at least you're appropriately dressed for our date."

I threw a rubber glove at him. "Make yourself comfortable in the family room or living room, but don't step on my kitchen floor." I wagged a finger at him. "It's still wet."

I took the steps two at a time to go properly get ready for my date. I showered in record time, dressed in jeans, a tight black sweater and a pair of black Timberland boots. I brushed my hair, pulled it back in a tight ponytail and grabbed my leather jacket.

"You look fantastic," Luke said when I found him watching ESPN in the family room.

"Thanks. I'm sorry I made you wait."

"You didn't take long at all, especially for a girl."

"Well, thanks," I said. I snatched my Coach bag off of the couch. "Ready?"

We decided to skip the pancake breakfast and hit up the drive-thru at Dunkin Donuts instead. We drove to Atlantic City talking, laughing, and arguing about what music to play on the radio. We were only forty minutes into our date and I was already finding myself attracted to Luke in ways I'd never thought I could be. Even though we had been friendly with each other for a long time, I was feeling a little fluttering in my chest, something I didn't feel in the past with Luke. I tried to wave off what I was feeling, and nearly succeeded until we were on the boardwalk.

It was late January and the temperature by the ocean was always much cooler, especially with the wind chill. I should have worn a warmer coat, but I wanted to look cute. Now I was paying the price. I was so cold that my teeth chattered violently, making a loud clacking sound.

Luke took off his coat and put it on my shoulders.

"Oh, no," I said trying to hand it back to him. "You'll f-f-f-freez-z-ze," I managed.

"I will be fine until we get into the casino." He again wrapped the coat around me. His hand brushed against my cheek and the fluttering returned four fold. He took my hand and led me down the boardwalk.

We sat side by side for a couple of hours, leisurely playing the fifty cent slots. At some point, we both turned in our seats so that our legs were entwined while we talked, played, and sipped on the complimentary drinks the casino supplied. We did a little shopping on the boardwalk and ate at the Hard Rock Café before jumping back on the expressway.

In the car, Luke drove with one hand on the back of my seat and the other on the wheel. I leaned in his direction as much as my seatbelt would let me.

"I hope I didn't bore the hell out of you today," he said.

"Don't be ridiculous. I am having a great time. I have to admit, I've never had a first date at a casino."

"It wasn't one of my better ideas," he glanced at me with a slightly worried look.

"No, it was fine - different. I like different sometimes. If we didn't already know each other, it could have been awkward."

He smiled at me, and we drove in silence for a couple of minutes. Every few seconds he would glance over at me, his smile unfading.

"I'm sorry I kept saying no," I said, breaking the silence.

"What?"

"You've asked me out before, a few times over the years. I said no, and now I regret it." I knew without looking that my cheeks were red. I looked straight ahead, hoping he wouldn't notice.

"It's okay. It took you awhile to realize what a fine specimen I am."

"I didn't say all of that," I gave him a warning look. I looked at the time on the dash. It was almost six, still early. We spent the whole day together, but I wasn't ready to end the date. "So, what are you going to do with the rest of your weekend?"

He looked at me with a slightly guilty expression.

"What?" I asked. When he didn't answer, I pinched his arm, making him laugh and pull away. "What?"

He replaced his hand on the back of my seat and sighed.

"I was hoping that you would have had such a great time that I would have my second date with you tomorrow."

"What if I wasn't interested or what if I am going to be busy washing my hair?"

"I would have to gracefully bow out and thank you for the one good day you gave me."

"Such a gentleman."

"And then I would go back to work and spread ugly rumors and write dirty things about you on the men's bathroom wall."

"Damn. I guess I should go out with you again. I don't need another story written about me on the bathroom wall."

"I'm cool with you accepting a date based on blackmail."

"I'm sure you are. What are you doing tonight, my blackmailing friend?"

"Whatever you let me do." He raised an eyebrow.

"That sounds dirty." I wiggled my own eyebrows.

His eyes widened and he chuckled. "I didn't mean it that way, although if you put on that outfit you had on this morning, I may not be able to control myself."

"You wish you had my pink rubber cleaning gloves."

"Don't forget your bleached short shorts. They would look hot on my legs."

"I will pay you a thousand dollars to wear only my short shorts and my pink rubber gloves."

"Whatever turns you on, baby," Luke said with a low, seductive voice that made me giggle because it was funny, because it was rather sexy.

"I'm about to pee my pants just thinking about it."

"Kinky."

"Do you want to do something tonight?" I asked. "Like rent some movies or something?"

"Sure. We can stop at the grocery store and pick up some junk food."

"I like junk food." I smiled, relieved that he agreed.

We hit up a Wal-Mart to pick up a couple of movies from Redbox and to grab our junk food before heading over to Luke's place. I instantly felt at home there. The décor was simple, but pleasant and it was clean and warm.

As we stood in the kitchen sorting through our goodies and drinking beer, I was suddenly overwhelmed with nervousness. I knew that eventually he would try to kiss me, and thinking about it sent adrenaline racing through my veins. I realized that I really, really liked Luke, enough where I was seriously ready to make the first move and kiss him in the middle of his rant about how Oreo cookies aren't what they used to be. He looked up at me, stuttered a few times, and then just seemed to forget what he was saying altogether. I didn't say anything, or act surprised that he stopped talking. I just stared at him, feeling my heart pounding in my throat.

"Wow," he said.

"What?"

"You just left me speechless."

"I didn't do anything," I gently shook my head and smiled a confused smile.

"I know," he said and moved in closer to me. "I love that you can do nothing and leave me speechless." He wrapped his arms around my waist and I linked my fingers behind his neck. We stood like that for a moment, staring at one another in silence.

"I have a confession," he said softly.

"Oh no," I sighed. "It's not about the gloves is it?"

"No," he grinned, and gave me a quick peck on the lips. "I've seriously been crushing on you for about three years."

"Really?" I was genuinely surprised. His asking me out a few times never equated to a crush to me. I knew he probably liked me a little, but I didn't think he had a crush on me.

"Okay, maybe more than crushing. I'm pretty sure I've had some pretty strong feelings for you for a long time."

Well, that was an even bigger development than a crush. Now I was speechless.

"Maybe I shouldn't be telling you this on our first date," he sighed and started to pull away, but I held fast to him.

"It's okay," I said, my voice shaky. I really liked Luke, but I wasn't sure that I was on the same level as him, but I did want him. Just maybe not as strongly as he wanted me, but I thought that could grow, easily. It's not like I had anything else going on, especially with Kyle.

I froze at the thought of him. Why had my mind gone there? Why did I think of Kyle in this exact moment? Why was I so hung up on something that meant nothing?

I didn't have time to think about it, because Luke kissed me. The kiss was so strong, fueled by three years of "strong feelings" and secret crushing, and hurt feelings from all of the times I turned him away. It was the sweetest, most sensual kiss I had ever had and I found myself completely lost in it. When I thought I would absolutely and happily drown in his wonderful kiss, he pulled away and groaned.

"What's wrong?" I asked, feeling a little alarmed until I saw the smile creep onto his face.

"I have to stop kissing you or I'm going to go too far."

I smiled a devilish smile and bit my bottom lip.

"Don't look at me like that," he said huskily, unable to take his eyes off of my face.

I pushed myself up on my toes and touched my lips to his. He couldn't help but to kiss me back. His hands gripped onto my ass as he pressed himself against me. He suddenly pulled away again.

"Oh my god, you're driving me crazy," he whispered. He backed away completely and started gathering our junk food. "I think we better go watch the movie before I drag you to my bed."

I couldn't tell you what was happening on the TV screen. My eyes saw the pictures, but could not register what was happening, especially since my eyes kept falling on Luke. I knew he knew that I was watching him, because he grinned and threw a cookie at me without taking his eyes off of the screen. Boldly, I closed the distance between us and kissed his neck. He pretended not to notice, but I heard a very quiet sigh escape his lips. I left a trail of kisses from his neck, across his cheek, and to his awesome lips. He kissed me back for a moment, but gently pushed me away.

"You have no self-control," he said with a lustful smile.

"You have too much," I countered.

He kissed me again, but only quickly.

"You're making this really hard for me," he said quietly, holding my face in his hands.

"So, maybe you should give in."

"I don't want you to think that's all I want from you."

"What else do you want from me?"

"Everything," he whispered and brushed his lips against mine.

Embarrassment flooded through my face. I carefully removed his hands and backed away to the other side of the couch.

"God, I must look like a complete hoochie," I said with a nervous smile.

I was mortified that I threw myself onto him like that. Of course I wanted more from him, too. I really liked him, strongly liked him, and I wanted to explore the possibilities, but my first inclination was to get him into bed. What a slut.

"You don't look like a hoochie," he said, moving closer to me.

"Oh, I'm so embarrassed," I leaned over and hid my face in my knees. "You probably want the first time to be special and I'm just like 'hey, let's bang on the couch.' Ugh…"

"Hey, hey," he said soothingly and rubbed my back. "Come on, sit up. I want to see your pretty face."

I blew out a huge breath of frustration and then sat up and looked at Luke. He trailed a finger across my cheek to my lips. He stared at my lips with concentration as he again held my face between his hands. His thumbs slowly ran over my lips and I had the inclination to suck on one. I really couldn't help myself. I was out of control as I slowly and seductively sucked on his thumb. He watched with heated fascination for a while, until he suddenly stood up and took me by the hand out of the room, and down the hall to his bedroom.

Standing in front of the bed, he kissed me harder than before, and reached up and cupped a breast in each hand. I groaned when I felt his fingers gently squeeze my hardened nipples through my sweater. He pulled back, and quickly removed my sweater and camisole under that. My bra was unhooked and thrown across the room.

"Take your hair down," he demanded.

I did as I was told and he kissed me again, gripping the back of my hair.

"Sit down," was his next command.

I sat down and watched as he unlaced my boots and threw them, along with my socks, to random areas of the room. He unbuttoned my jeans and allowed me to stand up only long enough to pull my jeans and panties off of my hips. I didn't see where he threw them, because I was watching him with anticipation as he kneeled before me, spread my legs, licked two fingers and slid them inside. In a matter of seconds he had me squirming and having an orgasm on his fingers.

Wrapping his arms under my thighs and putting his hands under my ass, he pulled me forward to the very edge of the bed and buried his face between my legs. I thought I was going to die with pleasure as I grinded against his face. When I was already feeling spent from multiple orgasms, Luke stood up and quickly removed his own clothes. I ran my fingers over his muscular chest, down his six-pack, and followed the line of hair from his belly button down to his throbbing manhood. I repaid oral for oral, except in a way it wasn't fair. He didn't have to worry about a gag reflex when he went down on me.

I started to rethink whether or not I wanted something that size inside of me, and I said as much out loud.

"Too late to go back now," he said with a grin.

I scooted back on the bed and he followed me with that monster, and hovered over me.

"I might walk funny for days," I objected.

"I'm not that big."

"Have you seen your shit?" I asked in a high pitched voice. "There are horses across the state that are jealous of you."

I gasped when I felt just a little bit slide into me.

"Do you want me to stop?" he whispered. "If you seriously want me to stop -"

"No," I whispered.

"Do you want me to go slow?"

I shook my head. Negative.

"I don't want to hurt you."

I pulled his face to mine and kissed him deeply and passionately. While our tongues and lips were busy with each other, Luke slammed into me. I cried out, not knowing if I was crying out from pain or pleasure. He pulled out slowly and then did it again, but a little harder. I had never felt anything so painfully good. I cried out for more, for him to go faster, and even harder though I knew my poor body would regret it later. At the end, we exploded together, both of us shouting out expletives and fiercely holding on to one another.

I woke the next morning in Luke's arms. He was sound asleep and I didn't mind watching him sleep for a little while, until I felt myself stirring for more action. I was sore as hell, but I wanted more anyway. I woke him by stroking him until he was not only fully awake, but fully erect. He didn't waste any time pulling me on top of him.

We made love a few more times throughout the day. By the time I made it home that night, I really was walking funny, but Luke was well worth it, and I couldn't wait to spend more time with him.

Chapter Ten

The gala I had studied so hard for was approaching. It was an annual event and all proceeds went to various institutions to aid the families that had chronically ill children. Anyone who could afford five grand a plate could get an invite, but it was a notorious occasion for big business, rich housewives having a chance to show off their bling and rubbing elbows with the occasional celebrity. Kyle and his father, whom I worked for before Kyle, always attended, and not because they cared so much for the children, but because they almost always met new business associates there or were able to further their business opportunities with current clients.

My parents have been attending the galas for years and flew in the week before the event. Luke went with me to pick them up from the airport and we were going to dinner afterward. I was nervous about my mom meeting him. I didn't want her to start asking questions about his family tree, whether or not he was ready for marriage, or boring him to tears with stories about the south. It was embarrassing. And even though I didn't love Luke or anything as deep as that, I didn't want him to see me in a different light because my mother was crazy.

"He's a very good looking man," she whispered to me in the back seat of my car. Luke was driving and my dad rode shotgun.

"How is he in bed?"

I took a deep breath to help resist the urge to push her out of a moving vehicle.

"I haven't slept with him, Mom," I whispered, lying through my teeth. I just didn't want to discuss my sex life with her. She would probably critique my oral skills or something.

"I should have known. You don't sleep with anybody. That's why you can't keep a man."

I glared at her but said nothing more for the rest of the car ride to the restaurant. I let her chatter on about the gala and what she was going to wear and what I should wear and a bunch of other things I didn't really listen to.

During dinner my mom badgered Luke about his family, his finances, and a long list of other things. He was clearly flustered. My dad tried to tame my mom as much as possible, but it wasn't enough.

"Did Emmy tell you we have a plantation?" she asked, moving onto talking about the south.

"Mom! Stop calling it that!" I was so embarrassed.

"What am I supposed to call it? That's what it was when my mama was young and it hasn't changed."

"A lot has changed, but you're blinded by your insanity," I said.

"Emmy did tell me your family still grows cotton," Luke said to my mom before she could say anything else to me.

I was thankful that she was leaving the day after the gala. She and my dad would be returning to Louisiana - back to the plantation - until the end of May or early June.

The rest of dinner went smoothly, as my dad wanted to discuss business and sports, two things my mom had no real interest in, so she had little to say.

"Your mom is a riot," Luke said later outside of my house. We were standing next to his car.

"Yeah. Sorry about that."

"Now I know where you get your gift for speaking bluntly." He laughed and then leaned in to kiss me.

"So I will see you at work," he said after a long kiss.

"Bring me a muffin, will ya?"

"Banana nut for the nut."

I giggled and went inside.

Chapter Eleven

When I got into work in the morning, I was surprised to find Kyle already there.

He wanted to go over the gala guest list every morning leading up to the event. I had other work I would have liked to get done, but I was able to juggle it around to another time.

I got us some coffee and he sat in the chair next to my desk while I quizzed him on who's who. He wasn't doing too badly. I was impressed with how much he knew. Before the office could get too packed, I wanted to say something to him.

"You're doing really well with the staff," I whispered. "Your attitude is so much better and it appears that everyone is responding so well."

He actually blushed!

"I'm getting to know everyone a little better. I didn't even know Eliza had three kids until a couple of weeks ago. And she's worked for me for a year."

"I understand you can't get too personal. It makes it hard to properly do your job, but you're doing well. I just thought you should know."

He smiled, started to say something else but then frowned. I was perplexed for only a moment. Luke was suddenly at my other side, holding what I presumed to be my muffin in a paper bag. I stood up but didn't hug him or kiss him. Those things aren't prohibited in the office but I needed to be an example, as an office manager slash assistant to Kyle.

"Sorry I'm late," he said. "Long morning. I have a long meeting today, so I can't meet for lunch. Maybe dinner?"

"Sure. Let me know later. Thanks for the muffin." I smiled, which made him smile, which made Kyle make a small gagging noise behind me. I didn't acknowledge it and Luke didn't seem to notice.

"Have a good day," he said, and despite my personal rules, he gave me a quick kiss on the lips. He then looked directly at Kyle and nodded a hello before walking away.

Feeling Kyle glaring at me, I took my seat again and looked at the clock on my desk.

"Don't you have a meeting in a little bit?" I asked lightly.

"Did your muffin bring you a muffin?" he asked with a smile that didn't touch his eyes.

"How's Jess?" I asked.

He gave me a sour look and left me without another word.

Ever since he figured out Luke and I were dating, Kyle had been making little snide comments or looking at Luke with disdain. At first I could hardly believe it. Was he jealous? I finally chocked it up to some kind of ego trip because he had slept with me and maybe he expected me to only want him. It didn't make things awkward, but it was annoying.

For the rest of the week, every morning Kyle and I would go over the guest list and sometimes just have a simple conversation about a movie or food or whatever. He never brought up Luke again, not that he was really given the chance. Luke had been working a lot lately and didn't really come to our floor after the muffin incident.

Friday night I didn't stay late at work. Kyle and I left at the same time. He offered to drive me across the bridge to the train station where my car was parked. I accepted, because I had a lot to do before the gala Saturday night.

"Is Luke coming with you tomorrow?" he asked as he navigated into traffic out of the parking garage.

"No. He will be on a cruise with some friends from Chicago. Besides, I'm more or less working."

He nodded but said nothing in response. Every now and then he would look over at me, but I pretended not to notice. After a while, he spoke again.

"So. Are you two pretty serious?"

"Why does that matter to you?" I looked at him.

"It doesn't matter to me." He feigned surprise by my question.

"What's going on with you? You act like a jealous teenage boy when he's around."

"I do not act like a teenage boy."

"But you are jealous," I said pointedly. "And I don't know why. You have your own life going on with Jessyca and it was only one weekend, Kyle. It's not like we had this elaborate love affair going on."

I know I sounded irritated. In a way, I guess I was. I'm not sure why. When I looked at him, he looked a little hurt and I instantly felt bad. He recovered quickly though, with bitterness.

"I apologize. I didn't realize it meant so little to you."

"You're wrong," I said, looking out the window. "It wasn't a 'little' thing, but..." I searched my mind for the words. "It doesn't matter what it meant for me."

We arrived at the parking lot for the high speed line. I directed him to where I was parked. The area was crowded with mostly people on their way home from work. In a few hours it would be busy with people going back into the city for a night out.

"Thanks for the ride." I said, opening the door.

"Wait. We're not done talking," Kyle protested, his hand on my arm.

"There's nothing to talk about. I'm sorry. See you tomorrow night." I got out, closed the door and walked to my car quickly before he could stop me.

Chapter Twelve

My parents made a striking couple when they weren't all dressed up for a gala, but the fancy clothes made them a remarkable couple.

My mom was almost sixty-eight years old and didn't look a day over forty-five. Her hair color, a honey blonde, was maintained by a hair dresser, but she had no other artificial work. She barely had wrinkles or sagging skin. Women her age envied her. Women my age envied her.

My dad was going bald, but was still a good looking man. He stayed in shape after retiring from the military. He was bulky, but not fat. He also had few wrinkles and no saggy skin. He looked twenty years younger than his seventy years. Women of all ages flirted with him.

For the gala, my mom wore a white gown by Dior and had her hair swept up in an elegant bun. I spent significantly less money on my dress, a long blue gown that fluttered when I walked. I wore a simple diamond pendant with matching earrings. My money well spent was on my Manolo Blahnik shoes. Heaven on my feet.

My mother wrinkled her nose when she saw me, and the whole way into the city she wouldn't shut up about how I wouldn't let her buy me a different gown and that I should have went to her hair dresser and why didn't I wear pearls instead of the diamonds.

"Can you stop?" I slapped my hand on my lap and glared at her from the backseat. "I'm really tired of hearing you. Don't you ever get tired of berating me?"

She turned in her seat to look at me, all shocked and surprised.

"I'm not berating you. I just -"

"Samantha," my dad said firmly. "Leave her alone."

"But - "

"It's over." He said it with such finality that she turned back around in her seat.

By the time we got to the gala, I was so wound up, I couldn't think straight. As soon as I could get away from my mother, I did. I found the bar quickly and was already on my fourth drink when Kyle found me. I drank them pretty fast and on a mostly empty stomach. It took everything I had to keep my composure and not look as tipsy as I felt.

"You look amazing," Kyle said, letting his eyes travel over my body.

"Thank you." I smiled. "My mother doesn't think so, but at least someone does. Where's your date?"

"She's running late. She'll be here soon, by the time dinner is served." As if it was natural, he put his hand on the small of my back and led me away from the bar. He then held out his elbow expectantly and I took it, looping my arm through his.

We walked through the reception area for the rest of the cocktail hour, greeting people we knew and introducing ourselves to those we didn't. Kyle was a freakin' social butterflying master. He remembered names without my help and spoke to others in a way that always made them feel flattered. Whenever we would move on, he would put his hand on my back.

"I love this dress," he whispered to me.

My back was fully exposed in my dress. What he was loving was touching my bare skin, the curve of my back.

Jessyca arrived just as seating started for dinner. I hastily released Kyle's arm and made my way inside with the rest of the crowd.

Galas sound like a lot of fun, but once someone gets on stage and starts talking, you can find yourself all dressed up and bored to tears. The food is always good and most of the time the entertainment is good, too. This year's entertainment was a cover band covering a number of songs from Frank Sinatra to Green Day. There were a lot of younger people this year, so the dance floor stayed busy with bodies. I loved to dance at any event, so I took to the dance floor with or without a partner. One of my frequent partners happened to be an up and coming film star. He was cute, but when he offered to take me back to his hotel room, I politely declined and went back to my table.

Kyle didn't really need my help all night, so I was free to roam and socialize and dance and drink to my heart's content. When he wasn't with Jessyca, he would follow me around. When he was with her, he would watch me as much as he dared from afar.

During dinner, whenever Jess wasn't paying attention, he would try to talk to me about something mundane. At one point he started talking to me about olives. I must have looked at him as if he were nuts because he stopped talking about it in mid-sentence, sighed and then stared at his glass.

Kyle's mother sat on the other side of me. I was nervous about it, because despite what Kyle had said about her, I still had the impression that she was a little snobby and cold. However, I noticed her husband barely spoke to her and even Kyle tended to forget she was there. Jess was so fake to her, it was shamefully obvious. She rarely left the table to go socialize or anything. I really believed she didn't want to be there. Maybe she was Walter Sterling's eye candy.

I was getting bored sitting at the table watching everyone else. Kyle and Jess were across the room talking to some people I knew, but didn't care for. I wanted to stay as far away from my mother as possible, and she was surrounded by a large group of women, and admiring men, as usual. I made my way over to the bar and started taking some shots. After my fourth one, I looked up and found Jess squeezed in next to me, ordering a cosmopolitan.

"Well, you do look like you're enjoying yourself," she said with her fake smile.

I hated talking to Jess, for obvious reasons, but also because she always talked to me as if she was some kind of princess and I was a lowly servant, even though we both came from wealthy families. I didn't know what her problem was with me.

"Actually, I'm bored," I said, not bothering to return the smile, fake or otherwise.

"I suppose this crowd is just a little too sophisticated for some," she tapped her manicured nails on the bar.

"Gosh, maybe you're right. I may not be sophisticated enough for this crowd." I threw back another shot and wiped my mouth with the back of my hand, showing her I didn't care how unsophisticated I was.

"Your dress is very nice," she said. "It is a little too...suggestive for my tastes, but it is nice."

Jess was wearing a red Gucci dress that was flattering, but not fantastic.

"Maybe it is a little suggestive," I said, throwing money on the bar for my drinks. "Kyle really likes it."

I walked away, but not before seeing the startled expression on her face.

Take that, Bitch.

A little while later, we all ended up back at the table again. Jess kept throwing me curious looks, wondering about what I said. I probably shouldn't have said it, but it was an easy way to get back at her for being an ass.

After a long boring hour, Kyle stood up and offered me his hand.

"Let's dance," he said.

I looked at Jess and she shrugged and forced a big smile.

"Jess doesn't like to dance at these things," Kyle sighed.

"I don't like to get all sweaty and yucky, but you don't seem to mind at all," she said with so much sweetness I was getting a toothache.

"You're right. I don't mind getting sweaty and yucky." I stood up and offered Kyle my hand.

As we walked to the dance floor I said to him "She has no idea how sweaty and yucky I've been with you before."

He tried to hide his smile, because I was clearly angry. We danced for two fast songs. I was surprised by how well Kyle could dance. When the band began to play *Wonderwall* by Oasis, I started to walk off of the dance floor, but Kyle held my arm. Instead of causing even a minor scene, I reluctantly gave in. He held me as close as he dared in front of all of those people and under the watchful eyes of Jess. He had his hand on my bare back, which I knew he really liked.

I wasn't prepared for the emotions that this very slow dance to this awesome song elicited. My heart pounded so fast I would be surprised if he didn't hear it. A large lump formed in my throat and I was finding it hard to breathe. It felt like any feelings I had for him during or after that long weekend that I had buried were coming to the surface. They sat in my chest like a bomb, threatening to explode out of me into the light for everyone to see.

Not very long ago I had hated him. Now trying to deny that I cared for him was useless. Was it love? Was it infatuation? Either way, it wasn't something that could flourish from here.

When the song ended, I turned away and left the dance floor as quickly as possible. As fast as I could, I navigated out of the ballroom. I barely made it to a stall before vomiting up all of the contents of my stomach. As I flushed the toilet, I wished I could get rid of my feelings for Kyle as well.

I rinsed my mouth out thoroughly for a few minutes and bummed a couple of mints from an acquaintance. When I returned to the ballroom, I discovered my parents had deserted me. They wrongly assumed that I had wanted to stay longer. I had made some mention of staying late earlier, but I was angry that they had not checked with me before taking my car.

"I told them I would take you home," Kyle said, searching my face for what I didn't know. It was kind of annoying.

"I'll be at the bar," I grumbled, and that's where I stayed until Kyle and Jess were ready to go.

"I have a four a.m. flight to catch," Jess reminded him on our way out. "I still have to pack." She nodded in my direction. "And you have to take your assistant home."

I stretched out across the backseat while Jess took the front. For the first few minutes, she berated various guests of the gala, people I had seen her hanging out with.

"Where are you going?" Jess asked Kyle after a few minutes.

"I'm taking you home. You have to pack for your flight, you've made that clear."

"I thought you were taking her home first."

"Does that even make sense? You want me to drive across the bridge, come back across, and then back again to go home myself?" Kyle was clearly frustrated with her. He had on his dick face.

"Well..."

"I'm exhausted, Jess. I'm taking you home first."

"Okay," she said grudgingly.

They spoke in low tones for the rest of the ride to the Main Line. If I wanted to pay attention, I could have eavesdropped on their entire conversation, but I tuned them out and stared out of the window the entire time. I felt weird being in the same vehicle with them, all things considered.

When we pulled into the driveway of the Venner estate, Jess turned in her seat and smiled a fake smile.

"Have a nice night, Emmy. Oh," her face scrunched up. "Your hair is messed up from all of that dancing."

So is your face.

"Thanks for noticing." I said dryly.

"Sorry. I am so used to keeping every hair in place and looking good at all times, especially for my man."

She whispered the last part as if it were some secret that she was a high maintenance bitch.

As Kyle made his way around the car I looked at Jess with loosely veiled disgust. "I don't think Kyle is that superficial. In fact, I think he appreciates those little imperfections. He's seen me all kinds of messy and has never complained."

She stared at me, started to smile but it faltered and then just faded. She wasn't sure what to make of what I just said. She didn't know whether to shrug it off as nonsense or to be worried, especially after the comment I had made earlier in the night about Kyle liking my dress.

Even after Kyle had opened her door, she stared back at me for another moment. She finally got out only because I got out first so I could take the front seat for the ride home, but Jess recovered quickly. She gave me a quick hug and told me to make sure Kyle picks her up from the airport next week. She didn't view me as any kind of real competition, not that I was even competing, I think. He was all hers, but it bothered me that she felt she was somehow above me.

"I will be out in a minute," Kyle said and closed my door. They walked inside with her arm linked tightly through his.

I waited for Kyle for almost five minutes. I didn't really mind, but I was getting pretty sleepy. I looked in the mirror at my hair. A few strands broke free of the French roll it was in, but nothing to get upset about. She was just trying to prove to me that she was better than me.

"Do you want to go get some coffee and pie at the diner?" Kyle asked as we drove away.

"I'm pretty tired and I have to take my parents to the airport in the morning." I wasn't lying, but the main reason I declined was because I was still trying to deal with the churning mass of emotions that struck me earlier.

"Em, it's only pie and coffee," he said with an exasperated sigh.

I was feeling a little hungry considering I had puked up my dinner a couple hours before, but my mouth felt icky and I was dying to brush my teeth and rinse with some strong mouthwash.

"My mom made a cake yesterday." I had forgotten about it. She had made it especially for me. Sometimes she wasn't so horrible. "It's chocolate cake with chocolate buttercream frosting, but it has white chocolate between the three layers."

He grinned, which made me smile. Stupid mouth.

I thought about the worse that could happen while eating cake with my parents in the house, and figured the worse that could happen is that one of us choked on a hunk of cake. I could handle that. It was just cake…

My mom was still up when we walked through the door. She was in flannel pajamas and Phineas and Ferb slippers (thanks to my nieces and nephews, she was a big fan of the cartoon). Her hair was pulled back in a ponytail and she was sitting at the kitchen table painting her nails and reading Vogue. She looked like an over grown teenager.

"Your hair is looking a little bent out of shape," she said immediately, and she had barely looked up.

I rolled my eyes, prepared to tell her where she could go when Kyle stepped in behind me. My mom's attitude quickly changed and she smiled at him with her beauty queen mouth.

"Thank you so much for bringing Esmeralda home safely. I hope she wasn't too much trouble." She waved her hands, trying to dry the paint on her nails.

"I'm not a toddler, Mom. He wasn't babysitting me." I angrily struggled to get out of my coat until Kyle gently eased it off of me. "Thank you."

"I'm going to bed now that you're home. Don't stay up too late." She smiled that ridiculous smile at Kyle again and patted his arm as she left.

"I understand now why some children throw their parents away to rot in nursing homes," I said, taking my shoes off of my sore feet.

"That's a horrible thing to say." Kyle took off his bowtie and jacket and unbuttoned the first few buttons of his shirt.

"Yeah," I admitted. "Maybe it is."

"She did bake you this cake," he said, uncovering the cake with a flourish.

There wasn't even one slice taken. When I urged my parents to eat some, my dad reminded me he wasn't a big chocolate fan and my mom insisted that since it was made for me, I should have the first slice. I didn't feel like eating it until Kyle started talking about pie.

"I suppose I can try to be a little nicer. Sometimes." I shrugged. "Only a little though."

I excused myself and quickly brushed my teeth and rinsed. My mouth felt much better and my stomach rumbled just thinking about my mom's cake.

It was delicious. My mom was the biggest pain in the ass, but she can cook and bake better than anyone I know. I've chosen her food over that of five star restaurants and world famous chefs. Even though she gave me ideas of suffocating her while she slept, she cooked banging meals almost every day.

I told Kyle about my mom's cooking and how she even prepared and froze several meals for me to enjoy in her impending absence.

"I will be here every night to help you eat it all," he said, dabbing my nose with frosting.

"Hey!" I scooped up some on my finger and smacked it onto his cheek.

"I really want to get you back for that, but I don't want to waste good cake."

"It would be like sacrilege," I said with a mouth full of cake. I washed it down with some coffee.

We sat and talked for over an hour. It was nice because we didn't discuss work or anything sensitive, like our feelings or the wild sex we had in the past or about Luke. Luke was a pretty sensitive topic. And Jess. Jess was a really sensitive topic. Instead we chatted about embarrassing moments, our favorite artists and old cartoons.

Like before, he helped me clean up and wash our few dishes. When I dried the last dish and turned around, Kyle put an arm on either side of me, trapping me between him and the counter. His face was only a few short inches from mine.

My heart began to race. Stupid heart.

"Did I tell you that you look amazing tonight?" he asked just above a whisper.

"You may have mentioned it once or twice." He had mentioned it several times.

I moved my hand towards one of my stray hairs, suddenly self-conscious, but he stopped me.

"No, I like it. It's sexy."

His lips brushed mine but then he pulled back some and then did it again, but then restrained himself once more. He was having some kind of internal struggle. He gripped the counter behind me and looked down at the floor between us. I couldn't help myself. I ran my fingers through his dark hair. He looked at me, searching my face for permission. As an answer, I locked my hands around his neck, bringing him closer. He responded quickly, kissing me deeply and slowly.

His lips drifted from mine to my ear. He nibbled on my earlobe, occasionally flicking his tongue across it, driving me a little crazy. When he started to kiss my neck, I got all jelly-like in the knees.

He had one hand on my back, pressing me to him. His other hand was entwined in my hair. I knew we weren't high school kids, and hickies were generally unattractive on a thirty something woman, but it felt so damn good as he nibbled and sucked on my neck. I moaned softly, completely lost in the moment.

His lips found mine again, but more aggressively than before. He pulled away again and kneeled before me. While staring up into my eyes, he slowly eased my dress up over my thighs. He tugged on my panties and I stepped out of them. His fingers found me moist and willing and ready. Without much trying on his part, I had an orgasm that almost made me fall over.

I thought he would stand up then, but when I felt his tongue on me I thought I was going to lose my mind. When he finally stood up he gave me another deep kiss. Without taking his lips from mine, he pulled my dress up again. While he held it up, I undid his pants and reached inside. He moaned into my mouth as I stroked him.

Suddenly, he stopped kissing me, adjusted himself with one hand while holding my dress up still with the other. In one fluid movement, he put his hands under my ass, lifted me up and then entered me. I gave a short shriek and wrapped my legs and arms around him, holding on for dear life.

Even though my parents were right upstairs, I couldn't help myself. I moaned and cried out. The faster and harder he went, the louder I got. My butt was up against the counter getting bruised, but I didn't care.

He grabbed the back of my head, forcing me to kiss him. He stopped kissing me, but tilted my head back so he could attack my neck again. He suddenly groaned really deep which sent me upward toward another climax.

"I love you, I love you," Kyle groaned into my neck. I started to scream as I came and he quickly covered my mouth with his to muffle it.

After a quiet minute with no sounds but the two of us trying to catch our breaths, I untangled myself from him and he eased me back onto my feet.

I didn't know what to say or do. This was an awkward moment for me. I stood where Kyle left me while he fixed his clothes. He had said he loved me, but that could have been just in the heat of the moment and maybe had no real meaning, but he had never said it before.

I was really too tired to think about it. I was tired before we started but now I was almost completely drained.

I could feel my hair on my neck, knowing that most of it had fallen out of the French roll. Jessyca would probably have a conniption.

I didn't know if it was because I was overly tired or slightly off balance, but imagining Jess's face if she saw my hair and me knowing how it got that way made me giggle. Once I started, I almost couldn't stop. Kyle looked at me as if I had completely come unhinged.

"What's wrong with you?" he asked in bewilderment.

"Nothing. I guess I'm just overly tired," I said after I managed to stop.

He raised his eyebrows, but he looked worn out, too. His eyes were red and sagging and he kept rubbing them.

"If you're too tired to go home, you can crash in Emmet's old room," I suggested. I still didn't know what else to say, how to address what just happened.

He looked at me blankly, as if he had not understood. Then he blinked hard and seemed to get it.

"Thanks. I appreciate that. I can't keep my eyes open much longer."

"I have to take my parents to the airport in a few hours, but you can sleep as long as you like."

Kyle followed me out of the kitchen and up the stairs. I walked him to Emmet's room and turned on the light for him.

"Goodnight," I said, but didn't immediately back out of the door like I should have. Instead, I found myself in a sleepy staring match with Kyle while I nervously bit my lip.

"Come here," he said, wagging his finger at me.

The strong emotion in his eyes should have sent me running the other way to avoid any further mistakes and trouble, but I found my feet willingly carrying me into his arms. He gave me a kiss that I could only describe as sweet.

"Goodnight," he said after releasing me.

I went to my bedroom with a crooked smile. I was feeling feverish and achy, probably from our sexcapades in the kitchen. I took a quick shower and then crawled into bed, really wanting to think about Kyle and imagine what was ahead, but a nagging guilt was building. Luke came to mind, and even though we never claimed to be that serious, it still felt like cheating. That was something else for me to ponder, but my brain was feeling rather murky. I had a long day and long night. Before I could think about it any further, I was asleep.

Chapter Thirteen

When I woke up in the morning, my head was no longer murky. I slept like the dead. I still felt like a cheater.

The first thing I did was go see if Kyle was still around. I stepped into the hallway and listened. I heard my mom moving around in the kitchen humming, and I heard the rustling of the newspaper from the formal living room from my dad. I tip toed to Emmet's door and carefully opened it. The bed was empty and made. There was no sign of Kyle, save for his wallet peeking out from under the bed.

Sonofabitch.

I grabbed the wallet and retreated back to my bedroom. I left it on my bed while I got ready to take a shower, but I kept looking at the wallet. I wondered what was inside of it. Condoms? Pictures of Jess? A lock of my hair?

"None of my business," I said out loud to the wallet. "Just because you were abandoned - again - doesn't mean that I can freely go through you. That would be wrong, you know?"

I took my shower, brushed my teeth and applied deodorant. When I stepped back into my room in a towel, the wallet was still there, enticing me. I turned my back on it, got dressed, and brushed my hair.

"Well, if you're just going to sit there and stare at me," I said afterward before picking up the wallet.

I carefully opened it, expecting what, I didn't know. I found a few credit cards, business cards for restaurants, car dealers, a few work-related cards, and I even found one for an upscale strip club with the name Tandi printed on it.

Hmm.

I counted a hundred and thirty dollars in cash. I didn't find any pictures, or condoms, or any of my hair, but I did find a piece of folded paper that looked promising. I carefully unfolded the paper. Written in Kyle's handwriting was the address of the bar he found me at, my bar. I owned the bar. I bought it just after my 25th birthday. It wasn't common knowledge that the bar was mine. My family knew, my best friend Donya knew, and Lilly the bartender knew. The rest of my employees didn't even know the woman who occupies the same stool a couple of nights a week was their boss. So, why did Kyle have it written down and when did he write it down?

I didn't have time to think about it. I heard my mom coming up the stairs and it was almost time to leave. I slipped the wallet into my tote bag just as my mom barged into my room. It didn't matter that I was thirty years old, she didn't care about invading my privacy or the dignity I craved just from a simple knock.

"I was wonderin' if you were awake or not. What time did that boss of yours leave? He's a good looking man. Too bad he's with that Venner woman." She had started making my bed, which was also annoying the crap out of me, but I chose to focus on her words instead.

"What? You don't like Luke?" I asked with a sigh. It was hard to say his name out loud after my night of whoring.

"I think he's great, but I like that Kyle, too."

"Kyle can be a dick," I said, edging toward the door.

"Well, honey, you're no angel."

"It doesn't matter. As you just pointed out, Kyle's with that Venner woman."

"Yes. Well." She stood upright, fluffed a pillow and put it back on the bed. "Since he is with that Venner woman and you are with Luke, he should probably be more careful how he looks at you when you're surrounded by hundreds of other people."

"What are you talking about?" I froze, half in the room and half out.

"He couldn't keep his eyes off of you last night, and I saw his face when you didn't want to dance to that slow song. If I saw all of that, then who else did?" She hummed lightly, as if this conversation wasn't as important as it really was.

"Maybe you're the only one who saw what you think you saw," I said, hoping to dissuade her. "I don't think it's as dramatic as you think it is."

"Yes. Well." She started opening the blinds with more humming before finishing her thought. "Maybe if it weren't for the enormous hickey on your neck that wasn't there when I left you two alone last night, I would be inclined to believe that I'm imagining things."

I raced to the mirror to look at my neck, nearly tripping over my own two feet.

"Shit!" I yelled. I didn't really look in the mirror when I was getting ready. I don't need a mirror to brush my teeth or my hair. "Fuck!"

"Don't let your daddy see that," Mom said before exiting my room.

After putting on a jacket that better hid my neck, I got my parents' loaded into the car and deposited them at the airport. I went over the bridge and raced up 295 to Cherry Hill. I parked outside of Kyle's apartment building, next to his Lexus. I had to put an end to this. No more hickies, because his lips couldn't touch me again. The truth is, my relationship with Luke was getting heavy, and I really felt something for him. Maybe love? I was in denial about it before, but I knew for sure that I didn't want Luke to see the marking on my neck.

After taking the elevator to Kyle's floor, I half hoped that he wasn't actually home, that Jess changed her mind about leaving and picked him up, or he was abducted by aliens. I punched the doorbell and he opened the door seconds later, wearing only a pair of pajama bottoms. So much for aliens.

I held up his wallet.

"Again?" He asked, plucking it from my hand.

"I'm starting to believe you're doing it on purpose, like you're leaving your mark."

His eyebrows went up. "I don't need to leave a mark. I'm memorable."

"I beg to differ," I said and pulled my jacket back at the collar.

"I do good work," he said, touching the hickey.

"Yeah, whatever. Have a good day, boss." I started to walk away, but he grabbed my arm and pulled me inside. He took my bag from me and put it on the floor by the door.

"Why don't you stay a little while?" He caressed my hand in a way that made me a little melty.

"I really shouldn't."

"Why not?"

"You know why."

"Because you can't resist me?"

"Funny." I started to pull away again, but he pulled me further inside and then closed the door.

"Why are you in such a hurry to leave?" He wrapped his arms around my waist, drawing me closer.

"Because you have a girlfriend and I have a boyfriend."

"Yeah...we should get rid of them."

"You don't mean that," I said, trying to break away.

"I'm not sure that I do," he whispered. "For reasons I don't want to get into. I don't want to talk about them. I want to talk about us."

"Us?" I raised one eyebrow.

"I love you," he whispered, staring into my eyes.

So, it wasn't just in the heat of the moment. I stared at him, startled, unsure of what to say. I tried to pull away from him again, but he pulled me even closer and held me tightly.

"Do you love me?" he asked.

"I can't..." I couldn't remember what I couldn't do. His gaze was so intense I lost my train of thought.

"You can't what? Love me? I think you already do."

I shook my head.

No. No way. Hell no.

He pressed me into a closet door.

"Don't lie to me. Don't ever lie to me." He kissed me so hard it hurt, but it hurt so damn good. "Tell me you love me," he whispered.

I shook my head. I couldn't breathe. My heart was in my throat and it was beating faster than I thought possible.

"Stop shaking your head. You love me, I know you do."

"I have to leave," I managed.

"No, you don't, but if you tell me you love me, I'll let you go."

"Sex does not equal love."

"I know that, but I loved you before I ever touched you," he said and ran his fingers over my cheek.

I stared at him with my mouth open. It felt like déja vu. Luke and I were wrapped in a similar scene not very long ago. What was it with men secretly carrying a flame for me?

I left my mouth open too long, because Kyle planted his mouth on mine. He kissed me for a long time, more tenderly this time. I reflexively kissed him back.

"I love you," he said again with his face buried in my hair. Then his mouth was on my neck, gently kissing where he had marked me.

I involuntarily moaned, but with all of the strength I had, I shoved him away from me. I felt tears burning in my eyes and did the best I could to blink them back.

I was sure I loved Luke. The problem was I was also sure I loved Kyle.

"I love Luke," I said weakly.

"Yeah. And I love Jessyca," he took a step closer. "But I can't help how I feel about you. I love you, Emmy. You love me, too or you wouldn't be crying."

"I'm not crying!" I wiped at my eyes.

"Just say it."

I hastily pushed past him to the front door.

"I have to go," I said and slammed the door behind me.

I marched down the hall and took the elevator all the way down and almost got to my car before I realized I didn't have my bag, therefore, I didn't have my keys or wallet.

"Crap!" I stomped my foot and went back inside.

Kyle opened the door before I could knock or hit the bell. He had a stupid grin on his face as he held my pocketbook up in one hand.

"It's not funny," I said, snatching the bag from his hand.

"It would have really been a great exit if you didn't forget your purse," he said. "I tried to look through it, but you have way too much shit in there."

"I feel violated."

"Like you didn't look through my wallet."

"Why do you have the name and address of the bar in your wallet?" I blurted out.

"I told you, I loved you for a while."

"That's not an answer."

"Why don't you at least come inside?" He stepped aside so I could get in.

I looked at him with suspicion.

"Chicken."

"I am not chicken." I stormed inside.

"Want a drink?" he asked, walking past me towards the kitchen.

"No."

"How about a bottle of water?"

"Okay." I accepted the water while he cracked open a beer. "Now, answer my question."

"What did you want to know?"

"Why do you have that address?"

"Oh, the bar. So I could punch it into my GPS." He said it casually, as if he stalked people all of the time.

"Why?"

"So I could find it. I thought you were smart."

I smacked his elbow just as he was lifting the beer to his lips. Beer spilled down his bare chest. He looked down his chest and when he looked up again he was grinning.

"Two of your favorite things. Me and beer. Wanna lick it off?"

"Why did you want to find the bar?"

"Because I wanted to see it."

"Stop being evasive!" I smacked him again.

"Emmy, you were going to be working directly under me, handling my professional and personal business. You have access to everything I have access to. I needed to know who you really were."

"Wait," I held up a hand. "You were 'interested' in me before I started working for you?"

"Professionally, yeah. Everything else soon followed."

"So, why did you suddenly appear at the bar that night if you had known about it for so long?"

"I was very mean to you that day, and I wanted to come apologize."

"You were very mean every day," I pointed out. "All of the time."

"Yeah, but I was meanest to you."

That was true. As mean as Kyle could be to his staff, I always took the brunt of it. Some days I felt like he was purposely trying my patience. Now I believe that was exactly what he was doing.

"Why?" I asked.

"Stupid guy thing," he said, shaking his head at himself. "I can't even explain it."

"Seems juvenile," I said. "Like the little boys who torture the girls they have a thing for."

"Yeah, I guess it's a lot like that," he said thoughtfully. "I'm sorry."

I didn't know what to say. I just stood there with my arms crossed, glaring at him. I thought boys grew out of that stuff by the ninth grade. Apparently not all do.

"I was going to order some lunch and watch some movies. Do you want to hang out?"

My eyebrows went up and he smiled.

"I promise I won't try to force you to say what I know you feel," he grinned. "And I promise I won't try to take you out of your clothes. We'll just chill and watch the movies and eat some food."

"What movies?" I asked suspiciously.

"*Lord of the Rings*. I've never seen them."

"Seriously, do you live under a rock?"

I followed him to the living room where he produced three different menus. Why I didn't just leave after I got my explanation, I don't know. I asked that question aloud while we sat on the couch debating what to order.

"Because you love me," Kyle said with a wink.

This time I didn't object or give him a reproachful look. Instead, I chose buffalo wings and onion rings off of a menu and made myself comfortable on the couch.

Three long ass movies, several buffalo wings and countless beers later, I was stretched out on Kyle's couch with my feet resting in his lap. The credits were rolling, but I wasn't moving. He was rubbing my feet and it was making me deliriously relaxed, and turning me on.

He held true to his word and didn't try to disrobe me all day, and didn't try to force his tongue down my throat. He kissed my cheek and the top of my head, rubbed my elbow when I hit it on the bathroom door and it was not funny. He cracked jokes about hobbits, made fun of my obsession with Orlando Bloom, and listened intently when I compared the books to the movies. Now he was rubbing my feet and I wanted him to rub me in a few other places.

I pulled my feet off of his lap and sat up.

"I love a good *LOTR* marathon," I yawned as I slipped on my shoes.

"You don't have to leave," Kyle said, looking as lustful as I felt.

"You know I do."

"I can take the couch, you can have my bed."

I stood up and stretched.

"We both know that won't work."

He followed me to the door.

"Why not?"

"You know why." I slipped into my jacket and opened the door.

"Tell me why," he said softly. He was grinning, so I knew that he knew why.

I bit my lip as I contemplated what I was about to do and say. I was going to say what he wanted to hear, but then I'd never get out of there. I wanted to kiss him, same end result.

I smiled and waved goodnight before walking away.

Good girl.

Chapter Fourteen

It was a busy work day the next day, leaving little time for casual conversation between me and Kyle. At least he wasn't being a dick. He was actually scaring the staff, smiling and being polite. They didn't know what to make of it.

Later in the day my phone rang and I answered it without looking to see who it was.

"Sterling Corp, this is Emmy."

"Hello, Emmy," Kyle said in a professional tone. "Mr. Kyle Sterling would like to know if you are available for dinner this evening."

"Dinner?"

"Yes, it's the meal after lunch but before dessert."

"Oh, that meal."

"Yes, that meal. Perhaps even a movie."

"Why? Is there another epic movie you have yet to see?" I rolled my eyes. Next thing I knew, he was going to say he had never seen Star Wars. Then I started to panic. What if he never did see Star Wars?

"I was thinking we can see something you would be more interested in, like a chick flick. I can do a chick flick if necessary," Kyle said, interrupting my disquieting thoughts.

"Totally not necessary. I don't do chick flicks."

"Maybe I like chic flicks. Maybe I am in the mood for some Pretty Woman or Sense and Sensibility."

"So you like getting in touch with your feminine side?"

"Do you think I have a feminine side?" he asked in a tone that made me squirm in my seat.

"No," I said. "So what movie did you have in mind?"

"How about a classic? Like Weird Science."

"That hardly classifies as a classic. Why don't we decide later? I have Netflix, we can watch something off of there."

"And what about dinner?"

"What do you want to eat?"

"You."

I squirmed again.

"Behave or you'll be all alone tonight," I reprimanded.

"I'll bring something."

"Okay. Now hang up. I have a lot of work to do and I don't feel like hearing any shit from my boss."

"That guy's a douche."

"Douche excrement."

"Right. Later."

I hung up the phone and looked around to make sure no one had witnessed our conversation. Everyone seemed hard at work, but you never know...

Kyle walked out of his office a minute later. Our eyes locked and he found a smile reserved just for me that almost made me fall out of my chair.

We ended up watching a chick flick after Kyle found one hidden in my movie collection. *Love Actually* is one of those movies I can watch repeatedly and never grow tired of.

"I think you secretly love girly movies," I said to Kyle afterward.

We were sitting side by side and his arm was behind me across the back of the couch.

"I will never admit to any such thing."

"You probably have every Jane Austen movie hidden under your bed. I'm going to check next time I'm over."

"Do you plan on being near my bed?" he asked softly.

Flustered, I looked away.

"No," I said. My eyes focused on a small opening in the curtains. I jumped up and swept them wide open and stared.

Kyle was standing very close to me, also watching. It was snowing pretty hard, although the roads looked drivable.

"Check your phone," I said. "See how much we're getting."

"My phone is in my car," he said and slowly eased his hand into the front pocket of my tight jeans. I held my breath until he pulled out my phone.

"Wow. We're getting eighteen inches," he said after a minute.

"How do we keep missing the news on these things?" I shook my head.

"I heard it was going to snow, but I didn't know we were getting eighteen inches."

He slid the phone back into my pocket, but when he took his hand out, he moved it to my lower belly and closed the inches between us.

"I guess we're not going to work tomorrow," I said and then sighed when I felt his lips on my neck. "I'm glad I went food shopping," I added in a shaky voice.

He gently moved my hair and his kisses landed on the base of my neck, making my knees weak. I gripped onto the curtains for some balance. His hand that had rested on my belly slid down between my legs. I gasped and tensed up. How he was able to hit that spot through my jeans on one try, I didn't know.

"At least you...unhh...can beat the storm home...mmm...this time."

"I'm not going home unless you're coming with me," Kyle said huskily.

"Mmm...why is th-th-th-aahh?"

"Because you're riding my hand," he whispered in my ear before flicking at the lobe with his tongue.

I couldn't deny it. I was grinding against his hand as if it were going to save my life. His other hand reached around and found a nipple through my tee shirt. My vision blurred and then I stopped seeing altogether when my head tilted back and my eyes rolled to the back of my skull. I climaxed so hard I almost tore the curtains down.

"I love hearing you come," Kyle whispered in my ear as his fingers expertly unbuttoned my jeans. Before I could even recover from my orgasm, his fingers were sliding into me. He forced my head back and kissed me while he fingered me to another orgasm.

He carried me away from the window, not bothering to close the curtains. In seconds, he had my jeans and panties off and was pulling my shirt and bra up over my head. He planted his mouth over a nipple and nibbled, licked, and sucked me into a frenzy while he thumbed my engorged secret spot. I screamed out his name, begged him to make love to me.

Kyle undressed himself quickly, poised himself over me while I kept begging him.

"No," he said, and slipped in only a little bit before pulling out.

"Please," I whispered.

"I can't make love to someone who doesn't love me. I can fuck you," he slammed into me, making me cry out, but then he pulled out again. "So, which one do you want, baby? Hmm?"

I stared into his eyes. I knew this was more than lust. I was risking everything with Luke for Kyle. I could have made him leave before this got started, but I really didn't want him to leave at all.

"I love you," I whispered. "You know I do."

He smiled. "Yeah, I know you do." He kissed me, and while I was wrapped up in his kiss, he slid inside of me and I melted into the couch.

Chapter Fifteen

"My god, I've missed you," Luke said, before kissing me.

It was Sunday afternoon, and he had literally just returned from his trip. He didn't even go home first. I found myself genuinely happy to see him, eager to hold him, and our first kiss after his absence was magical. I wondered if the experience had been lackluster, if I would have felt just as guilty.

The guilt was swimming through my veins, mingling with my strong feelings for Luke. I was practically choking on my guilt while he told me how much he missed me. He was on a cruise ship and on various islands, surrounded by gorgeous scantily clad women, missing me, and I was playing house with Kyle.

Bad Emmy. Bad, bad Emmy.

"I missed you too," I said, and it was true, but it was also true that I had not missed him as much as I would have had I been alone all week.

"Emails, text messages and short phone conversations weren't cutting it for me. I was tempted to swim home to be with you."

And I would have drowned you with grief.

"But you had a good time, right?" I asked.

"Yeah, I did. I brought you some gifts."

"I like gifts. Maybe I have a gift for you," I said, running my fingers across his muscular chest.

"Oh yeah?"

"Mmm hmm. How about I give it to you right now?" I kneeled before him and unzipped his jeans.

"Wooooooowwww," he said after a moment. "I really love your gifts."

***

Kyle was in a bad, bad mood Monday morning. He was in total dick mode, barking at everyone who fell into his line of sight, including me. I blamed Jess. She had returned Saturday afternoon, and Kyle had spent the rest of the weekend with her. All her fault.

Being Kyle's personal assistant, I had to talk to him more than most. I tried to not let his bad attitude get under my skin. I was still on a high from spending all day Sunday with Luke. I also avoided going into his office if I could help it, so I wouldn't be tempted to knock his lights out.

Early in the afternoon, I had just come back from lunch with Luke. I still felt guilty, but it was subsiding. I was daydreaming about him when Jeoff Urvin approached my desk. I recoiled when I saw him standing there. That was my usual reaction to Jeoff.

He was a junior executive, just under Kyle. Whenever Kyle's schedule was too heavy, Jeoff took the overflow of clients on top of the more minor clients he acquired. I didn't like Jeoff because he was a talentless hack, a brown nosing, sexist, snake who kissed ass, lied, and stomped on toes to work his way up in the company. He really didn't know very much about his work. I knew more than he did.

A long time ago, Jeoff tried to pull rank on me. If Jeoff was worthy of his title and not a puss filled zit, I would have conceded as I do with Kyle. Instead, Jeoff left the office that day without his balls. Ever since then, I was recognized as the second in command, and the HBIC (head bitch in charge).

"What?" I said, irritated to have him standing near me.

"I'm sick."

"Ew." I sprayed Lysol in his general direction. He was looking a little greener than usual. "So?"

"I'm supposed to have a meeting with Hernandez in an hour. I can't go."

"So?"

"So, I need you to go."

"I'm not going."

"You're going. Kyle wants this wrapped up last week."

"So, why didn't you wrap it up last week?"

"Hernandez is...difficult."

More like Jeoff was incompetent.

"It doesn't matter," I said. "I'm not qualified."

"Bullshit. Show him some leg and go get it done." He wiped at his face with a handkerchief. He looked like he was going to hurl.

"Are you trying to tell me what to do?"

"Look, if no one goes today, Kyle is going to be in one hell of a mood, and he will take it out on everyone. Besides, this came down from Kyle."

"Then why didn't Kyle tell me himself?"

"He told me to tell you on my way out. Look, I gotta go. Get it done."

He ran into the hall and turned toward the restrooms. Gross.

I got up and marched into Kyle's office without knocking. He was concentrating on something on his computer screen.

"What."

"Did you tell Jerk-Off Jeoffery to tell me to go to the Hernandez meeting?"

"Yes."

"I am not an executive or even a junior executive. I'm not qualified."

"You're more qualified than Jeoff." Kyle still had not taken his eyes off of the computer screen.

"I don't get paid to do what Jerk-Off Jeoffery does. You can go."

"I'm busy."

"Clearly," I said dryly. "Hernandez is a bigger pig than Jerk-Off Jeoffery. He gets handsy. Don't you remember how handsy he was when I accompanied you last time?"

"Threaten to taser his balls. You'll be okay for a couple of hours. Take someone with you."

"Okay. Right. Except, I don't have a taser."

"I don't have time for your whining, Emmy!" Kyle roared, finally looking up at me. "I need you to just do what I need you to do and stop crying about it."

I stood there in a stunned silence for a moment. Kyle has yelled at me before, but after all of the personal shit we recently shared, it felt very personal this time. He's never called me a whiner or a cry baby or any names at all. Then again, in the past I would have never approached him like this.

I turned on my heel to leave the room.

"Wait," Kyle said. "I'm sorry. It's just that -"

"Go fuck yourself," I said in a low tone so no one close to his office could hear and then left the room.

Late that night, five minutes after Luke left, Kyle appeared at my front door. I didn't let him in.

"What did you do? Circle the block until Luke left?" I asked, leaning against the door frame with my arms crossed in front of me.

"Actually, yes I did."

"What do you want?"

"Did you get my texts?" His eyes were hopeful.

"Yes."

"You didn't answer."

"I was busy. First I was busy trying to keep that creep Hernandez's hands off of me, and then I was busy with Luke."

He flinched slightly.

"I'm sorry I yelled at you like that. There's no excuse for it. Do you forgive me?"

"Sure." I shrugged.

"I don't believe you," he said with suspicion.

"I don't like to hold a grudge."

"Okay." He shifted from one foot to another. "Can I come in and show you how sorry I am?"

"No. We agreed to put 'us' on hold, remember?"

"No, you agreed. I adamantly disagreed."

"It will be easier for both of us if you go along with it. You're not ready to end it with Jess and quite frankly, I'm not sure I really want to let Luke go."

Another flinch.

"Did you say that just to hurt me or do you mean that?" he asked.

"Maybe a little of both," I admitted.

"Harsh."

"I'm sorry."

"Are you?"

"A little."

We stood there staring at each other. I really did feel sorry for being mean, but I had to keep on my game face.

"I guess I'll go."

"Okay."

He turned and started down the drive, but turned back.

"Did you get Hernandez to sign?"

"Of course I did."

"Good girl."

He continued on to his car.

"I love you," he called over his shoulder.
"Love you, too."
Stupid, Emmy!
"Shit," I said and slammed the door.

Chapter Sixteen

"My parents are having a cocktail party Saturday night and my mother invited you," Kyle said.

We were waiting for the elevator after another late night of work.

"Me? Why did she invite me?"

"You must have impressed her at the gala."

"We barely spoke ten sentences between us at the gala," I said, stepping onto the elevator.

"She told me to make sure you and Luke were invited," he shrugged. "I will be happy to see you there."

"As your friend."

"Yeah. Whatever."

I was trying to reinforce our friends only relationship. I was selfish, because I didn't want to give Kyle up completely, but I didn't want to be a sneaky hoe bag either. We "agreed" on a platonic relationship at the end of that long week after the gala. Since then, we have only hung out a couple of times, and I sorta missed him.

"What's the party for?" I asked.

"For nothing. A good time. A chance for the Main Line to show off in expensive clothes. Will you come?"

"Interesting statements from a man who spends thousands of dollars on a single suit. Do you want me to go?"

He gave a small smile. "Of course I want you there. Even if you will be with Luke, and I'll be with Jess."

I didn't say anything. Maybe it wasn't a good idea to try and maintain a platonic friendship after all.

"What should I tell my mother?"

Gah.

"Tell your mother I will be there," I sighed.

We stepped off of the elevator and walked through the lobby.

"Are you meeting Luke?"

"Nope. He's in Dallas."

"Want a ride to your car?"

I looked through the front revolving doors. It was pouring rain. Even with my umbrella, I would surely be soaked by the time I got to my car at the speed line.

"Yeah, I'll take the ride," I said.

We walked through the building to the attached parking garage reserved just for Sterling employees.

"Why don't you drive to work?" Kyle asked as we neared his car.

"Traffic is a bitch, and I like walking through the city, and if I want to do anything after work, I don't have to worry about finding parking. I just go."

The rain was falling in sheets and giving everyone a reason to drive like idiots - more than usual. Kyle didn't complain when he was cut off by cabs or when traffic gridlocked. He kept one hand on the wheel and one on my seat, not so much a position of comfort as it was an indication of possession.

"Do you have plans for dinner?" he asked me.

"I have meatballs in a crockpot at home."

"I could go for some meatballs."

Probably, it would have served me well to say no.

"I just have to stop at the bakery on my way home," I said instead.

Traffic eventually eased and we made our way out of the city. Every now and then Kyle's fingers would lightly touch my hair or brush gently across my neck. I didn't stop him or even acknowledge it.

"I'll meet you at your house," Kyle said when I was getting ready to depart.

"There's a spare key under that big rock in the front garden, if you don't want to wait outside for me."

"Cool. Now I can sneak into your house anytime I want to."

"Can you turn the crockpot off, stalker?" I asked, rolling my eyes.

"Sure. Be careful." He leaned over and kissed the corner of my mouth.

"Okay," I said, flustered.

The bakery was half way between my house and the speed line. I parked at the curb while I ran in for bread to go with dinner, and a cake for dessert.

When I got home, Kyle was draining pasta in the sink, with his sleeves rolled up to the elbow and the top of his shirt unbuttoned. His tie was on the table and his jacket was draped over a kitchen chair.

"Thank you, Betty Crocker," I said, pulling my shoes off.

"Julia Childs," he grinned.

"I'll be back, Julia. I have to change."

I went upstairs and after some thought I changed into unattractive sweat pants and an ugly purple tee shirt. Maybe if I looked a hot mess, Kyle would be less likely to want to throw me on the floor and make sweet love to me. The thought of it instantly made me horny.

I sighed and returned to the kitchen where Kyle had set the table and poured two glasses of red wine.

"Nice work," I said, impressed.

"Thanks."

We ate dinner with quiet conversation. It was pleasant and platonic, and I started to feel that maybe we could pull off this friendship thing after all. After dinner, we put the dishes in the sink and started on the cake while standing at the counter.

"I want to talk to you about something," Kyle said after we finished the cake and had washed it down with the rest of the wine.

"If it's about the cake, I'm sorry. We can't always have my mother's cake, and I'm not a good baker. My cookies burn and my cakes are crunchy."

His mouth curved up slightly, amusement danced in his eyes.

"I'll let it slide this time," he said.

"What a friend." I gave his arm a hearty, friendly whack.

"That's what I wanted to talk to you about."

"Oh?" I took a step backward, which was a big mistake because I literally backed myself into a corner. Kyle wasted no time closing the distance between us and trapping me.

"I don't want to be just your friend," he said.

"We had an agreement," I said feebly.

"No, you agreed. I didn't agree to something I knew I wouldn't be able to do."

"You have to accept my friendship or nothing at all," I argued.

"I don't have to accept either one of those options. You want to explore the possibilities as much as I do. You don't like this box you've put us in any more than I do."

"That's not true."

"Oh? It isn't?" He ran a finger over my neck, just under my ear, like he did in the car earlier. A grin appeared on his face. "See? Your eyes just glazed over. You love when I touch you."

I pushed his hand away, aggravated by his ballsy behavior, but he grabbed my hand and pinned it to my side. He pinned my other hand, too before leaning in to kiss me. I pulled my head back, turned so that he got my cheek instead. He let go of my hands and grabbed my head with both of his hands.

I was pressed into the counter, with nowhere to go, and he had a firm hold on my head. I could have hit him, or pinched him, but why bother? I probably would still cave.

Kyle's lips were warm, his tongue warmer. When it was apparent I wasn't going to fight him anymore, he used his hands to pull me into him and then held me extremely tight. I wrapped my arms around him and kissed back.

Minutes passed, judging by the numbness spreading through my lips, when suddenly Kyle pulled away. Entirely. He backed away from me, leaving me confused and wanting.

"I want you to think about that for a few days before you decide you only want to be my friend," he said and left me alone in the kitchen. Moments later I heard the front door close.

I was still reeling when my phone buzzed on the kitchen table. On weak knees I crossed the kitchen and plucked the phone off of the table.

"Hey, babe," Luke said.

"Hey," I said, breathlessly.

"You sound like you ran to the phone."

"I practically did," I lied and then mentally chastised myself for lying.

Well, I couldn't tell him Kyle left me breathless, could I?

"How are you?" Luke asked.

A little fucked up.

"Fine. Tired. How are you?"

"The same," he sighed.

He proceeded to talk about the suckish points of his day. I didn't mind. Luke doesn't complain much, so if something bothers him I want to hear about it.

"So, what's going on in your world?" he asked when he finished talking.

"The Sterlings invited us to a cocktail party they're having on Saturday."

"While that sounds painfully merry, I have a bachelor's party to attend Saturday night in Chicago."

I giggled. "Painfully merry. Funny. I forgot you weren't coming right home. You're flying to Chicago to get drunk and have other women shake their boobs in your face."

"If it bothers you, I won't go," he said seriously.

"No," I kicked at the table leg. "It doesn't bother me. Maybe I'm just jealous."

"Jealous? You're not the jealous type."

"Maybe I want boobs shaken in my face."

He laughed hard for almost an entire minute, a sound I loved.

"You're a riot," he said after regaining his composure.

"I know. Seriously, though, have a good time, be careful. Make sure you get a lap dance."

"I'd rather have you dancing on my lap."

"Well, you know where to find me."

He chuckled. "I'm going to get to bed. Talk to you tomorrow."

"Night. Miss you."

"Miss you, too. And..."

"And?"

"I love you," he said in a quiet tone.

"I love you, too, Luke."

We hung up. I sat down in a chair and let my head hit the table with a loud THUNK.

Chapter Seventeen

At work, I pretended that nothing had happened. Kyle did, too, which should have made life a little easier, but Kyle wasn't being friendly. He wasn't being a dick either. He was indifferent. It was as if he were saying "See, this is how it will be if you decide you only want to be friends."

At the end of late work nights, Kyle usually left with me, always offering to take me to my car. This time when I stepped into the elevator, he bid me goodnight and took the stairs. By the time the elevator picked up stragglers from other floors, Kyle was gone.

I decided that I was going to have to shake it off. Psshh, that kiss wasn't even all that. If he wanted it to be that way, that was fine. I can be indifferent, too. I was indifferent before he stalked me and found me in my bar that night.

When Saturday rolled around, I was mentally and emotionally exhausted from being indifferent. I almost didn't feel like going to the cocktail party. I lounged around on the couch, flipping through boring Saturday television and eating popcorn with too much butter. My mom called me half a million times, but I never answered. Judging from the voicemails she left, she wasn't calling about anything important.

The party was at six. At three, I had to make a decision. If I were to go, I had to shower, shave, wash and style my hair and do my makeup. My dress was still in the bag from when I bought it, draped over a chair in the living room, and my new shoes sat in a box by the couch. If I didn't go, the carefully selected dress and shoes would have been bought in vain, and I do not waste designer clothes and shoes.

I dragged myself off of the couch and went upstairs to get ready.

***

The Sterling Estate was off of the affluent Main Line, not far from stupid Jess's family estate. The enormous house sat on thirty acres of private land. During the summer, the property was beautifully landscaped with lush gardens and fountains shaped like naked little cherubs spitting water out of their mouths…and other things.

I pulled up into the Sterling's driveway a few minutes after six and handed my keys off to a valet. Upon entering the door, I checked my coat. Just outside the enormous dining room, a servant waited with a tray of champagne. I snagged one and drank half of it by the time I was a few steps inside the room.

I paused and took in my surroundings. The room was slightly dimmed, I suppose to give it a little ambiance. The bar, I quickly noted, was in the far left corner, and there were tables of food straight ahead, along with servants wandering the place with trays of booze and food. There were tables, couches and chairs set up throughout the room to make it look like an enormous lounging area. It didn't at all look tacky, but looked posh. Really, it looked more like an upscale club. I was impressed.

There must have been two hundred people in the room. I recognized some faces, but many were strangers. There was no sign of Kyle, his parents, or Dumb-Dumb Jessyca. I floated towards the bar, stopping to speak to a few people along the way.

One guy I knew, Trevor, followed me on my journey. I think he thought he was gonna get some. Trevor's had a crush on me since high school. He was good looking enough, but he was a pig. I was pretty sure I heard a rumor that he had the clap.

I was rescued from Trevor several drinks later when Kyle magically appeared at my side.

"Hello," Kyle said, openly letting his eyes wander up and down my body.

In my mind, while purchasing my dress and shoes, I told myself that I was buying the nude, backless, short dress because it was stylish, not because I knew Kyle would love it. The six inch red shoes were bought because they matched the dress, not because Kyle thought high heels made my legs look incredibly sexy. I wore my hair up with a few strands loose, because it was comfortable, not because Kyle had a thing for me exposing my neck in this way.

But let's be truthful. I did it all for Kyle.

Shame on you, Emmy.

"Hello, Kyle."

"My mother is looking for you," he said, offering his hand.

"Nice seeing you again, Trevor," I said, taking Kyle's hand and gracefully stepping off of the stool.

"Maybe we can talk somewhere more quiet and secluded later," Trevor said.

"Maybe not," Kyle said firmly and led me away.

"I don't know, maybe I'd like to talk to Trevor in a more secluded, quiet place later," I said.

"If I ever catch you with that loser, I'll beat him to within an inch of his life," he said seriously.

He had his hand on my bare back as we weaved through the crowd. I loved it. He loved it. We loved it.

"Well, that's drastic, coming from a man who has been indifferent to me for days."

"It wasn't easy."

"No kidding," I muttered.

"You look amazing." His fingers trailed down my back.

"Thank you."

"Every guy in this room wants you, and every woman is jealous."

"Whatever." I rolled my eyes and shook my head.

"It's true. Take a casual look around the room."

"I'm not vain enough to check. Even though I think you're exaggerating, I'll take your word for it."

"Where's Luke?"

"Bachelor party in Chicago. Where's Jess?"

"Around."

A moment later we reached his mother. Jess was with her. Great.

"Mrs. Sterling," I said reaching out my hand. "Thank you for inviting me."

She nodded with a brief smile and said "You look lovely."

She looked at me from head to foot and then had me slowly spin around. I felt like she was about to buy me.

"Beautiful," she sighed. I was beginning to wonder if she was a lesbian.

"Yes," Jess piped in. "Although, it is a little...skimpy." Her eyes flickered over to Kyle. Kyle was watching me.

"But you pull it off perfectly, Emmy," Mrs. S said. She gave me another brief smile and walked away.

"What was that all about?" I drew close to Kyle so only he could hear me. "That was weird."

"You remind her of what she used to be."

"She used to be an idiot?" I laughed lightly.

He flashed me his grin, but didn't answer because dumbass Jess interrupted by taking hold of his arm.

"It was nice to see you, Emmy," she said without meaning it. She tried pulling Kyle away, but he stood firm.

"Did you think about it?" he asked, ignoring Jessyca.

"The answer is no, of course." I looked at him like he was nuts.

"I don't believe that," he hinted a smile as he slowly let himself be dragged off by the succubus.

"Why not?" I crossed my arms.

He broke free of Jess and whispered in my ear "Because you dressed up for me."

He allowed Jess to take him away without a backward glance.

I wanted to go back to the bar, but Trevor was there, watching me from afar. I grabbed two glasses of champagne off of a moving tray and drank them quickly. I ambled over to a group of people I knew and allowed conversation to distract me for a while, but every now and then my eyes would float around the room in search of Kyle. When I finally saw him across the room, he was already looking at me.

His face gave nothing away, but there was something in his eyes that made my heart flutter. I peeled my eyes away, so no one in my group would get suspicious, but every time I looked in his direction, he was watching me.

Eventually, I got tired of talking to people I usually don't care about. I got tired of Kyle's staring and Jess's glaring. I felt like I should have never come, and especially should have never dressed to impress Kyle.

My heart really wanted to go where he was offering, but my mind knew better. A wise man once said "Anyone who can rationalize love through intellect, has no idea what love is, for it is an emotion, and cannot be rationalized. For love is crazy." I couldn't allow myself to plead insanity and run into Kyle's arms. Under the circumstances, rationalizing love through intellect was the right thing to do, even if it was crushing me from the inside out. I'm pretty sure the man who made that quote wasn't thinking about cheating in the name of love, but occasionally, my own mind went that way.

While Kyle's attention was elsewhere, I slipped out of the party. When I got home, I turned on the radio in the kitchen, took out a half gallon of Breyer's vanilla and chocolate ice-cream, a jar of peanut butter and a big spoon. I found some chocolate chips and mini marshmallows in the cabinet, grabbed a bowl to dump them in and sat down at the kitchen table. I ate right out of the carton, finding creative ways to get all of my ingredients into my mouth at the same time. This was my comfort food, but it wasn't working very well.

I had eaten half of the ice-cream when I heard the front door open. My heart skipped a beat. I sat stock still, wondering if I'd be able to defend myself with a sticky spoon. Footsteps sounded in the hall and I thought maybe I could convince the robber or rapist to sit down and have some ice-cream instead of committing their intended crime.

Kyle appeared, holding my pocketbook.

"You forgot this in your haste to leave the party," he said, setting it down on the table.

"Your bad habits are rubbing off on me."

"I thought maybe you were trying to lure me here." He took a spoon out of the drawer and sat down across from me.

"Don't you need to get back to the party?"

"Not my party."

"Hmm."

We ate in silence for a while. When it seemed like we were both done, I got up and started cleaning up the mess. Kyle helped and when we were finished we stood on opposite sides of the table staring at one another.

"You should probably go," I said.

"Why?"

Because I don't know if I will be able to say no.

"It's late."

"Never stopped you before."

I couldn't think of another excuse, so I just stood there looking at everything but him.

"Tell me you don't want me in your life and I will leave."

I opened my mouth to speak but he cut me off with "And you have to mean it."

I closed my mouth. I opened it again, sputtered out a few words, but not enough to say what I really should say and have this done and over.

"That's what I thought," he said, walking around the table.

I moved away in the opposite direction. We circled the table until I ended up where he had been standing and vice versa.

"Why are you running from me?" he asked in a quiet voice.

"I...I..."

Damn it.

"Stay where you are," Kyle said firmly.

I obeyed and watched with apprehension as he walked around the table. I seized up when he reached for me, and my feet dragged when he tried to make me close the distance between us. Roughly, he pulled me to him, but my arms stayed limp at my sides.

"No more of this just friends shit," he said, tilting my head back. "There's nothing platonic between us."

Just before his lips touched mine, I hurriedly said "But this is wrong!"

"Yeah, but it feels right."

Maybe that was true. Mentally and morally speaking, it was so very wrong, but when we were together it felt so right. But that didn't mean I had to give in.

"But Jess and Luke..." I said as his lips neared mine again.

"This isn't about them. Now shut up so I can kiss you." And he did.

I didn't immediately kiss back. I just stood there stiffly. He pulled away and pulled my arms up and put them on his shoulders.

"Hold on to me," he whispered before kissing me again.

His tongue teased mine, daring me to kiss back. I tried my hardest not to kiss him, but his lips on mine was like dangling a steak in front of a hungry dog. Even a well-trained dog would only be able to stand it for so long before he devoured it.

If I kissed back this time though, there would be no going back. I wasn't sure how this would end or with whom, or how many hearts would be broken. I was only sure of the way I was feeling at that moment, which is why I tightened my arms around his neck and kissed Kyle back.

__Chapter Eighteen__

It's been a month since I kissed Kyle back that night, and I've been living a TLC song. I spent the majority of my time with Luke and I loved every minute of it, but I secretly couldn't wait to see Kyle. I felt guilty for stepping out on Luke, but I couldn't help myself. Kyle was a drug and I was the addict. Every time I would try to break it off with Kyle, he would somehow convince me not to, and maybe I didn't really want to, or I would have stuck to my guns.

At work, I really tried to stay professional, but when I would find myself alone with Kyle in his office, I couldn't resist his advances. I would come out looking flustered, but my office mates attributed it to Kyle's remaining ability to occasionally be a big dick.

At least three times a week, Kyle and I would see each other outside of work. We even started going on real dates - way out of the way, of course, where we were unlikely to run into anyone we knew.

Our biggest obstacles were Jessyca and Luke. Kyle's situation was more complicated than my own. I know we aren't living in the 1500's and this isn't a country that practices arranged marriages, but in essence, that is what it was. Jessyca sat on a fortune, as did Kyle, and both of their families owned or had a big stake in very successful and lucrative businesses. Bringing the two families together made it appear the two businesses were together, or have a big chance of coming together. Somehow that translated into more money for both, and sometimes, as in the case of Kyle's parents, the two businesses actually do merge.

While I work for Sterling Corporation, I don't pretend to understand all of that shit I just told you. I just take Kyle's word for it. The bottom line is that he was expected to marry Jess for those reasons, and until he found another way to appease his dad, Jessyca's dad and a bunch of other people things would remain the same.

I didn't just accept this. It wasn't okay with me. In that fourth week of our new "relationship" it spurned a pretty heated argument.

We were in Baltimore for the day, strolling through the aquarium, one of my favorite places. I had always known that his relationship with Jess was more business than love, but I had asked for more explicit details regarding the situation because I was already growing tired of being sneaky. He had just given me the run down.

"So, eventually you will propose." I said rather unkindly.

"I didn't say that. I said that it is expected of me."

"What happens if you just break up with her?"

"You've asked me that before," he said, looking down at the floor.

"You haven't given me a straight answer."

He hesitated, bit down on his bottom lip like he was thinking.

"My father will disown me and find some reason to fire me."

"Is that all?" I almost laughed. "You'd have to go earn a living like a normal person?"

"It's not just that," he looked at me cautiously.

"What else is there?"

"Jess has possession of...some pretty sensitive information."

"Regarding what?"

"Regarding Sterling Corp and some of its business associates."

"Sounds like a lot of trouble. I hope it's not an Enron situation."

"No, but if the information came to light at the wrong time, a lot of shit will go down that no one is prepared to deal with."

"So, Jess is blackmailing you into staying with her?"

"Not exactly. She doesn't know that I know."

I sighed extra loud. "So much drama. How long do you expect to have to play along?"

"I don't know. I can't give you a time frame. Just know that I'm working on it."

"This is ridiculous," I huffed. "I wish I understood the circumstances before I 'committed' to this dysfunctional relationship."

"I gave you an opportunity to back out," he argued.

It was true. That night, after literally sweeping me off of my feet kissing me and whispering sweet things in my ear, he asked while we were having sex on the kitchen table.

"I've been pretty pushy about this," he had said. "If you want to back out, I'll respect that."

Now at the aquarium, I said "You presented that opportunity while we were sexing on the kitchen table! You can't ask me that during an orgasm!"

A mother with three small children gave me a look so dirty I felt like I should wash my mouth out with soap. I apologized and led Kyle away from the cluster fuck of families we were in.

"What do you want me to say, Em?" He threw his hands up.

"If you are going to just propose, why are we doing this?"

"I love you. You love me. We want to be together, and I didn't say I was going to propose."

"What we have isn't togetherness. It's sneakiness," I hissed.

"Well, if you break up with Luke, that will be one less person to worry about."

"Why should I break up with him?" I put my hands on my hips. "Am I supposed to just sit at home alone on the nights you're fucking Jessyca?"

"You have nothing to lose by breaking up with him," he said, and I could hear Kyle the Dick surfacing.

"I would actually lose a lot. He's a good man and cares about me, which is another reason this is so fucked up. He doesn't deserve this."

"Then let him go."

"You're so selfish, Kyle. Maybe I should let you go."

His eyes flashed with anger and he crossed his arms, looking like a real tough guy, but said nothing. He only glared at me.

"And I'm tired of coming to you after being with him, staying up so late. My work - your work - is suffering."

"What do you mean being with him? You're sleeping with him? You told me you weren't."

I bit my bottom lip and watched a young couple a few yards away, holding hands and totally carefree.

"Emmy." He said my name in a way that made me take a startled step back. He was seething with anger and I had not said anything yet.

"I never said I wasn't," I said quietly. "For some stupid reason, you assumed I wasn't sleeping with him and I didn't correct you."

"So if you love me, why would you sleep with him?" That tone again. It was low, but firm, strong, and so infuriated.

"He doesn't know that I have another boyfriend, Kyle. So I can see why he thinks it's okay to sleep with his girlfriend."

"But you know differently." He opened and closed his fists.

I never thought that he was going to hit me, but his anger was unsettling nonetheless. My own anger was about to boil over, though.

"You don't have to make me feel any dirtier than I already feel." Tears threatened to spill out of my eyes.

Stupid tears.

"You're still sleeping with Jessyca, I know you are, and I know you love her. I know it's more than 'just business' like you say. Until you are ready to choose, don't you dare judge me or tell me who I can and cannot see or sleep with."

I walked away from him.

"Where are you going?" he said from a few feet behind me.

"I'm going home." I glanced over my shoulder at him. "Alone."

"I'm not ready to leave," he said it as if that gave him some kind of control, which made me angrier.

"Stop following me."

"How are you going to get home?" He didn't ask out of concern. He was taunting me.

I stopped and turned around. He almost ran into me.

"I know you think I'm inferior, Kyle, but I'm not incompetent. Dick."

He looked surprised, started to speak, but I walked away. This time he didn't follow.

It was well over an hour before my phone started blowing up. I sent each of his calls straight to voicemail. He texted several times, too, but I didn't answer them either.

I was lucky enough to find a train to Philly. I didn't care if Kyle was angry or worried. We have had disagreements in the past, and once at work when he was in a sour mood, I told him off in front of Eliza. It was a work related situation, but it's not something I would have done before we started our affair.

I refused to cry, even though I had a strong urge to do so. I intended to stay angry so that I could break this shit off. I really did have strong feelings for Kyle but I couldn't continue down this path. It wasn't going to end well for me.

In a cab back in Jersey, I finally answered one of thirty-three of Kyle's text messages (he called forty-seven times, I shit you not. Who does that!).

I'm in Jerze for now. I don't want to see you or talk to you right now.

Whether or not he answered, I don't know. I turned my phone off. When I got home, I quickly packed a bag and left before Kyle could show up. I couldn't just lock him out since I was stupid enough to give him a key.

Stupid Emmy.

***

I decided that I needed to get a lot of stuff off of my chest. I turned my phone on long enough to again lie to Luke.

Having phone issues. Will call you soon. Xoxo

"What is that?" Donya pointed at my duffel bag.

"I need to stay here for a night, maybe two." I said, walking past her into her house.

"Is your crazy mom in town already? There should be posters up across the county to warn people she's coming."

"It's not my mom, but if it helps you and the rest of the county to know, she will be here the first week of June."

"That's good to know. What are you doing here?" She wasn't being mean. Donya was always straight forward.

"I have proverbial skeletons in my proverbial closet." I said with a heavy sigh.

We sat down on her couch. I propped my feet up on her coffee table and sighed again.

"I'm sleeping with Kyle."

"Your boss? The dick?" She gaped at me. "Shut up!"

"Okay. Reactions like that...not helping."

"I'm sorry, but...damn, Emmy!"

"Not helping!"

"Okay, okay. I will try to contain myself through your story." She stared at me expectantly.

"Okay. It all started the Thursday night before that big storm, in December."

"That far back? Shut up!"

I glared at her. She quickly apologized.

"It started that Thursday, at the bar..."

It took me awhile to sort through the sordid details aloud, and even though D didn't yell "shut up" anymore, she still asked a lot of questions.

"Wow," she said when I had finished.

"I feel like such a dirty whore," I said, unable to keep the trembling out of my voice. I didn't stop myself from crying this time.

D rubbed my back for a few minutes, letting me cry.

"Emmy, you're not a whore," she said softly. "Whores get paid."

"Kyle's my boss. Technically, he's paying me."

She looked thoughtful. "You're right. You are a dirty whore."

Chapter Nineteen

"I love how Lafayette is always calling someone a bitch," I said, with a mouthful of ice-cream.

Donya was doing homework on the living room floor while I had myself a True Blood marathon.

"Bitch, shut up. I'm doing my homework."

"Sookie's a pussy though. She's always screaming. Stop screaming, bitch!"

Donya gave me a death stare, so I didn't say anymore. She was in her final semester of school, majoring in business. Before starting college three years before, she was a model. Not a small time model, but a world class model. She's modeled for Versace, Oscar De Lorenta, Dior, Dolce and Gabanna, Marc Jacobs, and more. She's been in all of the top magazines and even graced the cover of a few. D has been in movies and on various television shows. She's been all over the world, has met and befriended all sorts of influential people and celebrities. She was the most beautiful person I knew with her long legs, perfect, yet unusual face and chocolate brown skin.

An agent had found her on the boardwalk as she walked beside her ordinary, plain friend (me), eating cotton candy when we were only 15. The agent said she even ate her cotton candy like a model.

I was lucky enough to go with her to Paris, London, or meet her in Italy or Australia, and of course at a few locations in the U.S like Hawaii or L.A. She didn't always have time to actually hang with me, and she was often overwhelmed, stressed out and frazzled or even down right depressed. The designers were often extremely picky and obnoxious, although they deserve to be. Their fashion was their art and it should be displayed how they wanted it. One time a designer not to be named told her she looked bloated and fat and sent her off of the set. I had felt so bad for her, but she shrugged it off and said it wasn't the worse thing that's been said to her.

On her 28th birthday, Donya stopped taking work. She finished any contracts and followed through on prior commitments, but hung up her runway shoes when all was done.

"I want to quit while I'm still good at what I do. I don't want to be a washed up has been." She explained on the phone to me from Japan.

"You lead such a fabulous life, though," I said.

"I lead a lonely life, E. I want to have a somewhat normal life. I want a family, a permanent home and a minivan."

I gasped. "Now you're going too far. A minivan? Unbelievable."

"I knew that would hit you hard. Anyway, I gotta go, but in a few months I will be free and I get to spend more time with you and my family. Girl, I even miss your nutty mama."

"Now I know that job is making you crazy. Call me when you get to India."

That was three years ago. D had earned enough money to take care of herself for a very long time, but she was frugal with it, and still worked part time. She found the man of her dreams, Jerry who happened to be a major league baseball player. They lived well below their means and stayed under the radar, which was admirable. They agreed that when they started having kids, they would buy the big house and big cars. They lived a fairy tale life, like my parents and siblings.

There was a knock at the door. Donya looked at the door as if just by looking at it the person on the other side would go away. When the knock came again, I said "I don't think they can feel your death stare through the door."

She threw down her pencil and got up to open the door. "Get your boots off my table," she told me before opening the door.

I was wearing a black skirt and a pair of Louis Vuitton boots, taken from D's closet. So technically, she wanted her boots off of her table. I wanted to live another day, so I didn't argue the particulars.

"Hi, Donya?" I heard Kyle's voice. I froze with the spoon in my mouth. "I'm Kyle. Is Em here?" He sounded really hopeful.

I was hoping that she would say no and slam the door in his face. Instead she said "How did you get my address?"

"Samantha Grayne."

"Son of a bitch." Donya stomped away from the door, but left it wide open. She snatched her cell off of the coffee table and quickly found the number she was looking for. "Sam! Why are you giving my address out to complete strangers?" She yelled at my mom. "I don't care if he's the pope! I don't know him!"

She walked out of the living room, arguing with my mom like I would. Donya was an extension of my family, so there was nothing disturbing about her behavior towards my mom. If circumstances were different I would have laughed, but as it was, Kyle was standing before me. I still had the stupid spoon in my mouth.

He didn't say anything, but he sat down on the couch next to me. He took the spoon from my mouth, put it in the bowl I was holding and put them on the coffee table. Before I could object, he kissed me. I jerked away before I could fall under his spell.

"You can't hurt me like that and then make it up by kissing me," I said bitterly.

"I'm sorry," he whispered and kissed me again. I pulled away again.

"No, Kyle! Go home. Go back to Jess."

He winced, but didn't back away.

"Fine. I'll leave." I jumped off of the couch before he could stop me. "D I'm leaving!" I called out.

She came out of her room, still holding the phone. She and Kyle both watched me as I cursed trying to get into my jacket and dig out my keys.

"I'll get my stuff later," I told her.

As I opened the door, I heard her ask Kyle "Where the hell is she going?"

"I don't know."

I slammed the door and ran to my car. As I pulled away, I was surprised that Kyle had not come out behind me. I sped through Cherry Hill, intent on going home but reconsidered and took a detour.

I was feeling so angry and the pain from our argument also felt fresh. I was feeling such a broad range of emotions, I thought I was losing my sanity.

How dare he think he can make up with me so easily! What made him think that I would just let it go and fall back into his arms? And to track me down and come to Donya's door - what balls!

Life would be so much easier if I just let him go.

***

I didn't have to wait for him as long as I thought I would. He must have known that I wouldn't go home, because he walked through the door of his apartment only a few minutes after me.

I had parked in the visitor's area, not far from his parking space, but he would never think to look for my car there. I have had a key to his apartment since soon after I started working for him. He had left his briefcase at home and was in an important meeting. I had to go get it for him. After that, he made sure I had a key and every now and then I would have to use it.

He didn't notice me right away. He put his keys down on the table by the door and took his coat off. I came out of the dark kitchen and into the light of the living room.

"Shit," he said when he saw me.

"I'm rarely allowed to be here incase Jess comes by. You invade my life on every level and I can't even spend the afternoon in your home." I sniffed and quickly wiped away a tear. "That makes me feel like trash. I let you into my home whenever you feel like it, and the circumstances are the same. Luke could show up anytime and I take that risk. You're hardly risking anything. You're so careful that you don't get caught, but have no concerns about me getting caught."

He sighed and looked at the floor, but said nothing.

"That's what I thought." I said after a minute. I wiped my tears and I took his key off of my key ring and threw it on the coffee table.

He was standing in front of the door and once he realized I was going to leave he stood up a little straighter. I boldly moved towards the door, but he put his hands on my shoulders when I tried to go around him.

"Kyle, let me go."

"No way. If you leave now I know you won't ever come back to me."

"If Jess shows up you're going to have a problem," I gave an exasperated sigh.

"I want you to be here." He held onto me tighter when I again tried to leave.

"I can't be here, because of Jess," I said lamely.

"I don't give a fuck about Jess right now!" he roared.

I stared at him, startled. He put his hands on my face and apologized.

"I'm sorry. I'm sorry. I didn't mean to yell. I just don't care about that right now. I really don't want you to go."

I took a few steps back out of his reach, and crossed my arms.

"Kyle, let me go."

"I don't want you to leave," he said pathetically.

"I mean...let me go."

He stared at me and shook his head.

"I can't." He took a step towards me.

"You have to, because I am letting you go," I said softly.

"No." He shook his head.

"Yes." I started around him for the door again.

"No!" He grabbed me by my wrists.

"Kyle, let go!" He did and I looked at him as if he was crazy. Maybe he was and I trapped myself here with him.

"Emmy, please," he pleaded, stepping towards me again. He again cradled my face in his hands and then kissed me. I pulled away.

"Kyle! You can't make everything okay with a fucking kiss!"

As if he didn't hear me, he tried to kiss me again. I slapped him hard across the face. My hand hurt from hitting him and I wasn't sure how he was going to react but I stood my ground. He looked a little stunned for a few seconds but shook it off.

Too quick for me to react, he threw me over his shoulder. I yelled at him and punched him in the back as I tried to get down, but he didn't put me down until we reached his bedroom. He threw me on the bed and pinned me down.

I started to scream, but he quickly covered my mouth. He didn't say anything, he just stared at me. He held me down easily and I fought for a long time before I relented and went slack.

He waited until he knew I wasn't going to scream and uncovered my mouth.

"I didn't mean to hurt you," he said. "You're not trash and I don't want to let you go. I will try harder to find a way to make things right, but I don't want you to go."

I didn't speak right away. I wasn't sure what to say or how to feel. Part of me wanted to leave and never come back and another part of me wanted to believe him.

When I still didn't say anything after a while, he gave me a closed mouth kiss while keeping his eyes locked with mine. When he tried for a more serious kiss, I turned my head. Aggravated, he forced my head back and kissed me more aggressively than he's ever kissed me.

I really fought it at first, but the truth was he knew what he was doing. I was a huge sucker for his kisses. From day one, whenever he kissed me he would disarm me completely. No one had ever kissed me the way that Kyle kissed me. Not Luke, not anyone. That's why I kept trying to get away every time he would try.

The more I relented, the harder he kissed me. I involuntarily moaned a little and pushed my body into his. He took my arms and pinned them above my head without ever taking his lips from mine. He pressed himself against me and moaned into my mouth.

I struggled against him as he became more aggressive, but I didn't want him to stop. He used one hand to hold my wrists down and with the other he tore open my shirt. I heard buttons hitting the bed, the wall, and who knew what else. I cried out in pain when he initially grabbed at my breast but then I sighed with pleasure.

He slid his hand down my stomach and then between my legs. He went around my panties and sent me into a frenzy. He was being so rough, but I was enjoying it.

He started to fumble around with his belt and jeans, never releasing my wrists with his other hand. Once he freed himself, he again reached between my legs and tore my panties off of me. He entered me with such force I was pushed half a foot across the bed. He released my hands long enough to pull me back to the edge of the bed and again pinned me down as he slid into me again.

I really thought we were going to break the bed because we were going at it so hard. He used both hands to pin my arms now and the harder he squeezed my wrists, the closer I knew he was getting. Just when I thought he was about to break my wrists, he moaned my name and it was over.

Chapter Twenty

Luke lazily caressed my bare leg. We were relaxing in his bed reading. He was reading a paperback and I was reading on my Kindle, but Luke had put his book down and turned his attention on me. I was wearing a pair of boy shorts and a tee shirt, my standard sleeping gear in warm weather.

I liked sleeping at Luke's. I could get completely comfortable without any concerns of another woman walking in and wondering why I was there or why I was in bed with her boyfriend. It had become like a second home, which was really important since my parents' return from Louisiana. Whenever I felt like punching my mom I went to Luke's. I had clothes there, a toothbrush, deodorant and other necessities.

"I love hairy legs on my woman," Luke said, still caressing my leg. "I love getting my fingers all tangled in your long, coarse leg hair."

"Stop!" I smacked him with his book. "I just haven't felt like shaving."

"At least your legs will be warm and protected when it rains."

I gave him the most evil stare I could muster and then went back to my book.

"How is your book?" he asked, resting his head on my lap.

I ran a hand through his light hair and sighed a happy sigh.

"Amanda Hocking is my hero," I said about the author I recently discovered after Luke gave me the Kindle as a gift. "I want to have her babies," I said dreamily.

"Well, that sure ruins my plans."

"What plans?" I put the Kindle on the table next to the bed.

"I was hoping maybe you would want to someday have my babies." When I looked surprised, he said "I didn't mean like tomorrow or next year, but someday."

I stared at him and shifted uncomfortably. He sat up and looked at me, but I couldn't meet his eyes.

"I'm sorry. I didn't realize you felt so differently than I do..." He looked so deflated and I instantly felt bad.

"Oh, no. It's not that." I turned to look at him. I couldn't tell him the main reason I reacted that way, but I could tell him something else that was true. "I'm just not sure that I would be a good mother..."

"What? You would be an excellent mother. You're nurturing, caring, and responsible."

I winced at "responsible." My actions over the past several months were not responsible. To cover my reaction, I smiled and said "You know I drink way too much."

"You don't drink and drive, you don't drink at work, and you know your limit. I've never seen you out of control. Besides, I haven't seen you pick up a drink in weeks."

Oh, you poor man. I've been out of control for months.

"Now that my mom is back, that may change." I rolled my eyes, but Luke took me into his arms.

"You can come here whenever you want to get away from that old bag."

"Thanks," I laughed.

"And while we're on the subject..."

"What's up, doc?" I looked up into his face, which had grown serious.

"I'm thinking of moving back to Chicago, and soon."

"What?" I broke free of his embrace so I could look at him better. I must have looked as stricken as I felt, because he put his hands up as if to calm me down.

"I want you to come with me," he said in a rush. "I mean, you don't have to decide right now."

"Oh," I said softly. "How long?"

"By October, at the latest." He took my hands in his. "I really want to be with you, but my family is in crisis and they need me. And to be honest, I need them, too."

I nodded in agreement. His family did need him. His parents were way older than my own and needed looking after. He had two sisters, but not only did they have their own families to worry about, one of them just found out she had cancer. I felt really bad for reacting the way I did.

"I understand," I said. "I promise to deeply consider it."

"I'm going home in two weeks for a few days. Think you can get away?"

I considered it a moment. I had plenty of vacation time saved up and even if I didn't I wasn't worried about losing money. Kyle was a problem. He was insanely jealous of Luke.

"I'll go," I said, deciding that Kyle couldn't be my first priority.

Luke grinned and kissed me. I locked my fingers behind his head and pulled him closer. I had told my mom I would be home for dinner, but once Luke slipped his hand under my shirt I didn't feel confident about making it on time.

<u>Chapter Twenty-One</u>

I did make it to dinner on time. My mom was her usual annoying self, but for the most part I was able to tune her out. My mind was already heavily weighing on Luke's proposal. I could decide to go, and it would be the end of the triangle I was in, but the thought of letting Kyle go made my chest ache.

"You're not paying any attention to anything I'm saying!" My mom's voice snapped me out of my thoughts.

"Sorry. What did you say?"

She sighed dramatically and rolled her eyes. "I said I wish you would consider coming back with us in the fall. I hate that you're up here all alone."

"I'm not alone, trust me." If only she really knew how much I was never alone.

"Yes, I know you have Luke and you've become friendly with your boss, but you ain't got no family here."

"I have cousins and aunts and uncles."

"I meant none that you talk to."

"I talk to Mayson all of the time and sometimes I may run into Tabitha at the store."

"You know what I mean!" she snapped.

I put my fork down and looked from her to my dad. "If you guys want me to move out of the house so you can stay down there, just say so."

Now my dad put down his fork and looked at me. "No one is saying that, Emmy. We would never make you leave here if you didn't want to."

My mom looked at my dad with a look of surprise. "I am saying that!"

"Oh for crying out loud," he grumbled, throwing down his napkin. I pushed my plate away and crossed my arms.

"I'm too damn old and tired to be coming back and forth," my mom pouted. "I would rather use this time to maybe take a cruise or visit my cousins in France."

"News flash, mother," I said. "You don't have to keep coming back and forth. I can take care of the house just fine."

"If we didn't come up here, no one would ever see ya!" she said in a high pitched voice. "You never come down to see us or the rest of the family."

I couldn't argue that point, because she was right. I didn't feel all that close to my siblings or their kids, but it very well could have been my own fault.

"Fine. If you want me to move out, I will." I got up and carried my plate to the sink and started stuffing the contents into the disposal.

"You don't have to go anywhere," my dad said to me, and then to my mom he said "She doesn't have to go anywhere. If you're too tired to come back and forth then stay in Louisiana."

"What are you going to do if I decide to move further away?" I asked my mom. "Not visit me? Is that all I have to do to be rid of your incessant nagging?"

She wrinkled her nose at me. "You're a devil of a child."

"I'm thinking of moving to Chicago," I announced. "With Luke. In October."

They both looked at me quietly for a moment. My mom tried to be casual, but failed.

"Will you be moving there as a married woman?"

"No," I said defiantly.

"You're gonna live in sin?" she shrieked.

"Oh stop it!" I yelled. "Don't act like you're all about that because you're not."

"What are you doing wrong? You should have a marriage proposal by now! Not a wanna-live-together proposal!" She slapped the table.

"Samantha!" my dad yelled.

"She's thirty-one years old and isn't even close to bein' married! Maybe you need a makeover. I can send you to New York and you can get your hair done so it won't be so plain."

"She is fine the way she is." My dad was trying to be patient.

Ignoring him, my mom continued on. "You can get a new wardrobe - a good one. You can go to the gym and maybe work some of that belly off."

"Are you finished insulting me yet?" I asked quietly.

"Is it the sex?" Her eyes widened and even as my dad tried again to stop her mouth, she talked over him. "There are books you can buy and maybe you can be better in bed. Maybe you need all of it - the make-over, the clothes, the gym, and the sex stuff."

"That's enough!" my dad boomed. My mom jumped and even I was a little startled.

"Thank god I have some confidence in myself, because if I had to depend on my own mother I would be in sore shape," I said bitterly and stormed out of the kitchen.

Later that night when I met Kyle for ice-cream, I was still fuming from my mom's idiocy, and at the same time I was trying to think of a way to tell him I was going away with Luke.

"You're quiet," Kyle said, looking at me carefully. "What's up?"

"Nothing," I said quickly. I was tapping my spoon on the table instead of digging into my sundae, and under the table my leg bounced.

"You're quietly freaking out, I can tell. What's going on?"

"You mean in addition to this four way love story?" I asked, irritated.

"Forget it," he said, tossing his own spoon down.

"Don't ask me stupid questions."

"Whatever. Are we done here?"

I put my spoon down as a response. Kyle rolled his eyes as he pulled out his wallet. He threw some cash on the table and we left the ice-cream there to melt.

Chapter Twenty-Two

I don't know what my problem was. I was so distracted by the current events of my life I could not function correctly, even at work which I tried hard to keep separate from my personal life. That wasn't an easy feat since one of my boyfriends was also my boss and the other one worked a few floors down.

Monday morning after our failed ice-cream social, I still wasn't really in the mood to deal with Kyle. He wasn't much in the mood to speak to me either judging by his extra dickness.

My sulkiness came to a head that Thursday. I had been taking constant bull from my mom all week and even though Kyle attempted to make up with me, I couldn't get my shit together. Luke was giving me a hard time because I still had not asked for time off and our trip to Chicago was only days away.

"Just forget about it," he had said, not really trying hard to hide his anger. We were in the elevator on our way into work.

"I'm sorry, okay? I've been distracted."

"Clearly! For once, I want you to focus on me and not..." For a half a second, I thought he was going to say Kyle's name. "Forget it." He glared at me for a moment and then stepped off of the elevator and didn't look back before the doors slid shut.

I was thinking about that and other things while I stood at the shredder, shredding a pile of documents.

"What are you doing?" Kyle said, suddenly at my side. "Please tell me that's not the Carlton-Lauglin paperwork."

"What?" I stared at him. "You told me to get rid of it."

"I said to get rid of the Happerson documents!" he yelled. "Why would I tell you to destroy documents of our biggest current client?"

We were in a small room away from the main office, but I was sure someone probably overheard.

Kyle opened the door to the shredder and picked up a pile of shredded paper and held it before me.

"This deal was about to close and you have single handedly set it back by weeks, and that's if they don't back out again or try to change shit because there's no paperwork for them to sign tomorrow!"

"I'm sorry," I said stupidly, but then blinked out of my stupor. "I still have it backed up on a few CDs."

"How long is it going to take you to get all of that shit together again, Emmy?" He threw the shredded paper into a trash can and walked out of the room.

I took the rest of the file and after a few deep breaths went to my desk. Looking through the CDs I realized that it was going to take a while. I delegated my daily responsibilities to a few other people in the office and gathered the CDs and the rest of my things. I would get more done in one of the private offices reserved for traveling associates. I wouldn't be disturbed by anyone and I would have more work space.

After closing the door to the available office I found on the next floor down, I let myself cry for a moment, but only a moment because I had a lot of work to do. I worked through lunch, through the afternoon and evening. Eliza brought me some dinner, but didn't stay and distract me. No one else came by or texted or called, which was sad, but I was too busy to worry about it.

Somehow I had pushed myself to stay up all night and work. When I finally finished, it was a little after ten in the morning. I looked like hell and I knew it. My dress was wrinkled and looked sloppy on me. My hair was tangled, my eyes were bloodshot, and I needed a shower. I walked into Kyle's office and put the time sensitive documents in front of him.

He looked at me and then at the stack of files.

"I'm taking a vacation, effective immediately," I said tiredly. "Eliza is perfectly capable of doing my job while I am gone."

He sighed and rubbed his eyes. "I agree you need some time off, but what is going on with you?" He was asking as my boss, not my boyfriend.

"I'm just distracted. I'll feel better when I get back."

He got up from his desk and closed the door. He came and stood in front of me, but didn't touch me.

"You worked on that all day and night?" He nodded at the files.

"Of course I did. It was my fault."

He reached out and rubbed my cheek with the back of his hand, back in boyfriend mode.

"I am sorry I yelled at you," he said softly.

I let him touch me for a moment, but then stepped back toward the door.

"It's fine. I was wrong. I need to get some sleep."

"Okay." He was obviously hurt by me pulling away, and it really pulled at my own heart. "Are you just going to hang out with D or at home? Maybe we can do something fun."

"Actually..." I bit my lip.

His eyes widened and then narrowed. "You're doing something with Luke?"

"I'm going to Chicago with him for the week," I said carefully.

Kyle's face fell into a million pieces. I couldn't stand to look at his face a second longer, so I opened the door and rushed to the elevator. I didn't have time to consider Kyle's feelings or my own, because it was only seconds to Luke's floor. I found him in his office, working so diligently he didn't look up when I walked in. He assumed I was his secretary Tracy.

"Not Tracy," I said, making him look up at me, surprised.

"Forgive me for saying so, but you look like crap."

"Forgiven and I agree. I worked all night in a spare office. Listen, I want to apologize," I started, but he cut me off as he stood up and came over to me.

"No, I should be apologizing to you." He took my hands into his. "I shouldn't have talked to you that way."

"It's totally understandable. I came here to ask if it's too late to go with you Sunday."

He grinned and then gave me a slow kiss. When he released me, he said "I get to kiss your morning breath mouth every morning for a week."

I hugged him tight, but not so far back in my mind I thought about the expression on Kyle's face. I hoped he would be okay. Hell. I hoped I would be okay.

Chapter Twenty-Three

We arrived in Chicago late in the afternoon. We checked into our hotel before heading to Luke's parents' house for a quiet dinner. I was nervous about meeting his family and kept asking him questions like "What if they don't like my hair? What if they think it's too Jersey?" and "What if they don't like me?"

"They're going to love you," Luke had promised. "It's not like you to be so nervous."

"It's not every day I fly half way across the country to meet my boyfriend's family." I sighed and sat down on the edge of the bed. "Maybe I'm just a little wound up from traveling. I get cranky when I travel."

He leaned over me, kissed my lips and whispered "Let me help you unwind."

I let him push me back on the bed as he kissed me. He pushed up my skirt and pulled my panties down. I unbuttoned his jeans and pulled them down just enough to let his monstrous penis out. I guided him until he was inside of me.

Nothing like a quickie before we go off to meet the parents.

Grace Kessler baked an apple pie for my visit. I was flattered and fattened, because I think I ate more pie than anyone else. My mother was the best cook and baker I knew, but even her pie couldn't compete with Mrs. Kessler's pie. I was in pie heaven.

"You really like that pie," Luke whispered to me while his Mom poured us some coffee.

"If I had to choose between you and the pie…" I sighed and shook my head.

"I'd rather you choose pie over me rather than another guy," he said with a smile, but I saw a hint of something else in his eyes I couldn't place. It made me uncomfortable for a little while.

Luke's mother was disappointed that we would not be staying in her home during our visit. Luke explained that there would be several late nights for us and we didn't want to disturb them, but what he told me was slightly different.

"I don't feel comfortable with my parents hearing you scream my name," he had said, grabbing my ass.

Luke's sisters immediately treated me as part of the family. Lena, the oldest one, and the sister with cancer, handed me her baby within moments of meeting me.

"I really gotta pee and it's hard to pee holding a baby," she said and rushed off.

"She looks so healthy," I whispered to Luke.

"Yeah, well you know, she won't always look that way," he said sadly.

Lena had the same light brown hair Luke had, and the same shocking blue eyes. She was a thick woman, boisterous looking and lively, like her personality.

"You look good with that baby." Luke grinned.

I forced a smile. The baby, a little girl, wasn't even six months old yet and her mom had cancer. Lena also had two other small children. I felt bad for Lena's family. What would happen to them if she didn't make it? Her husband worked hard to keep them comfortable. How would he work and take care of the family? No wonder Luke felt he needed to be there. I looked over at Luke and felt an overwhelming sense of appreciation for him.

The other sister Lorraine had six kids of her own. Lorraine was pretty, but looked a little frazzled. I guess with six kids, anyone would look frazzled. We had visited her first but didn't stay long. Four of the kids were sick and she was very busy. Besides, I definitely didn't want any kiddy sicknesses.

Despite the health issues and other typical family drama, Luke's family was great. They were close and kind to one another, and even if they did fight they made up quickly. His dad was a little boisterous, but made me laugh, and he really appreciated and loved his only son. His mom wasn't anything like my mom. She was meek and treated her children with dignity and they treated her the same way. It made me sad to not have a very close relationship with my own siblings and to have a mother who thought so lowly of me.

We didn't spend our entire time with his family. Luke took me out to museums and bars and to meet his friends. I had a much better time than I ever expected. More importantly, I fit in well with his life in Chicago. I felt at home immediately and I was sad to leave, especially Lena who I connected with more than anyone.

As much as I knew I fit in with Luke and his life, on the flight home I couldn't stop thinking of Kyle. Throughout the week I had a gnawing ache for him, but the ache only intensified the closer we got to home. I had not spoken to him since the night before I left. We met in a Wal-Mart parking lot that was the half-way point between our homes. We stood a few feet apart, both of us feeling uneasy.

"Are you all packed?" he had asked with his hands jammed into his pockets.

"Yeah. I never go anywhere anymore so it took me some time to get it right - at least I hope it's right."

He nodded and stared at the ground between us. I shifted from one foot to the other. I was still on edge after everything that had happened that week.

"Do you have to go?" he asked.

"I want to go, Kyle. You shouldn't make me feel guilty for it. That's really not fair."

"I'm sorry," he said.

"Maybe we should..." I bit my lip and looked at the customers going in and out of the behemoth store, oblivious to us and our problems. I wished I was oblivious.

"Maybe we should what?" he pushed. "What?"

"Maybe we should stop this." I said quietly, and it hurt to say it.

"Is that what you want?"

"What I want is apparently irrelevant, but maybe this is best."

We were quiet for a long time. Finally, he said "I don't want to make any decisions right now. I want you to go to Chicago and have a good time."

I looked at him with suspicion, but he said it again. "I won't bother you while you're there and you don't have to feel obligated to contact me."

After more discussion, I agreed. He kissed me and held me for a long time that night.

***

As soon as I got home from Chicago I texted Kyle. After a brief exchange of texts, I took a quick shower and drove to his apartment. He was waiting for me when I got into the lobby. At first I thought he was just that excited to see me, but the look on his face wasn't that of excitement.

"What's wrong?" I asked immediately.

"Jess. She just showed up minutes ago. She was supposed to be in the Hamptons."

"Okay," I said and started to leave.

"Wait. I can get rid of her I think or tell her I need to go to the office."

I sighed and rolled my eyes. "I'm really not in the mood for this tonight. I'm going home. I'll just see you at work on Monday."

"Em, wait." He grabbed my arm. "What about tomorrow?"

"I think I'm going to stay in and hang with my dad tomorrow." That wasn't my original plan, but I suddenly didn't feel much like talking to any other man. "Besides, what's another day?"

"But I really miss you. I really want to see you."

"Not enough," I said softly and left him standing there.

Chapter Twenty-Four

I dialed Luke's number and counted off the rings. It went to voicemail after the fourth ring like it did the other six times I called.

"How many times are you going to call him?" Kyle asked, irritated.

"Until he answers," I said, ignoring his attitude. I chewed on my lower lip, worried.

I was in California with Kyle for three days. Truly, it was mostly business, but at the end of the working day, it was just us. No work, no Jess, and no Luke, but Luke wasn't answering my phone calls. My departure from his house the night before my trip did not go well.

"I don't understand why you need to go," he had argued when he found out about the business trip.

"It's part of my job. Sometimes I have to travel with my boss. It's not the first time."

Before I even had eyes for Kyle, I went away with him twice. It was hell and I stayed as far away from him as my work would let me. This time it would be different, but Luke didn't need to know that.

"Why can't he take Eliza?"

"Eliza isn't qualified," I said absent mindedly. I was working at the kitchen table.

"How qualified do you have to be to look pretty and follow your boss around like a servant for three days?"

I looked up at him. "It's not like that."

"It is exactly like that. You're there specifically to wait on him hand and foot. It looks good to the clients, except in your case it's an incentive that you're good looking."

"I actually happen to know a lot about the business and about the clients," I argued. "You make it seem like I'm just a dumb bimbo."

"No one is going to ask or care for your opinions."

I stared at him. He was being such a dick.

"You're being such a dick," I said out loud.

"You don't have to go."

"I do have to go, Luke," I sighed, rolling my eyes.

"Lawyer, remember?" He pointed to himself. "It's not in your job description to go anywhere with Kyle."

"Okay, so you being an attorney makes you smarter than me?"

"I didn't say that. I am just very knowledgeable of the employment policies in the company."

"So, what? You want me to tell Kyle I can't go?"

"Yes."

"You're on crack."

"I tolerate all of the time you spend with him here, but going away with him is unacceptable."

"All of what time?"

He gave me a knowing look, and when I looked at him with a blank expression, he growled.

"You 'work late' with him at least twice a week, and you two go drinking at the bar often."

"Would you like to go drinking with us at the bar, Luke?" I asked contritely.

"I don't want to hang out with that dickhead."

"Then you want me to stop hanging out with the dickhead?"

"Actually, yeah."

I stared at him with my mouth slightly open. When all we could do is glare at each other, I saved my work and started packing up my laptop.

"What are you doing?" he demanded.

"I can't work here. I need quiet, and since it's impossible for you to shut the hell up, I guess I need to leave."

He followed me through his tiny house as I collected some of my things.

"Where are you going to go? To Kyle's?" he asked tauntingly.

"What is wrong with you?" I snapped after several more similar comments.

"If you were half as smart as you say you are, you'd have that figured out already." He picked up his keys and started out the door. "Lock up my house when you go."

The door slammed behind him and I stood there for a few seconds, shocked and anxious. By the time I had enough sense to go after him, he was gone.

I gave Luke the rest of the night and the following day to cool off, but after all business was conducted for the day, I called him three times, and three more times on the second day. I never got an answer or a call back. He answered a couple of my text messages, but they were short and cold.

My mood was not at all cheery. I couldn't enjoy the fact that I was in L.A or my alone time with Kyle, and Kyle was losing his patience with my unhappy attitude. We ended up fighting for almost the entire trip. The flight home was silent between us. When we landed, we went our separate ways with few words. Now both of my boyfriends were mad at me, and what was worse was that I had to go home to my mother.

Ugh.

When I stepped outside of the terminal to hail a cab, I saw a familiar face on the sidewalk approaching me.

"I thought you could use a ride home, if your boss doesn't mind."

"My boss left already," I said.

His eyes narrowed and he took a deep breath to try to shake away some of his anger.

"What a standup guy," he muttered and took my bag from me.

"Wait," I said, stopping him. "I'm not going anywhere with you if you're going to be all growly and mad. I'd rather risk my life with a crazy cab driver."

Luke sighed and looked like he was really trying to find a way to calm down.

"I will be...cordial."

"Cordial? Really..."

I really had no right to give him a difficult time. This was ultimately all of my fault, and his anger was just one of many results of my dumb actions, but that didn't mean I had to sit in a car with him for a half hour if he was just going to treat me like dirt.

"I'm really trying here," he said a little less harshly.

I sighed and relented. He was a little less angry when we arrived at his house and he threw me on the bed and gave me an angry screwing, relieving much of his tension.

I hit the shower afterward, much needed after a day of travel and then angry sex. When I came out of the shower, my stomach dropped. Luke was holding some lacey undergarments that had been packed away in my bag.

"What did you need these for?" he asked darkly, clutching a pair of red, lacey underwear and a matching bra.

"To wear," I said it as if it were obvious, but they were items a girl definitely wears to get laid, not items a girl wears for a long day of work.

"For whom?"

"For myself," I said as casually as possible and rooted through a drawer for some clothes.

"Doesn't seem like something you wear unless you're trying to impress someone."

"Am I not allowed to feel pretty under my work clothes?"

He sighed and dropped them back in the bag.

"Is there anything...you think I should know?"

Here was my opportunity to come out with it all, to tell the truth and spare the grief that will surely come from waiting too damn long to tell him I've betrayed him. Pain was inevitable, but this was my chance to somewhat lessen the blow.

I opened my mouth to speak...and chickened out.

"Just know that I missed you," I said, wrapping my arms around him. "And know that I love you and I don't ever want to be without you."

Reluctantly, he held me, and then less reluctantly, he threw me on the bed again for round two.

Chapter Twenty-Five

Before my trip to California, Luke and I had minor disagreements and a couple of heated arguments over things I can't even remember now, but life always reset itself and it was never long before the argument was left in the past, forgotten. After my trip to California, nothing was ever the same again.

Arguments disrupted peaceful Sunday afternoons. Silence replaced conversation during meals. Kisses goodbye fell away to slammed doors and abruptly ended phone calls. It was breaking my heart, but then again, I could only point the finger at myself.

A stronger, less selfish woman would have been forthright. She would have told Kyle to fuck off, admitted her transgressions to Luke and begged his forgiveness. A stronger woman would not have found herself in this situation to begin with. I was weak and selfish. Getting rid of Kyle was like going into detox. Letting go of Luke was like kicking a puppy. Maybe drowning a puppy.

I was in an endless, sick cycle. I was unable and unwilling to make important decisions, allowing myself to be stretched thin between the two men. I didn't need a soothsayer to tell me this was not going to end well for me.

Sometimes I would sit alone in my bedroom, mentally beating the shit out of myself. I entered into my current state with no thought about how I would exit. At times, I foolishly believed that either Luke or Kyle would give up with ease, wish me well, and move on with their heart intact. Sometimes I imagined that I would choose one of them, but we would all become good friends. So many happy endings in my idiot head.

Summer floated on in slow motion. Not much changed between Kyle and me; meanwhile I felt Luke drifting further and further away from me. He still kissed me with everything he had. He still tried to treat me with honor and respect, and he still told me he loved me, and I believed it. But I could feel him slipping anyway.

I woke up one morning and knew that I had to tell Luke the truth, even if it meant losing him. Everyone always deserves the honesty of the people they love.

Luke was out of town for work that day, and he didn't expect to be back until late in the evening. I wasn't going to tell him over the phone or through text messages. I wanted to tell him face to face. I was supposed to go away with Donya for the weekend. Jerry had a double header in Florida, but she called me a few hours before our flight.

"Yeah, I'm not going," she said casually.

"What? Why? I'm all packed!"

"We had a fight. He doesn't deserve my support. He can roast down there with his teammates."

"Wow. Harsh."

"He'll be fine."

"What about the tickets? There's no way you're getting your money back."

"Eh. There's more money in the bank," she said, her tone bored, but I knew my friend was irritated.

"That's so wasteful," I sighed. "At least have the decency to give the tickets to someone less fortunate."

"Hmm. My cousin Kera is less fortunate."

"D, butt ugliness does not count for less fortunate."

"Do you want me to give away the tickets or not!" she snapped.

"Yeah okay, sheesh. Give them to Kera."

"You wanna do something else? Maybe Vegas? We haven't done Vegas in a while."

"No. I'm actually glad you canceled. I want to come clean with Luke. He's not home now, but I figured I'd go over there and make him a nice dinner."

"Do you think a nice dinner is going to cover your ass, Emmy?" Donya asked. "Seriously?"

"No, but I hope it helps."

"And what about the other one?"

"What about him?"

"What happens after you come clean to Luke? What if Luke says to dump the dick or he rolls?"

"Then I dump the dick," I shrugged.

"You love the dick," she said doubtfully.

"I love Luke."

"I feel you're in for some shit."

"Maybe so."

"Well...good luck with your shit."

"Thanks."

Donya had no idea how right she was. I was in for some shit.

The first thing I noted when I got to Luke's was that his car was in the driveway. I thought it was strange, but then I assumed he caught a ride with a coworker or took the train or something. The second thing I noticed was the rental car parked on the street in front of house. Curious, yes, but not suspicious. There were a lot of houses on the street, and sometimes parking was tight.

I started up the sidewalk to the front door, but realized I had mud on my sneakers. It had been raining a little earlier and I had stepped right into a puddle of mud when I went into my back yard to talk to my dad before leaving. I turned around and walked around the house. The plan was to leave my sneakers on the back steps and wash them down with the hose later.

After kicking my sneaks off, I used my key to let myself in the back door. The television was on, I could hear it. Okay, no big deal. It deters would-be robbers. However, the low girly giggle and the chuckle that was unmistakably Luke's was not on the television!

Thanks to my socks, I moved quietly through the kitchen without being heard. What I found in the living room on the couch was Luke and a blonde haired woman about my age. They were sitting very, very close. Too close.

"Hello." I said, making both of them look up in surprise.

Luke quickly got to his feet.

"Babe, I thought you would be on your way to Florida by now."

"Yeah and I thought you were in D.C.," I said tightly.

"The meeting was postponed late last night."

"Why didn't you tell me?" My eyes flickered to the woman. Her hair was ugly.

"I didn't want you to change your plans for me. You don't spend a lot of time with D."

I raised an eyebrow and again looked at the hoe on the couch. She looked nervous.

"This is Claire," Luke waved her over. "She's one of my Chicago friends. Claire this is Emmy."

I shook her hand, but couldn't match her smile.

"I thought I met all of your Chicago friends," I said to Luke.

"Not all of them."

"I'm out here with some friends," Claire explained. "Doing the Jersey shore thing. It was dumb luck that Luke became free while we're here."

"Ohhhh," I said, not really sure what to say.

"Where's your shoes?" Luke asked, looking at my feet.

"So...can I talk to you in the bedroom?" I asked, completely ignoring his question. I walked away before he could answer.

"Where are your shoes?" Luke asked me again, closing the door behind him.

"What's going on here?" I asked, crossing my arms.

"Claire is visiting the Jersey shore from Chicago."

"This isn't the shore!"

"No, it's not. When my schedule opened up, I asked her if she wanted to catch up."

"So you're catching up on your couch? Two inches apart?" I yelled.

Luke crossed his arms and his eyes darkened.

"What is it you want to know, Emmy?"

"I want to know what the hell is going on between you and Claire!"

"Is that what you want to know?"

"Yes!"

"No big deal right? Just a straight answer?" He was patronizing me, but I was too blind with anger to see where it was going.

"Right," I said, standing my ground.

"Okay. I will tell you what's going on between me and Claire."

"Okay!"

"Right after you tell me what's going on between you and Kyle."

Well...I wanted to come clean. Here's my chance. Maybe not this way, though.

I deflated, my anger floated away.

"N-n-nothing," I stammered. I was on the verge of wailing, but bit my lip to keep it back. "Sorry I jumped on you like that. I'm...." I started towards the door. "I'm going to go."

Luke followed me out of the room, calling my name.

"Nice to meet you, Claire," I said absently. I went out the front door, forgetting my sneaks.

"I'll be right back," I heard Luke say.

"Emmy," Luke got in front of me and stopped me.

I let out an exasperated scream. "Everything SUCKS!" I yelled.

The Lab in the next yard answered with barking and whining and a few kids playing in the street looked over at us. Even Luke looked at me with apprehension.

"Give me an hour or so and I'll come pick you up from home," Luke said.

"I don't want to go home," I grumble. "My mother is there."

"Okay then stay here."

"I don't want to stay here with Claire."

Luke put his hands together in front of him, like he was trying not to flip out.

"Emmy," he said with controlled quietness. "Go do what you have to do to get yourself together. I will call you soon."

I sighed noisily and got into my car. It wasn't until I was a couple of miles away that I remembered my sneakers.

An hour later my cell rang. I dug it out of my pocket and answered.

"Where are you?" Luke asked.

"At McDonalds," I said pitifully. "Eating the entire menu."

"I have your shoes. Why don't you come get them?" His tone was light, almost playful.

"Is Claire gone?"

"Yes."

"Why did it take you an hour to get rid of her?"

"Actually, you kind of got rid of her, and she left fifteen minutes after you. I was outside washing your sneaks."

"Sorry and thank you," I said with a sigh.

"Come home," he softly commanded.

I finished my fries and milkshake and drove back to Luke's. He was waiting for me at the door.

"In a few minutes, I'm going to take you to the bedroom and make you scream my name," he said as he closed and locked the door.

It wasn't really what I expected to hear. I didn't know what I expected, but it wasn't screaming orgasms.

"But first," he continued. "I dated Claire years ago. Nothing was going on when you came in today. We were just talking."

"You were cozy," I blurted out.

"Yeah, we were cozy, but nothing more. I would never hurt you like that."

The way he said that made me believe that he thought that I could hurt him like that, and he wouldn't be wrong. I felt like a douche puddle.

"There are some things in our relationship that need to be fixed," he said carefully. "I'll do my part, but you have to do your part, too, Emmy."

"Okay."

I was confused. Sometimes I thought that Luke knew more than what he was saying about Kyle, but then I thought there was no way that he would just stand aside and let some other guy do as he wished to his woman. There's no way he would stand for my divided heart. I believed that maybe whatever vibe I was giving off was the culprit. Maybe it was my own guilt surfacing on my face that registered in his mind and not some other solid fact. After all, I had been very careful with Kyle.

For me to do my part, Kyle had to go, but before I could begin to think of how to do that, Luke scooped me up in his arms and carried me to the bedroom. My screaming orgasms overshadowed any thoughts of Kyle.

<u>Chapter Twenty-Six</u>

As summer neared its end, my parents started discussing their travel plans back to Louisiana. My mom harassed me about getting married, and gave me ridiculous suggestions on how to accomplish it. I couldn't tell her I wasn't in any position to accept anyone's proposal. My dad reminded me that I didn't have to go anywhere if I didn't want to, but said he may not spend the whole summer in Jersey next year.

"It's not that I don't want to be up here with you," he explained one morning. "But I am old, and I want to spend time with my grandkids and great grandkids while I still have time."

It made me sad to remember that my dad was getting older, and I felt bad for keeping him away from the rest of the family. I told myself that I would have to make a bigger effort to go back to Louisiana more often. Their life down there was important to them and I shouldn't negate that.

Luke and I had made plans to go to Wildwood on Labor Day. I was excited about stuffing my face with boardwalk fries, pizza, funnel cake, enormous pretzels and salt water taffy. I couldn't wait to get on a few rides, play a few games, and to whip him at mini golf. I was even more excited just to spend the day with him. While things had not necessarily improved, they had not worsened.

I drove over early that morning. I was going to drag him from bed if I had to. I let myself in and headed towards the bedroom, but a slight noise from the kitchen caught my attention. I found him already dressed, leaning against the kitchen counter. My happiness and excitement instantly began to fade. The look on his face was serious, dead serious.

"Lena's not doing as well as we had hoped," he said so quietly that it unnerved me.

"I'm sorry," I said, unsure whether or not to reach for him.

"I'm going to leave sooner than I planned."

"How soon?" My heart began to race because I knew which conversation was about to take place, even though I had put it off for the entire summer.

"Next week. By the end of next week." He was speaking so stiffly to me that I took a step backward without thinking about it. "I've decided I don't want you to come with me."

I swallowed hard and offered the smallest of smiles. "I understand. You have a lot going on with your sister and family."

"This isn't about my family, it's about you. I don't want you."

Even though I knew I didn't deserve him, it was still harsh. My smile instantly vanished and I took another involuntary step back.

"I thought if I gave you some time, you would make a decision," he started in a firm voice, but I could hear the anger and hurt behind it. "I thought you would stop stringing me along as a backup and really commit, but you haven't. You're still seeing Kyle."

I closed my eyes, dizzied and stunned and scared. I didn't give Luke any credit. I totally took him for a fool, but all along he could see right through me.

I didn't have a defense and I didn't think he wanted to hear my apologies yet, so I stayed quiet, head hung in shame, tears tickling my eyes and waited for him to berate me - rightfully so.

"I'm not sure which part bothers me the most, the fact that you've been lying for months or the fact that you thought I was too simple minded to see what was going on. I can't count how many times you've lied about where you were or who you were with, or the times that you climbed into my bed still reeking of him. How many times have I kissed you and your mind was with him? I've given you opportunity after opportunity to come clean, but you never did."

He made an exasperated sound and paced the floor for a moment and stopped inches from me.

"At least give me the courtesy of looking in my fucking face while I am talking," he said so quietly, it was terrifying.

I slowly raised my head and looked at his face. He looked so damn angry, so damn hurt.

"I looked like the biggest idiot at work, committing myself to the girl who was obviously fucking Kyle Sterling."

My mouth hung open, and I started to ask what he meant, but the look on his face suggested I stay quiet.

"Everyone knows, Emmy. Despite your sneaking around, people still know. You both think everyone else is too inferior and dumb to figure it out."

I shook my head, denying what he was saying. There was no way people could know. We took great precautions, didn't we?

"Don't you fucking shake your head," he grumbled through gritted teeth and pointed in my face. I backed up, but he just kept closing the gap until I was against the wall.

"You're more upset that everyone else knows than you are about me knowing!"

When he yelled, I jumped, hitting my head on the wall.

"No, that's not true," I argued, wiping at my tears.

"Like I can believe anything you say now!"

"I'm so sorry,"

"Maybe you are, but I don't forgive you. I can't even forgive myself for falling in love with you, knowing that you were Kyle's whore." He said the last word with such vehemence I thought he must have injured his tongue in the process.

Luke was one of the mildest mannered people I knew. Even though he was in the right, his current state was something to fear. Looking in his eyes, I could see the absolute fury and pain swimming around. Just as I began to think it was time for me to go, Luke's fist landed in the drywall next to my head as he let out a scream of anger. I, too screamed, shocked, and afraid he would hit me, but instead he backed up. His hand was bloody, but he didn't seem to notice.

"Luke, your hand!" I reached for him, but he pulled away. "Let me at least help you take care of your hand," I insisted. I approached again, cautiously, and this time he let me take a careful hold of his injured hand.

Silently, he allowed me to clean and bandage his hand, staring at me the whole time. When I finished, I was reluctant to let go, and dared to lightly touch his wrist.

"I didn't know how to let go of either one of you," I whispered.

"Fortunately for you, I made that decision for you," he said, still angry, but now I could definitely detect sadness.

I felt like such an asshole. I didn't feel like I deserved to really cry, but I could not stop myself. The floodgates broke and I was trying to remain on my feet, as my whole body just went weak.

I gently released Luke's hand and started to turn away, but he caught me with his good hand and pulled me into a teary, desperate, heart breaking kiss. When he broke it off, he held my face in his hands, wiping away tears with his thumbs. He had tears of his own, but I was afraid to touch him again.

"Listen to me," he said. "I don't ever want to see you after today. Don't call me, don't text me, don't email me. Whatever relationships you were building with my family, it's done. They've already cut you off at my request.

"I love you, Emmy, but you fucking broke my heart. I know I am part to blame, I know, but..." He paused and stared at me really hard. "I hope Kyle Sterling rips your heart out of your chest and makes you choke on it."

Chapter Twenty-Seven

The week after Labor Day always marks the beginning of a very busy period at Sterling Corp. I can't pretend to understand the logistics of why that is, I just know that my work load builds up quickly, so that by the time Halloween arrives, I have triple the work I would normally have. Usually, I shut up and take the work and Kyle's bullshit and fight my way to the finish line (with plenty of alcohol in between), but this year I wasn't really feeling it.

"I need an assistant," I told Kyle one morning, handing him his coffee and a stack of files.

"Use Eliza," he said, not even looking up at me.

"Eliza has enough work to do for Jerk-Off Jeoff. You have to hire someone new, just to assist me."

"You usually do pretty well on your own." He wasn't even paying attention to me really. He was blowing me off.

"Kyle, can you please pay attention?"

"I'm listening,"

I wanted to throw his coffee in his face.

"I need an assistant," I repeated, sighing.

Finally, he looked up at me, perplexed.

"Why again?"

"Because I am only one person with the work load of six people."

"But you always..."

"I know what I always do!" I snapped. "But not this time." I shook my head and sighed.

It dawned on him, finally. I could tell by the irritated expression on his face.

"You have to stay focused, Emmy. You can't keep thinking about him and what happened or what could have been."

"Focused or not, I'm always overwhelmed. Every year. This year is one of the busiest I've ever seen and it's only the last week of September. You know what my work load is like without a busy season added in," I argued. "I need help, and I need a new person. We can't spare anyone else."

Kyle looked at me for a long time before speaking.

"Okay," he relented. "I'll sign off on hiring up to three new people on a temporary basis and if productivity rises we will keep them. If nothing changes, they're out."

"Thanks," I turned to leave.

"Em," he called. "Come back here a minute. Why don't you look satisfied?"

"I am," I said, not convincingly.

"You're not," he said quietly. "Maybe we need a getaway?"

I glanced over my shoulder to see if anyone was milling around close enough to hear. Ever since Luke told me that everyone knew, I'd been extra careful not to get caught in any compromising positions, or conversations.

"We're too busy," I said.

"Yeah, but we're not as busy as we will be in a month. Let's go now while we can."

"To where?"

"Mexico?"

"No. Too far."

"Nowhere is too far when we can fly."

"We don't have to go anywhere," I shrugged.

"Yes, we do."

"How about Miami?"

"Why Miami?"

"I have a friend down there, kind of." I gave half a shrug.

"Kind of?"

"He used to hang out with my cousin, Tabby, dated her best friend for a long time. I ran into him in the summer while he was visiting."

"Oh," he leaned back in his seat. "You've never mentioned him before."

"Wasn't worth mentioning before," I rolled my eyes at his jealousy, which was so hypocritical.

"If that's where you want to go, we'll go."

"It is."

"I'll make reservations."

"Good. Talk to you later. Send May an email, please. Now," I demanded on my way out.

"Yep."

I felt a little better, knowing I'd have Kyle all to myself for a couple of days, but honestly, I was more excited about hiring new people.

I bypassed my desk and took the walk to the HR department. My cousin Mayson worked there, a job she obtained by my recommendation a couple of years back. I found her at her desk, seriously enjoying a chocolate bar. Even though she was...curvy, or full figured, I, nor anyone else in our family ever mentioned her junk food habits. At least she was eating, unlike when she was younger...those were some dark and scary years.

"Dickhead just emailed me," she said, barely glancing up. "Write out what you want the ad to say and I'll post it in the three big papers."

"I don't want it posted in all of the papers. Can't you just post it on the company site? I don't have time to weed through all of those resumes."

"Yeah, okay. Whatever. I'm so glad to put my PR degree to good use for you."

"At least you have a job. Shut up."

She started to slowly spin in her chair while I wrote out what I wanted the ad to say.

"Tell your mother to stop calling me," Mayson said.

"That would require me talking to her and I don't want to talk to her."

"She keeps trying to give me sex tips for the sex I'm so not having. She should be giving you the sex tips."

"Trust me, she does."

"How is he in bed?" She stopped spinning and stared at me questioningly.

I stared back at her. "Do you really want to know?"

"No," she made a sour face. "My stomach is churning just thinking about it."

Mayson, much like I did at one time, hated Kyle with a passion. She knew about our relationship, but not through the grapevine like everyone else. She actually caught us making out. May rarely dropped by unannounced, but she was literally in my neighborhood. Kyle and I were standing in the kitchen, totally tongue tied to each other, when I heard a shriek, startling us apart.

"Oh...my...god!" Mayson had yelled. "Not him!"

"What are you doing here?" I cried.

"I was in the neighborhood!"

"You can't tell anyone, Mayson," I plead.

"I would never tell anyone your personal business, Emmy," she was hurt by my command. I knew she could be trusted, but I had said it in a panic.

"I know, I know." I took a long, deep breath.

"But Kyle Sterling is a dick."

"Is this a genetic thing?" Kyle asked, with a smirk. "Is it in your DNA to hate me?"

"No, but hating you is so easy since you're such a dirty penis head," Mayson huffed.

"Mayson," I took her by the elbow, leading her away. "Maybe it's not wise to call one of the owners of the business you work for a dick."

"A dirty penis head," she corrected. "It's probably not wise to screw your boss either."

"I have no defense for that," I sighed.

"What about Luke?" she whispered.

"Can we talk about it later?" I had asked.

But we never did talk about it, and after Luke left I gave her the bare minimum of details. My pain was obvious, though; so she never bugged me about it.

"Here," I handed her the piece of paper for the ad. "I only want this listed until Saturday."

"Okay. So what are you doing this weekend? Working, no doubt. Workaholic."

"DH convinced me to go away for the weekend."

"What for?"

"I guess he thinks it will cheer me up."

"Sounds like he's trying to make you forget about Luke."

I didn't say anything to that. What could I say? She was most likely right.

We talked a little more about mundane things, but I insisted that I get back to work and left Mayson spinning in her chair.

The rest of the week was uneventful. I was busy with work and Kyle was busy with work and of course obligations to that bitch Jess. Outside of work, we only saw each other for a few minutes a day, long enough for an embrace and a short kiss.

Our flight for Miami left at four-thirty Friday afternoon. Kyle had a fake business meeting at three and I had a fake doctor's appointment at one-thirty. I really had no one to explain my whereabouts for the weekend; Kyle, however, had to come up with an elaborate excuse for Jess and his parents.

"I know it's not a long time," Kyle said later that night at a bar near our hotel. "But hopefully you unwind a little this weekend."

"I didn't realize I was wound up," I said before downing my third drink. I motioned to the bartender to bring me another.

"You're definitely wound up," he said, rubbing my arm lightly. "You haven't been yourself for weeks."

I almost laughed in his face. Myself? I hadn't been myself in almost a year, unless this was who I really was, a woman who was in love with and sneaking around with another woman's man, while carrying on a relationship with another man. Well, at least the last part was over.

I downed another drink. I didn't want to think about Luke. Sure, he was pretty harsh, and I did feel hurt by how it ended, but I deserved it. The guilt I felt for hurting him was weighing me down, killing me.

Kyle reached out and stroked my hair, which was mildly comforting.

"When do I get my girl back?" he asked softly.

"Which girl is that?"

"The one who wore SpongeBob underwear and shined on the dance floor at the gala."

I looked at him curiously. "Shined?"

"Yeah, you were radiant. Me and a hundred other men couldn't take our eyes off of you. Don't tell me you didn't notice?"

"I didn't. What else do you love about me?"

"Everything, Em. Everything." He leaned over and kissed me softly, but with so much power behind it, my toes curled in my flip-flops.

"Specifically, what do you love about me?" I asked a few minutes later.

"I love that you're too humble to notice that you were the center of every man's attention at the gala and my parents' party, and every woman's envy."

"You're exaggerating," I shook my head.

"I wish I were."

"Doesn't that just make me self-absorbed?"

"Not at all. You didn't act like you were too good or below anyone. You never do, and I love that about you."

"Hmm. Okay, what else?"

"Hmm. I love your lips," he leaned in and kissed me again. "I love your tongue," this time with a lot of tongue. "I love your eyes and how I feel when they're looking at me." He quickly kissed each eye.

"What else?" I gently pressed.

"I love this spot on your neck," his lips were quickly on my neck. I sighed softly. After a few more seconds, I was feeling rather hot, and it had nothing to do with the weather. I pushed him away, but not entirely. We were both on the edge of our seats, my legs between his, his hands on my upper thighs, my hands laced behind his neck.

"It's hard to really break down into words what I love about you," he said softly. "But I know that I love the way you make me feel. You make me feel like I am more than someone's business venture, more than a trophy to drag around. You make me feel like...I don't know. Like a real man, I guess, or that I can be a real man anyway."

"You are a real man," I insisted.

"No real man would do to you what I've done to you," he whispered. "A real man wouldn't do anything that could potentially hurt you. I manage to hurt you every day, every minute. I can see it in your eyes, Em."

I couldn't deny it, but at the same time, I didn't like that he was feeling so badly about himself. I opened my mouth to speak, but he started before me.

"If I were a real man, a good man, I would have let you go the second I knew you really loved Luke. He was good to you and he really loved you, and..."

I cut him off, with a finger to his lips. I didn't expect Luke to be brought up, especially like this.

"I don't want to talk about Luke," I whispered. I still felt like that topic was an open wound, highly sensitive and easily infected.

He took my hand, kissed it, and apologized, but he still looked like he was beating himself up inside. I ran my fingers through his hair, calming him.

"You always make me feel better," he said, staring at me. "Even when I don't deserve it."

"You almost always don't deserve it," I chuckled, fluffing his hair.

"Let's get out of here," he said and threw some money on the bar.

"You want to know something else I love about you?" Kyle asked a half hour later in our hotel room. We were on the bed, kissing.

"What?" I panted.

Instead of answering with his words, he reached into my jeans and answered with his fingers, making me moan.

"Mmm, I love hearing you moan, too." He grinned and then covered my mouth with his as I moaned even more.

As my moans grew louder and I was on the verge of screaming, he said "And I love hearing you scream."

He pulled my pants and panties off and practically ripped my shirt and bra off.

"And I love this," he said before burying his face between my legs. My eyes rolled back in my head as I gripped his hair.

Later, spent, exhausted, laying in Kyle's strong arms, I maybe should have or could have felt a sense of security, but I didn't. I only had another day and a half with Kyle before I had to resume sharing him with Jessyca again. There was nothing secure about that.

The next day I just tried to enjoy the beach and sun and Kyle's company. Sometimes I was able to forget our circumstances, but whenever we spoke about home, or anything related to home and work, it was a reminder of what else - or who else was waiting there. Plus, twice a day Jess and Kyle would check in with one another. I didn't ask Kyle to get out of the arrangement because I felt that I shouldn't have to ask. Wasn't it obvious that it was like salt on an open wound?

"Are you okay?" he asked Saturday night. We were getting ready to go meet the old acquaintance I told Kyle about earlier in the week. He owned a restaurant not far from our hotel.

"Yeah," I said and turned away, pretending to look for something in my bag so that he couldn't see my face.

"You're still not yourself. Maybe we should stay in tonight."

"I'm fine," I turned to face him. "I'm fine and Leo is expecting us. Okay?"

He didn't look convinced, but said "Okay."

"Okay," I breathed.

Leo dated my cousin Tabitha's best friend throughout high school. I only hung out with him a few times, and okay, I made out with him a few times, too, but not when he was with the other girl (they were always breaking up). I'm not a chronic boyfriend thief. I never told anyone but Donya about it, though, and I wasn't about to mention it to Kyle.

Leo looked better with age. His Italian genes were prominent head to toe, with his dark hair and dark skin. His light blue eyes were breath taking. I had to cough to cover the fact that his eyes had indeed taken my breath away. Back in the day, Leo had a nicely toned body, but all of these years later, he had muscles bulging from his chest and his arms that were not there before. He looked like someone had carved him from stone.

He lifted me off of the ground when he hugged me, and planted a big kiss on my lips.

"You look great," he said.

"Thanks. So do you." I grinned like a stupid school girl. He was incredibly hot. It was probably illegal in thirty states to be that hot.

"Hi. I'm Kyle, her boyfriend." Kyle reached out his hand. That was the first time he introduced himself as my boyfriend.

"Oh, yeah. Yeah, this is Kyle," I said, shaking my head out of a daze. "Kyle, this is Leo."

They shook hands and said their hellos.

"I have a table ready for us over here," Leo waved us on.

"This is a great place you have here," I said appreciatively.

"Thanks. I've put a lot of hard work into it."

There was already a bottle of chilled wine at the table. Leo poured some in each glass and asked me about Tabitha.

"I don't talk to her that much," I admitted. "She travels a lot. We haven't really been very close over the last few years."

"Oh. I'm sorry to hear that. I haven't seen her in years. I would love to see her again. Between you and me, I always had the biggest crush on her."

"Really?" I asked, eyebrows raised. "Is that why..." I didn't finish the question. My eyes fell on Kyle's for a mini second. I had forgotten he was there.

"What?" Leo looked confused for a second and then understood. "No! One had nothing to do with the other, I promise." His smile was so awesome, I blushed.

"What?" Kyle asked, looking from me to Leo. "I'm feeling a little lost here."

Leo looked at me with that winning smile and shrugged. I took a deep breath and smiled myself.

"Leo and I...hung out a few times back in the day."

"Hung out?"

"Made out." I cleared my throat.

"Huh." Kyle nodded. I felt his body tense up beside me.

"It was a long time ago."

"It's cool," Kyle smiled, but his eyes weren't happy. "So, how did you end up in Miami?"

And so the conversation moved away from my past with Leo, much to my relief.

The food Leo had his staff prepare for us was top notch. Even Kyle was impressed. I went through a bottle of wine by myself, but even that wasn't enough to numb me from the ache I felt when Kyle's phone rang and he excused himself from the table. I had forgotten about Jess while laughing and chatting with Leo. My mood must have shifted significantly, because Leo noticed.

"Who's on the phone?" he asked.

"His girlfriend." I said simply.

"Ohhhh..."

"Yeah."

"How long have you been with him?"

"Almost a year."

"I don't want to butt in, but..." he started carefully.

"But?"

He reached across the table and took my hands into his.

"Coming from a guy who wasn't always nice to women, he's only going to treat you the way you let him. If you continue to be tolerant of your circumstances, he's not going to have a reason to change."

I stared at him as if he just said the most remarkable thing I'd ever heard, and maybe he did. It was something I already knew deep down, but to hear it vocalized by Leo really put things in perspective.

I was still gaping at him and he still had my hands when Kyle cleared his throat beside us before sitting down beside me. I let go of Leo, reluctantly, when Kyle put his arm around me.

About a half hour later, after making sure that I had all of Leo's contact information and vice versa, Kyle and I headed back to our hotel.

"That was an interesting night," he said sourly as we walked into our room.

"Yes."

"What was with the hand holding?"

"Just a friendly gesture."

"What were you talking about?"

"Nothing important."

I quickly changed into a pair of pajamas and went into the bathroom to brush my teeth. Kyle followed me.

"Your demeanor was weird."

"When?" I asked with a mouth full of toothpaste foam.

"When I came back and you two were holding hands."

"Maybe it was because you were gone in the first place."

He said nothing to this and I was able to finish brushing and rinse my mouth out.

"You never told me that you hooked up with him before."

"It wasn't important. It was a long time ago." I sighed and sat down at the table in the corner of the room. I felt like I was being interrogated. I rested my head in my hands, feeling the effects of too much wine.

"How far did it go?"

"What do you mean how far did it go?"

"How far did it go? Just making out? Third base? Homerun?"

"I hate when people use baseball to discuss sex," I said, disgusted.

"Fine," Kyle said tightly. "Did you just make out with some light petting or did you fuck him?"

I looked up at him. He was standing in the middle of the room, arms crossed, smoldering.

"I thought you were cool with it?"

"Maybe I'm not."

"Well, that's becoming very obvious, Kyle."

"You haven't answered my question."

"Maybe I don't want to answer your stupid question."

"Maybe that's an admission of guilt."

"Guilt? For something I did before I knew you existed? You can't be serious."

"So, you did fuck him."

"Yes, you hypocritical dick," I snapped. "I fucked him. Not once, not twice, but three times."

His face contorted into shock, then pain, and then anger.

"So was this trip a guise to see him again? To get some kind of revenge on me?"

"Are you listening to yourself?" I jumped up. "You sound crazy - crazy and obsessive. This trip was your idea!"

"You chose Miami, specifically because of Leo!"

"I didn't come down here to sleep with Leo, Kyle. But you know what? If I wanted to, I would, because I don't belong to you."

He flinched as if I had slapped the shit out of him, and I wish that I really had. We stood there staring at each other for a minute.

"I'm going to take a shower," he said quietly, and disappeared into the bathroom.

I was having a hard time finding a sense of inner control. I didn't want to fight with Kyle all night. In fact, I didn't want to see Kyle for the rest of the night. I redressed, grabbed my purse, and escaped into the night.

<u>Chapter Twenty-Eight</u>

When I got to Leo's restaurant, he was just leaving.

"Hey, what are you doing back here?" he asked. "Where's your stud muffin?"

"I needed some air and he's back at the hotel. Are you leaving?"

"Yeah, I'm just going home though."

"Want some company?" I smiled.

He smiled back. "Of course. Let's go."

Leo's house was neater than I expected for a bachelor, neater than his bedroom was many years ago. It was tastefully decorated and he had pictures of friends and family, past and present, all over. Tabitha was in quite a few of them, many with Leo. It made me wonder if they had ever had anything going on, but I didn't feel like it was my place to ask.

"You want a drink?" Leo asked from the kitchen.

"Always. I think I was born with a tequila bottle in my hand."

He laughed and a minute later he handed me a pretty big, strong drink. "So why did you run away tonight?"

"Oh, you don't want to hear all of the gritty details."

"Actually, I do. Maybe I can help."

He wanted to know, and I actually wanted to tell him, and I'm not sure why. We sat down on opposite ends of the couch, and I started from the beginning. Throughout the story, Leo refilled my glass several times. By the time I got to the part where I told Kyle I didn't belong to him, I couldn't walk in a straight line, not even in a nice zig zag.

"I mean, I'm right, right?" I slurred. "I don't belong to him. A matter of fact, I don't belong to anyone!" I leaned in close to Leo, which didn't take much. Somehow, we had both ended up in the middle of the couch, dangerously close. "I don't belong to anyone," I repeated.

I wrapped my hands around his neck and climbed into his lap, straddling him. He ran his hands up and down my back.

"You sure you want to go there?" he asked and took a nibble of my bottom lip. "You may regret it later."

"I won't be doing anything wrong. I'm technically single," I said, slowly gyrating on his lap.

"I don't think Kyle sees it that way."

"Can you shut up?" I kissed him hard on the mouth before he could answer.

After a hot minute, Leo gently pushed me away.

"What's wrong?" I asked, baffled.

He patted my thigh. "I'm just not that guy anymore, Emmy."

"You mean you're no longer an easy lay."

"I guess that's right," he chuckled. "You're really attractive, and I really wouldn't mind revisiting the past, but I don't want to take advantage of you at this moment of weakness."

"It's not a moment of weakness," I argued. To try to prove him wrong, I kissed him again. It lasted a little longer than before, but he pushed me away again.

"If you still want me when you're sober, I'll comply," Leo said and eased me off of him.

I sat back on the couch, sulking.

"Why do you have to be so...kind?" I growled.

I fell asleep on Leo's couch, but he woke me up at dawn and drove me back to the hotel. In the car I checked my phone, which had been on silent through the night. Kyle had called me thirty-two times and sent so many text messages that I didn't have time to read them all by the time we arrived the hotel.

"Sorry for throwing myself on you like that," I told Leo before getting out of the car.

"I hope I didn't make you feel...unwanted. I just didn't want you to regret anything."

"I wouldn't have regretted anything," I said firmly. "Thank you for being so cool about everything." I gave him a kiss, a full tongue on tongue kiss and got out of the car. As I walked away, I could hear his laughter behind me.

When I walked through the door, I found Kyle sitting in the chair I was sitting in last night when we started arguing. His face was unreadable, but I knew this wasn't going to go well, and I knew that I was not going to play nice either.

"Where were you?" he asked quietly.

"Leo's." I stood on the other side of the room, leaning against the dresser.

"The restaurant?" he asked, looking a little dazed. "I checked there."

"His house."

"Were you drinking?"

"Yeah. Got pretty drunk." I shrugged.

He was silent for a moment, but his next words seeped out like venom.

"Did you fuck him a fourth time? Maybe a fifth?"

"I didn't have sex with him," I rolled my eyes.

"Why should I believe you?"

"I have no reason to lie, Kyle. I have nothing to lose," I pointed out.

"Me. You can lose me, or does that not matter to you anymore?"

"I don't have you, Kyle!" I yelled. "Jessyca has you! I don't have you and you don't have me."

He sat there, just as stunned as he was when I said that the night before. I couldn't stop myself from talking, making things worse.

"For the record I did try to sleep with him, but he didn't want me to regret it when I sobered up," I started throwing various items into my carry-on bag. "I'm sober now, and I wouldn't have regretted it."

One moment I was standing beside the bed and the next I was pinned down on it with Kyle's face in mine.

"Why are you trying to fucking hurt me!" he roared. "Are you satisfied now?"

When I didn't answer, he started violently shaking me, repeating the question.

"Get off of me!" I tried to push him off and it started a struggle.

Kyle was crazy with rage, obviously not thinking clearly as he fought with me. My wrist erupted in pain. I cried out, begging him to stop, but it took a moment for him to register that I was hurt. He jumped off of me, staring in disbelief as I held onto my wrist, crying.

***

My wrist was fractured. Kyle tried to follow me into a cab to the emergency room, but I screamed at him with such vehemence, he backed off.

I told the doctors I fell. I don't think they believed me, but they couldn't do anything about it if I didn't tell the truth. I realized this was part of a cycle of abuse, which scared the hell out of me. Was Kyle going to hurt me again? And if so, would I cover for him again?

In the time I'd been with him, he had been a little rough during arguments, but for my part, so had I, but was this just the beginning? Would it escalate?

When I returned to the hotel, Kyle was tearfully apologizing the second he saw the cast on my wrist.

"I didn't mean it," he insisted, and I believed him.

"I know," I said quietly. I let him hold me for a minute and even kissed him back when he put his lips on mine.

Love, I decided on the plane ride home, can make people crazy. Love can make us do things we never meant to do. Kyle wasn't trying to hurt me when he broke my wrist. I wasn't trying to hurt Luke when he was around, and surely I never meant to find myself in this position in the first place. It happened accidentally on purpose - my heart accidentally started loving two men, but I purposely (and stupidly) acted on it instead of walking away from one of them.

Love can also borderline obsession and lunacy. Kyle was obsessed with me even though he had no right to be, and I was crazy to stay with him, even though I had no right to do so. The whole situation was craziness, and Leo was right. As long as I allowed things to proceed this way, the circumstances would remain the same.

Chapter Twenty-Nine

Fall pressed on, as did my scandalous, dysfunctional relationship with Kyle. As I predicted, our busy season turned into the busiest ever, but I was able to hire two assistants and three temps, greatly reducing the stress and turmoil that would have been. This was especially helpful due to the fact that I was in a cast for five weeks.

More and more of Kyle's time was being sucked up by that succubus Jess. Where I used to be patient and not complain (much), my patience was now as thin as thread.

"What time do you think you will be over next Thursday?" I asked Kyle in the elevator one night after work. It was a week before Thanksgiving and I had a grand meal planned for us.

"Uh..." He said with a guilty look on his face. "I thought you were going to go visit your family in Louisiana."

"I never said that," I was sure that I not only didn't say it, but never even implied it.

"I'm sorry. I just assumed..."

The elevator doors slid open on the ground floor. I waited until we were outside, beyond earshot of the security guards before speaking again.

"So, you made an assumption and then made other plans with Jess," I said, making an assumption of my own.

"I honestly believed you were going down south."

I took a deep breath, trying not to go ballistic. "So, fit me into your day somewhere. Maybe you can come over at the end of the night?"

He winced, and I knew he wasn't going to be able to fit me in.

"I'm leaving Wednesday afternoon for Fiji."

"Fiji." I gaped at him. "With Jess."

"I'm sorry, sweetie," he reached for me, but I took a step back.

"That's why you asked me to keep your schedule open Wednesday," I said accusingly. "If I didn't ask, would you have told me about Fiji?"

"I guess so," he shrugged. "It's not that big of a deal. It doesn't mean anything. It was her idea..." He stopped talking, probably realizing how ridiculous he sounded.

"Yeah, okay," I said, taking another step back. "You enjoy your fucking trip to Fiji." I was supposed to be walking with Kyle to his car in the garage, but I turned in the opposite direction and stepped to the curb to hail a cab.

"Em, wait," he rushed over as a cab pulled up.

"Stop telling me to wait!" I yelled and stomped my foot, halting him. I opened the door, and before climbing in I said "Don't talk to me. Don't call me, don't text me, don't come over."

"Throwing a fucking temper tantrum isn't helping anything," he snapped. "You make this harder than it has to be."

I wanted to punch him, but instead I slammed the cab door and didn't even turn to look at him when we pulled away and zoomed down the street.

***

"You look like hell," my mom said a couple of days later. After my last falling out with Kyle, I decided to take a vacation, beginning immediately.

I had let myself into his office in the middle of the morning, wearing jeans and a tee shirt instead of my usual business attire.

"We're still in the busy season," he had argued.

"I don't really care," I shrugged. "You can either sign off on it or fire me."

"You're over reacting."

"I'm under reacting, trust me. Are you going to sign it or not?"

"No. We're too busy, and today is not a casual day, so I suggest you go find something work-appropriate to wear." He went back to his work, dismissing me.

I left his office, slamming the door behind me. Everyone looked up at me. I forced a smile and strolled out of the office. When I didn't return that day, Kyle sent me a text.

I signed off on your vacation, brat.

The next morning, I was standing in front of the family home in Louisiana, facing my mother, already ready to tape her mouth shut.

She stood on the porch, in a powder blue dress, wearing an apron and drying her hands on a dish towel. She looked as beautiful as ever, which made me a little sick.

"Do you think you can prescribe me some valium?" I asked my brother-in-law, Eric, a successful ob-gyn in a nearby town. He was the one who fetched me from the airport.

"If I have to deal with her drug-free, so do you." He carried my bags into the house.

"Come up here and give your mother a hug, girl."

Several children appeared out of nowhere, screaming and laughing. They were playing some kind of get away game, oblivious to the fact that I was there, running around me, bumping into me and yelling close to my ear.

"Hey!" Mom pointed at them with the dish towel. "Don't you kids see your Aunt Em trying to get into the damn house? Get the hell out of the way."

The kids took off across the yard, several yelling "get the hell out of the way!"

I didn't pay attention to whose kids they were. My family is enormous. I am one of five children, six if you count Donya. I have fourteen nieces and nephews with one on the way, and some of my nieces and nephews have children. Then there were my mother's siblings and their kids and grandkids and great grandkids, and various friends and their families that were adopted into our family, like my brother in-law Eric. His family and my family go way back. Way, way back.

My mom and his mom were best friends growing up, despite what people thought about a white woman befriending a black woman. My oldest sister Lucille and Eric were born only a few days apart, started dating in their senior year in high school and married a year later. His family and extended family became our family, and Lucy and Eric made a family of their own. And then there were Tabitha's and Mayson's families from my dad's side.

"Mom, stop cursing at the children," I said as I climbed the steps. I hugged her and planted a kiss on her cheek.

"I missed you, honey," she smiled, and held me at arm's length so she could check me out. "You put on a little weight, didn't ya."

Actually, I had, and I didn't understand how or why. I was definitely thicker in the waist, but I didn't need my mom calling me out on it.

"What is that on your wrist?" My sister, Charlotte demanded as she stepped outside.

I mentally punched myself in the face for not taking off the bracelet Kyle gave me. I couldn't tell them he gave it to me and why. I'm sure they wouldn't believe the "I fell down" story. I'm not even sure Mayson believed it, but I didn't have a good lie ready and both Charlotte and my mom were staring me down, waiting for an answer.

"Kyle gave it to me," I sighed. Now my eldest sister Lucy and my two brothers Fred Jr. and Emmet joined us on the porch. They all stared at me as if I had lost my mind, and of course, it was possible.

"What on earth for?" Charlotte asked, sounding a lot like my mom, but my mom met my eyes and I already knew I was caught lying before I started. But if she wasn't going to say anything now, I may as well charge forward.

"I work my ass off, like really work my ass off." I said, which was true, but not true to the question asked.

"Didn't you say he was a dick?" Lucy asked, confused.

"Well, I guess he was making up for that, too." I shrugged.

Lucy held up my arm, turning it back and forth, causing the bracelet to sparkle in the sunlight.

"Are those real diamonds? This thing must be worth thousands."

"Oh, for heaven's sake!" Mom snapped. "Can your sister get the hell in the house sometime this year?" She pushed Lucy out of the way and opened the door for me.

"Thanks," I said to her and stepped inside to greet more family.

I made a mental note to take off the bracelet, and soon.

I had a long day, traveling and then reacquainting myself with my family, meeting new babies and spouses and boyfriends and girlfriends. Eric's mom, Allie Mae and my mom made the best dinner I've had since my last visit, well over a year ago. Even when I was past stuffed, I kept nibbling. By the time I waddled to my bedroom, I was sleepy beyond all that was reasonable, but I'd been that way for a couple of months. I was probably burning out.

I lay in bed looking at the bracelet on my wrist, thinking about the night I got it.

I have something for you," Kyle had said the night the cast came off.

We were at The Cheesecake Factory for dinner. It was the first night in weeks that we were able to go out for more than a fast food run or diner food. Work had been hectic and Jess had demanded more of his time.

Half way through dinner he slid a small black, velvet box across the table. The box was a little too big to contain a ring, but for about six seconds my hopes were up, and then I remembered the impossibility of such a thing happening anytime in the near future.

"What is it?" I asked, my hand on the box.

"Open it and see," he grinned.

Carefully, I picked it up and opened it. Inside, sat a bracelet of leaves in yellow gold, white gold, and rose gold. On each of the yellow and rose leaves were at least a dozen and a half diamonds (I later looked up the price of the bracelet - it was more than my annual salary).

"Kyle, this is so beautiful," I breathed.

"I want you to know," he said, putting the bracelet on my now healed wrist. "That I will never hurt you again."

I stared at my wrist. I should have been like "aww" but I didn't feel mushy like that. I knew he meant to make up for what he had done, that this was an apology, but that's not how I took it.

"What's wrong?" he asked, reading my face.

"Every time I look at this, I'm going to be reminded that you broke my wrist." I didn't mean to say it, but the words fell out of my mouth anyway.

We sat there, staring at the jewelry on my wrist, the moment ruined.

Chapter Thirty

"Wake up, sleepy head," my mom sang, waking me up from a solid sleep.

I peeked out from under my quilt. She was opening the curtains, letting sunshine in.

"I'm on vacation," I grumbled. "Let me sleep."

"It's nearly noon. Get up and make yourself useful."

"Sometimes I really dislike you."

"I can say the same about you, kiddo," she chuckled. "Get up, take a shower. I have a list for you."

It took me some time, but I was able to drag myself out of bed and into the shower. I had been in Louisiana for five days now, sleeping in daily, relaxing more than I have in over a year. I haven't done an ounce of work for Sterling Corp, even though I brought my laptop in case I felt the need to do something. I should have felt well rested, but I still felt run down, and for three nights straight, I couldn't sleep due to a series of anxious flutters in my belly. I didn't realize I was anxious about anything, but I suppose the body acts in mysterious ways sometimes.

Surely, it wasn't my lack of communication with Kyle. I spoke to him once a day, and since I was still angry, that was all I needed.

After I was showered and dressed, I got my orders from my parents, snagged a few teenagers for help and took off in my mom's car. The days leading up to Thanksgiving were always very busy. It was the biggest holiday for my family. Not only was the entire, enormous family present, but so were co-workers, neighbors, friends, and a large group of people who couldn't afford a dinner of their own.

The event was held outside on the extensive grounds surrounding the family mansion. There were countless tables and chairs, and even blankets spread out on the ground. Turkeys were roasted, smoked, and deep fried. Most years there was a whole pig roasted, sometimes two. There were yams and potatoes, various greens and beans, potato salads, pasta salads, and macaroni and cheese. Cranberry sauce, dressing, and various breads. The dessert list was even bigger.

All of this took days to prep and everyone had to help, including my burned out self. Even with the kids' help, I was dragging. Before Eric left for the night, I stopped him and pulled him aside.

"I've been feeling totally run down lately," I explained quietly. My family was so nosey; I didn't want to share my personal issues with anyone else. I told him everything I'd been experiencing and asked him if he could just check me out, maybe order some blood work.

"Friday morning, come to my office early, like around seven-thirty. We'll start with some basic stuff. It's probably nothing." He gave me a reassuring smile and I felt a little better.

Somehow I made it to and through Thanksgiving, tired as hell, but well fed. I almost slept through my alarm Friday morning, but the urge to pee was so strong I wasn't sure I was going to make it.

When I got to Eric's office, a receptionist had me fill out paperwork for my chart. When I offered my insurance cards, she waved them away, stating that Eric said not to charge me, which was ridiculous because I could more than afford it.

I sat down in the waiting room. Only one other person was there, a very pregnant woman in a sundress and flip flops. Her eyes surreptitiously fell on me a few times before she finally said something.

"Is this your first baby?"

"What?" I stared at her, confused.

"How far are you?"

"How far?" I turned my head like a confused puppy and then it dawned on me. "Oh! I'm not pregnant," I laughed. "Doctor Jonson is my brother-in-law."

"Oh," her eyes fell on my belly fat. "I am so sorry for assuming..."

The nurse appeared in the doorway and called me back. I gave the pregnant woman a small smile and hurried after the nurse. She did my vitals, asked me some questions, and then left me alone in the examination room to wait for Eric.

I hated going to the regular doctor, but especially hated the gynecologist. Even though I knew Eric wasn't going near that area, just the sight of the stirrups and anatomically correct pictures on the wall was enough to unnerve me. By the time Eric came in, I was ready to run.

"Okay, Emmy," he said and sat down on a stool across from me and asked me to repeat my symptoms. He asked me about work and if I had anything, besides my mother, in my personal life that could be a stressor.

I wasn't sure how to answer. My relationship with Kyle was always a point of stress for me, but I couldn't tell Eric that, could I?

"Am I protected under doctor patient confidentiality?" I asked.

"Absolutely. Anything you say to me may go in your chart, but I can't go tell Sam or Lucy or anyone else."

I closed my eyes and took a deep breath.

"I've been having an affair with my boss."

"The dick?"

"Yeah, that's the one. It's been going on for almost a year I guess. He's had a serious girlfriend the entire time. My relationship with Luke ended because of my relationship with Kyle. Would you say those are stressors?"

He ran a hand over his head, speechless for a moment. "I would say so," he answered finally.

"So the flutters could be anxiety and stress."

"Possibly. We'll run a few tests to rule out other things," he stood up and took out a cup wrapped in plastic.

"You want me to pee in the cup," I said flatly.

"Yes, please, if you can."

"Ew, you're going to see my pee," I laughed and took the cup from him.

As it turned out, I had no trouble peeing. I returned minutes later and placed the cup on the counter. His nurse had returned.

"I will be back in a little while," Eric said and left me alone with the nurse, who had nothing to say.

She hummed at the counter while testing my urine, for what, I didn't know. When she left, she took the tests with her. Eric didn't return for another twenty minutes.

"Sorry, Em." He flipped open my chart. "Em, when did you say your last period was?"

"I don't know. A few months ago," I answered, growing nervous.

"Is that normal for you? To skip months at a time?"

"Since I was a kid, yeah. Why?"

"Are you on any kind of birth control?"

"When I remember, I take the pill. Why?" I asked again.

"Your pregnancy test -"

"Whoa!" I held up my hands. "You gave me a pregnancy test?"

"Yes, and it came back positive."

<u>Chapter Thirty-One</u>

It was late afternoon when I pulled up in front of the family house. I sat in the car a moment, counting. Again. I forced myself out of the car, numbers flying through my head, and by the time I plopped down on a chair on the expansive porch, I had reached the same dates I had reached the forty other times I counted that day. The door opened, and my mom stepped outside, the scents of a home cooked meal wafting out behind her.

"Where have you been? Eric said you left his office around ten."

In response, my arm extended towards her, and my hand reluctantly and painfully un-clutched the paper I was holding. I heard a sharp intake of breath as she took in what she was holding. I couldn't look at her, I could only look straight ahead at the yard, at the weeping willows swaying in the warm breeze. She sat down beside me, held my hand, and touched my face.

"It's going to be fine," she said softly.

"I did the math," I said, looking at her finally. "Luke hates me, Mom, and I don't know how Kyle is going to feel about raising someone else's kid." There. I put it out there, even though I was sure she already knew it.

"Luke doesn't hate you, honey."

"Yes, he does, and I don't blame him."

"Emmy," she said firmly. "Luke does not hate you." She said it with such assurance, I suddenly became suspicious.

"How do you know?" I whispered. "You know something and you're not telling me."

She sighed, stared at the floor for a moment, as if she was thinking about how to tell me something, which bothered me. My mom was so blunt and never had a filter, so I couldn't imagine what would make her hesitate to open her big mouth now.

"I talk to him every now and then," she said, with another sigh.

"You what?" I started to stand up, but she firmly pushed me back down.

"You two broke up, and I was honestly really concerned for his sister Lena, you know because of the cancer."

After my trip to Chicago with Luke, my mom went out of her way to introduce herself to Luke's family. I mean she really went out of her way. It started with phone calls and letters (my mom is computer stupid), and when Luke and I went again for just a long weekend, my mom tagged along. She charmed his parents, gained the trust and admiration of his sisters, and wooed the children with gifts and her grandmotherly ways. When I told her we broke up and that Luke didn't want any contact between the families, I thought she had ceased speaking to them. Apparently I was wrong.

"Wait. You were allowed to have communication with his family, but I wasn't?" The idea hurt me to the core. It was like I was being cut off from my own mother in a way, and of course I had really fallen in love with his family, and I had never quite gotten over losing them.

"Not at first. He wouldn't tell me what happened, but you know I already knew. I'm old, but not stupid," she gave me a knowing look. "I had to promise not to tell you, and I had a big problem with that, but then..." she suddenly looked so sad. "You're never here. You barely call anymore, so I didn't see where I would really have the opportunity to tell you anyway, and the truth is I really couldn't turn my back on that family."

I blinked back tears, knowing that she was right. I sucked at being a daughter, just as badly as I had sucked at being a good girlfriend to Luke, especially when he was going through so much. I wanted to be angry, but I couldn't find it in myself to be angry when I knew that my mom was doing what she does best when her stupid mouth wasn't in the way, caring for other people and their needs.

"Is Lena..." I couldn't bring myself to ask the question.

"She's doing as well as we can hope for. Their father passed away last month, though. Your dad and I flew up there for the services, helped pay for some of the expenses."

"That's so sad." I felt bad for Luke and wished that I could have been in my mom's position to go see and comfort him. "So, how do you know he doesn't hate me?"

Again, she looked as if she didn't want to release some information to me. Guardedly, she said "He's hurting, and he's sometimes bitter, but never hateful. It's going to take some time..."

"Mom, you can't tell him." I squeezed her hands. "You're still holding secrets from me and I'm your kid. You have to keep this from him."

"Why don't you want him to know?"

"I don't think that it will help anything right now. Mom, please!"

"Okay…" She was reluctant to withhold the information from him.

"Besides, until there's some DNA testing done, we can't know for sure. You can always use that as an excuse if it comes up later."

"I won't say anything, Emmy," she sighed.

"Thanks," I stood up. "I'm going to go pack."

"You want your ultra sound picture?" she offered it to me.

"No."

I dragged myself upstairs to my room and threw myself onto the bed. I should have felt better after the conversation with my mom, but I felt worse. I felt as if I had thousands of pounds of weight sitting on my chest. I couldn't find an ounce of happiness about the situation. I wasn't sure what it meant for me and Kyle, and I wasn't sure what I was going to do in a few months when the baby was born. Would I be waiting around for Kyle to leave Jess still, while caring for a baby? Or would I be alone, with no father around at all? I know there were single parents in the world, but I never ever thought that I had whatever they have inside of them to do it. I wasn't even sure if I would be a decent parent with someone else. I felt that no matter what, I was going to fail. I mean I couldn't even figure out I was pregnant! How was I going to raise a child?

If I had paid attention to my symptoms, I probably would have figured it out sooner. What I thought was an extended case of a stomach virus soon after Luke's departure was probably morning sickness. The morning sickness slowed down, but at least once a day I had the urge to vomit. I thought it was anxiety, as well as the fluttering in my belly. The sleepiness I had been feeling, I thought was a result of the busy season at work. My sudden extreme interest in bacon and cheese curls (together) should have been a clue, but I didn't think it was weird at all. While my face and hips had definitely gathered some extra weight, I thought my slightly rounded face was attractive and as for my hips, I thought maybe I had to cool it on the bacon; however, the fact that the weight sat mostly at my midline didn't even hint to me that there could be something growing in there. I figured when the busy season was over, I would spend more time at the gym, and cover up in bigger clothes. I was so freaking stupid.

I packed my suitcase for my early morning flight, and went downstairs for some dinner. I hoped there was bacon in it.

***

Kyle returned from Fiji late Sunday night. He dropped the succubus off and then came straight to my house. I wasn't expecting to see him until work the following morning, and he didn't text or call to let me know he was coming. I was lying on the living room couch, with the television on, absent mindedly rubbing my belly. The fluttering had begun again, and now I knew it wasn't anxiety, but fetal movement. I didn't even hear the door open, and I wasn't sure how long he watched me before letting me know he was there by saying my name.

Automatically, my hand flew away from my belly and my head snapped back to look at him standing in the entrance way. I tried to sit up, but learned I couldn't do that as quickly and easily as I had in the past. How did I not notice these things before?

"I wasn't expecting you," I said.

"I know." One thing Kyle was not, was stupid. Where some men would probably think that I had a stomach ache or ate too much, I could almost see Kyle's thoughts. He knew, and I didn't have to break the news to him.

He stood where I found him, staring at me, and I stared back. Either of us knew what to say. After several uncomfortable seconds had passed, I finally spoke, to break the ice.

"A pretty good number of girls in my family are pregnant or just recently had a baby. I didn't know it was really contagious."

"It's like the fart touch," he said, and finally we had an open dialogue for this momentous conversation.

Chapter Thirty-Two

"It doesn't matter to me. I already love this baby like my own, and we're going to raise him together, as a family."

Kyle had said that a month ago, the night he returned from Fiji, and found out I was pregnant. I had suggested a DNA test and explained why, but he had objected. He was disturbingly excited about the news, and started spewing off all kinds of plans for our expected child. I couldn't take it anymore and cut him off.

"Yeah, you know we're going to have a great time," I said with over the top enthusiasm. "You, me, the baby, and Jessyca."

He bit his lip, glaring at me as if I had just said the most offensive thing in the world.

"Give me some credit, Em, will you? Jessyca isn't going to have anything to do with our family."

"I really want to believe that, but I've been an idiot for all of this time," I said.

"Here we go," he said, throwing his hands up in the air. "You know why things have had to be this way."

"That does not make it okay!" I banged my fist on the table, making the plate holding my hot bacon rattle. I took a deep breath, and a piece of bacon. "My point is I have a hard time believing you're going to do what you say you're going to do, and I don't know if I want to wait for it to happen."

"So, what…you're just going to cut me out of your life?" he asked.

"I would rather be alone, depending on no one, than to depend on someone who is clearly undependable."

"You've given up on me – on us." It was not a question, but a well-placed guess.

"Every day that I have to share you with Jess, I lose more and more of myself. I'm so knotted up inside from this relationship, Kyle, I'm not sure if it can ever be fixed."

He stared at me stupidly, speechless.

"You get so pissed off when I make comments about your lack of action, but that's really not fair. I'm the one who should be pissed off, and if I were the old Emmy, I wouldn't be standing here with you, like at all. You don't understand, Kyle, you are breaking me." I choked on the last few words, unable to hold back the onslaught of tears and sobs.

Stupid hormones.

He held me for a long time, murmuring empty promises into my hair, begging for my patience and understanding, and insisting that the triangle would soon be dissolved and we would be able to get on with our lives. I know that he believed what he was saying, and that he really thought that things were going to change now, but I didn't have any faith in his words, and it was harder to admit the truth than to delude myself.

A week passed, two weeks, and then finally a month. It was almost New Years and nothing changed. Kyle said he was trying to settle some business before he severed his relationship with Jess. From a business perspective, I understood, I really did. From a personal perspective, though, I simply saw it as another delay, another link in the chain that kept me bound to him.

I didn't visit my parents for Christmas because I had plans with Kyle, which he significantly altered at the last minute. I didn't bother to make New Year's plans with him, and instead tried to make plans with my parents, but they were going to Chicago. I wasn't supposed to know about it, but my mom "slipped" in conversation. She offered to stay home or to come see me so I wouldn't be alone, but I lied to her, telling her I wouldn't be alone, that I would be okay.

I was feeling more and more depressed about my situation and I thought of Luke a lot more than I ever had in the past. I wondered if there would ever be a day when I didn't think of him, now that I was going to have his flesh and blood with me for the rest of my life. I was losing sleep, this time with actual anxiety, not just the fluttering of the active child growing inside of me. My appetite was lacking, bacon and cheese curls weren't even doing it for me anymore. When I should have been gaining a little bit of weight, I was dropping it. I was always good at hiding my emotions in public, especially at work, but I was so overwhelmed, so weighed down by it all, I didn't have the strength anymore to put up appearances. It was also becoming impossible to hide my swelling belly, and I knew that people were looking at me, wondering first, what the hell was wrong with me, why I looked so miserable, and second, who the father was.

My work started to suffer, so much that Kyle delegated most of my tasks to Eliza, and delegated her tasks to the assistants I had hired. I didn't even know why I was showing up anymore, I barely did anything. So, one day when Walter Sterling called me to his office, I really thought that he was going to fire me, or take away my position and put me back in the mailroom.

"Would you like a drink, Emmy?" Mr. Sterling asked, pouring himself a drink.

In the past, I wouldn't have dreamed of accepting a drink from him, in his office. I would have been ridiculously professional, stiff as his drink. But that was then. I couldn't drink the alcohol, I had done enough of that before I knew I was pregnant, just another thing to worry about. Had I damaged my baby? Eric couldn't give me a positive answer.

"I'll have water," I answered.

"Well, that's different."

He handed me a glass of cold water, and silently we watched the streets below out of his floor to ceiling, wall to wall window.

"How is your family?" he asked.

"Fine, I suppose."

"Did you see them on Christmas?"

"No."

We stood in silence again for a minute or so. I thought about leaving, but Walter Sterling didn't call me to his office to look out of the window and ask me stupid questions.

"You have been having an affair with Kyle for, hmm...about a year now." And there it is. He said it so casually we could have been speaking about the weather.

"About a year," I confirmed, still watching the streets below. "Another water, please." I held out my empty glass, but he was reluctant to take it. I was well aware of the irony of the situation. I should have been catering to him, not the other way around and we both knew it, but he said nothing and refilled my glass.

"I really like you, you know, Emmy. You are the best administrative assistant in this building. I gave you to Kyle because I knew he needed you to get on track and stay there. You've done a damn good job."

I stared at him, not because he complimented me, but because I wanted to know where this was going.

"I am confused as to where this is going," I said, not too kindly. "How did we get from my affair with Kyle to my work? Are you firing me?"

"Fire you? No, of course not. Firing you would bring questions and unwanted attention and we don't need any more of that right now," he said and nodded to my pregnant belly. "Besides, I've always wanted you to stay with the company, to grow here."

"Then what do you want, Walter?" I've never in my life addressed him by his first name.

"You're making Kyle lose focus of what's most important. He should already be married by now, having children with Jessyca Venner, not you." His tone was still so casual, that it was making me a little queasy. I never thought that this man who I had always thought well of could be so evil under it all.

"What if he doesn't want the bitch?" I asked.

"It doesn't really matter if he wants the bitch or not. There is a lot of money riding on their inevitable nuptials, a lot of money and the birth of a whole new era here at Sterling Corp."

"Don't you think that's a lot of pressure to put on one person?"

"He was fine until he started screwing you. You've got him all wrapped up in you, he can't see or think straight."

"Some may say the man is in love."

"And I would agree, but he has a duty to two families."

"Does Jess know she's someone's duty?" I spat out.

"Yes, she does, but she truly loves Kyle, and in some ways, Kyle loves her, but not the way he loves you."

"It doesn't matter," I said, putting my glass down. "His 'duty' will win."

"With you and the bastard child around, he could delay this thing for an extremely long period of time. Timing is everything."

For the first time, I felt an emotional response directed at my baby. I put a protective hand over my belly, offended, and hoping his little ears did not understand the word bastard.

"I have to admit, I'm jealous," Walt chuckled lightly. "You're a gorgeous woman, with a fantastic personality, and I would bet thousands that you're an animal in bed."

"Don't tell me you want to take me for a test drive," I said dryly.

"Who wouldn't want to? Even in your current state," he laughed. "But that would only further complicate matters, would it not?" He strolled away to the other side of the room, where he pulled a picture off of the wall, revealing a safe. I snickered, thinking it was cliché, obvious.

I stared out of the window while Walt rambled on about the good of the many outweighing the good of the few, or something. I vaguely remembered Mr. Spock saying something like that in a Star Trek movie, and thought how unoriginal Walter Sterling was.

"So," he said, with a finality that made me turn around. On his desk were stacks of cash. I thought maybe he wanted me to go to the bank for him or something, but then it hit me.

"You're trying to pay me off?"

"There's one million dollars here. I will keep you on the payroll, also, so you won't be losing anything. You can eventually return to the company, or if you like you can just go work at one of our other locations, or not come back at all. I would understand."

"You realize that my own family is wealthy and I'm not in need?"

"Even the wealthiest of people aspire to acquire more money."

"What if I refuse your offer?"

"It never once occurred to me that you would refuse." He said it with unbreakable confidence.

"You're a little too confident, don't you think?"

"Not at all. Let's be frank, Emmy. You don't like being Kyle's side piece. You know in your heart that he isn't going to commit to you. You're probably falling apart inside, wishing you could escape, just disappear. It's better that you leave on your own than to be forced."

"You're forcing me." I whispered.

"I am providing you with a means of escape."

I was angry that he was offering me a bribe. I was even angrier that I was thinking about accepting it.

"I don't trust you," I said to Walter. "And your ideas are total Swiss cheese, anyone could see through them, and who does this?" I pointed at the pile of money. "There are hungry children throughout the city and you want to pay off your son's mistress. I feel like I'm in the middle of a daytime soap. That money is probably company money anyway, which means you'd just nail me for embezzlement. You're crazy."

"You thought about it," he said, not hiding his animosity for me. "You were going to accept my offer."

"I don't want your money, Walter."

"I have a confession, Miss Grayne," he said, pouring himself another drink. "It's really not my money or company money."

Now it was really turning into a soap, except I didn't need the TV guide to let me know who the possible culprit could be.

<u>Chapter Thirty-Three</u>

The bracelet sparkled in the sunlight, as I turned my wrist back and forth. Back and forth, back and forth, sparkle, sparkle. I twisted and sparkled until my arm got tired, and then I regressed to absent mindedly fondling the bracelet, while staring at the rolling green French country side, dotted with the occasional house.

I spoke French as well as I spoke Klingon, and I only knew some very bad Klingon words. Fortunately, the family that I was staying with spoke fluent English and wasn't at all offended by my lack of language skills. Helene and Marcus were friends Donya had acquired in her travels as a model years ago. When I literally needed to escape my life in America, Donya brought me to Helene and Marcus.

Helene was a photographer by profession and for kicks. Often, when I wasn't paying attention, she would snap pictures of me. There were several pictures with my hand resting on my pregnant belly, and just as many of me looking at the bracelet on my wrist. I didn't look happy in any of the pictures. I didn't look sad either, but I didn't look like my mind was anywhere in the country.

Helene's husband Marcus was from old money and didn't really have a profession, but he tinkered with various things: painting, writing, trying various musical instruments and during my stay his hobby of choice was designing clothing for my unborn child. Usually the item was missing something fundamental to wearing it, like an arm, or the hole for the head. One time the shirt had an extra arm. I always kindly pointed out the mistakes to Marcus. He would curse in Italian and sometimes try to rip it apart. I didn't take it personally. I once witnessed him destroy a flute because he couldn't master a certain song, and there were a few paintings around the house that had obviously received a swift kick from a hefty foot.

My time in France wasn't anything to marvel at, nothing exciting to report. Even though I had Helene and Marcus and their occasional visitors, I felt completely alone. I was very pregnant without a father for my baby. No Luke and no Kyle. I was financially able to care for my baby, but raising a child isn't something that I ever wanted to do alone, at least not under these circumstances. My heart was shattered and I sometimes wondered if there was enough of it left to care for a needy child. I was sure that I loved my baby, but I always questioned whether or not my feelings would shrink into resentment. The thought was unnerving, but I could not succeed in completely pushing it out of my head.

Sometimes I didn't really want to go back to the states, back to the nightmare I created. I didn't want the stares of pity or to hear the sighs of disappointment, but my return was inevitable. My family and doctor insisted upon it, and truthfully, I didn't think Helene and Marcus wanted to deal with a screaming infant and the child's depressed mother. So, two and a half months after I arrived, my mother came to retrieve me. After more than half a day on a plane with her, though, I was ready to face whatever was on the ground for me in America.

I missed Kyle. I missed kissing him, with his fingers entwined in my hair, pressing on the back of my skull, reminding me that he was in control, and I always conformed with weak knees and bated breath. I missed his hand on the small of my back, guiding me in whatever direction he wanted. I missed his laughter, his smile, and his perfect brown eyes. I even missed the way he would look at me in a crowded room, in a way that only I understood: "I love you...I want you" and when times were rough "I miss you, I'm sorry."

The last time I saw Kyle was New Year's morning. At the company New Year's party, he had given me those looks, loaded with unspoken words and emotions after kissing Jessyca at the stroke of midnight. When she put her hand on his face, a dazzling diamond ring that could be seen from the moon nearly blinded me with grief. I had turned away, weaved through the bodies of people kissing or singing Auld Lang Syne, pressed through the drunkards and the single lonely people and flung myself out into the night. I stood on the sidewalk, watching people on the street celebrating the New Year, listening to cars honking. In the distance, at Penn's Landing, fireworks were booming in the sky.

I had forgotten my coat in my haste to get out of the party, and shivered violently in the night air while I waited for the valet to get my car. The coat was expensive but I wasn't going back in that place. I didn't want to run into Kyle or Jess or anyone else for that matter. People were already looking at me lopsided before, but the baby bump I was sporting gave people reason to openly stare at me and whisper with me in hearing range. Now Jess was rocking that rock, and I wasn't going back in there unless I wanted everyone to see how humiliated I was.

I dug my ticket out of my purse and handed it to the valet who was standing nearby.

"Do you want to wait just inside until I bring your car around?" he asked kindly.

"Oh, hell no. I'm not going back in there. I'll be fine."

He shrugged and trotted off to retrieve my car. I hoped he wouldn't take too long so that I could leave before Kyle came out. Other party goers came out, some to smoke, others to also leave. No one paid me any mind, and I was fine with that. My car appeared at the same time Kyle stepped up next to me.

I glanced at him, but said nothing before stepping off of the curb and squeezing myself behind the wheel. He leaned on the door, preventing me from closing it. I stared straight ahead, swallowing constantly, trying to keep the lump in my throat from exploding.

"I'm sorry," he whispered so no one out on the sidewalk could hear. "There's a lot you don't understand, that you don't know about. Jess has me by the balls -"

"Clearly," I said, my tone sharp and insensitive, even though his was genuinely pained.

He inhaled deeply and let it out in a huff.

"Look, I will come over around nine and we'll talk."

"I won't be there."

"What time is good for you then? When will you be home?"

Looking at him with hard eyes, I said "Whatever time I had for you has been used up, sucked dry. You're out of time. I won't be there when you get there." A horn blew behind me. "Consider this my resignation - from my job, from you, from all of this. I'm done. Now step away from my car."

He stared at me open mouthed, holding on to the door, until someone blew again, longer, and louder. He stumbled back and watched me drive away.

When I got home, I immediately started packing. I was only taking necessities now, and would have to return later to retrieve other items. While I packed, I had the airline on speaker phone, trying to book a flight to Louisiana. I didn't necessarily feel like dealing with my mom, but I needed to take a couple of days to figure out what to do next, and doing it here was impossible. I knew Kyle wasn't going to just leave me alone, and I knew I was virtually defenseless in preventing him from having me. He was my drug, and I his. The only way to solve the problem was to remove the source.

I managed to book a nine-thirty flight. It wasn't as early as I wanted, but I took it anyway. When the call ended, I saw that I had several text messages and missed calls from Kyle. I was surprised and relieved when they didn't continue, and after another hour when he had not shown up, I relaxed a little. I didn't look at the texts or listen to the voicemail. It wasn't going to help anything to see or hear what he had to say. If this was the only self-control I could have, then I was going to keep it.

I couldn't sleep. My mind was racing, and my heart was breaking off piece by piece every minute that passed. I let a few tears slip by, but I refused to bawl. I would allow myself a good cry at a later time. I found some empty boxes in the garage and decided to start the tedious task of packing up some of my personal items that I could have someone ship to me later. I turned some music on and lost myself in the task for a couple of hours. I was so involved in what I was doing that I never heard the front door or his approach. I was in my bedroom, standing at my bed packing some things from my closet when he spoke, making me drop everything I was holding and jump backwards, frightened by his sudden appearance.

Kyle stood in the doorway, clearly drunk. He reeked of alcohol, the smell easily wafted across the room. His bowtie was gone, several buttons unbuttoned on his shirt, and parts of it hung out of his pants, wrinkled.

"What are you doing?" he quietly demanded.

"What are you doing here?" I asked, trying to slow down my heart with a few even breaths. I picked up the things I had dropped and resumed packing.

"What are you doing?" he asked again, staggering into the room.

"What does it look like I'm doing?" I said, not looking at him.

"I wanna talk to you."

"I don't want to talk anymore."

"Look at me!" he bellowed, gripping my wrist.

I looked at his hand on my wrist, the same wrist he had broken not that long ago. I wasn't getting a good vibe from him, and for a few seconds, I thought he was going to break it again.

"What is this?" He used his free hand to start rifling through the box. "What is this shit? You're trying to leave for good?"

When I didn't answer, he yanked me away from the box and then threw it on the floor. Yelling, most of it incoherent, he grabbed my open suitcase and dumped it out on the floor.

"What are you doing!" I yelled, grabbing his arm.

"You're not leaving!" he yelled in my face.

I stepped around him, picked up the suitcase and mindlessly started to reload it. I felt a panic surging inside of me, but struggled to keep it contained.

"No!" he yelled, and grabbed me from behind by my shoulders, and spinning me around.

"Stop being a dick!" I yelled in his face as I slapped his hands away from me.

At first, I couldn't figure out why I was seeing stars and why the left side of my face stung and hurt so badly. Not until my vision began to clear did I see Kyle standing over me, with his hand still raised and breathing erratically, with an animalistic expression on his face. I tasted blood and then I realized what had happened. He had hit me.

End of Part One

Dear Luke,

I have rewritten this letter a dozen times already, but I feel there is no smooth way to lead up to what I have to say, so here it is: You are the father of a five month old, beautiful baby boy. His name is Lucas, in honor of his father, and he was born May 18th.

I didn't tell you because I know you hate me, and my biggest fear is that you will hate my son, too. Maybe that fear is unreasonable, but I have had a very hard time getting past it.

I am in Chicago for a day or so, at the Fairmont, room 317. If you would like to meet your son, I will be here all day today.

I am sorry for keeping this from you, and I am sorry for forcing my mother to keep this from you. Please don't be angry with her. It is my fault entirely.

Sincerely,
Emmy

Chapter Thirty-Four

The letter was sent off first thing on a Friday morning through a carrier service. Luke had to sign for it, so that I would know it was received, and he had signed for it an hour after I sent it.

I waited with jumbled nerves for the better part of the day. I didn't leave the room at all and ordered room service if I was hungry. Lucas kept me grounded with his need for entertainment and diaper changes and other things babies needed and wanted. I was happy to oblige.

He was a good baby. (are there really bad babies?) He rarely cried, and was always happy. He talked a lot, and I pretended to understand what he was talking about. I was never without him, he was my whole life, and if Luke chose not to come, my baby would always have me.

By the time night fell upon us, I knew Luke wasn't coming. I was sadder than I thought I would be about it. At ten o'clock that night, I went to bed feeling grief stricken by Luke's lack of response. I wanted to call my mother and tell her I told her so, but I didn't really feel like talking to her. Somehow I found the resolve to go to sleep.

In the morning, I decided to get Lucas out of the room for a little while before making any plans to leave. We had been cooped up there all of the day before and even though it was cold out, the fresh air would be good for both of us. I bundled him up and we left for a morning of shopping.

Just after noon, when Lucas and I walked through the doors of the hotel, Luke appeared in front of us, holding a little stuffed whale. My heart caught in my throat when I saw him. He looked better than he did the last time I saw him and I was tempted to run to him, but I didn't. I kept cool and slowly approached him.

He looked at me with a mixture of disdain, sadness, and awe for a moment before registering the smiling baby boy in my arms. He inhaled sharply and stared at Lucas with absolute wonder and astonishment. He couldn't deny that he was his, he looked just like him. They both had the same shocking blue eyes. Lucas's hair was dark blonde now, but like his father's it would darken over the years to a medium shade of brown with some natural blonde highlights. I had seen Luke's baby pictures, and Lucas was the spitting image of what Luke had been as a baby.

Luke offered his son a finger and Lucas promptly started to put it in his mouth, but Luke pulled back, mumbling about dirty hands.

"You didn't come," was all I could muster out.

"Yeah, I'm sorry. I was out of town. My sister just happened to be in my apartment dropping off some things I left in her basement when the letter came. I didn't read it until this morning when I got in." He looked at me for approval, to see if I believed him.

"I understand," I said, shifting Lucas from one arm to another.

"Can I hold him?"

"Of course," I said and gingerly passed him his child and he passed me the stuffed animal. My heart lurched in my chest watching his face light up as he held Lucas. I felt such an overwhelming sense of guilt for keeping father and son apart that I had to try very hard not to collapse to the floor in a fetal position and cry. Maybe suck my thumb.

Instead, I suggested we go back to my room. I pushed the stroller and Luke carried Lucas.

Luke, apparently, was Super Dad. He talked to Lucas and answered when all he got was baby babble. He fed him, burped him, changed his diapers, got spit up on, held him, played with him on a blanket on the floor, and took picture after picture. When Lucas took a nap in the middle of the afternoon, Luke sat nearby, working on his laptop and making phone calls, virtually ignoring me and the conversation we needed to have. When he finished, he looked at me as if he just remembered I was there.

"You let your hair grow out," was all he had time to say before Lucas was up from his nap and he was back to being father of the year. He was in his glory, but I was feeling funny about sharing my son's attention.

It must have shown on my face, because after Lucas was down for the night, Luke looked apologetic.

"I'm sorry. I totally took over today."

"I'm not used to sharing him," I said, looking at my hands in my lap. I found it difficult to meet his eyes. My immense sense of guilt never faded, not even a little.

"I'm going to go pick up some dinner. We'll talk when I get back."

"Hold on," I said and shuffled into the bedroom. I returned with a second key to the suite. "You can let yourself back in. I'm going to take a shower."

When he took it from me, our hands touched, but he quickly pulled away and walked out the door. I exhaled for what must have been the first time since I first saw Luke in the hotel lobby. I checked on Lucas before getting into the shower, with the door open so I could hear him if he cried. I had such a long day, and my muscles ached from being so tense. I stayed in the shower much longer than I meant to. When I stepped into the bedroom, dripping wet in just a towel, I was startled to find Luke standing over Lucas watching him sleep.

"Sorry," he said, glancing over at me. "I'm just...amazed. He's perfect."

"Yes, he is," I agreed.

He looked for a moment longer and disappeared into the living room. I dressed in a tee shirt and pajama bottoms quickly, and brushed the tangles out of my hair. I found Luke seated on the couch with a few cartons of Chinese food on the coffee table. He handed me a carton. I didn't have to peek to know that it was Chicken Lo Mein.

My body knew it was time to eat, but my mind and emotions were playing tricks on me. I sat as far away on the couch from Luke as possible, picking at my food with my chopsticks, never actually taking a bite.

"I'm conflicted, Emmy," Luke said after a few minutes. I gave up trying to eat and put the container on the table and waited for the onslaught of angry words.

"I am so angry with you for keeping this from me," he continued. "But at the same time, I understand how you must have felt, I think. I could never hate Lucas, even if..." He didn't finish his sentence and looked away from me, but I knew what he was going to say.

"You mean even if you hate me," I said.

He inhaled slowly and let it out even slower.

"I don't hate you," he said softly. "But I haven't forgotten what happened. I'm not going to lie and say that it's okay or that it doesn't still bother me. It's been over a year and I still get bitter about it."

I squeezed myself so far into the corner of the couch, it may have looked like the couch was eating me. He was speaking in a soft tone, but his face was bitter and his eyes were hard.

"I still blame myself, too. I had this inflated idea of who you were and misjudged. It's not entirely your fault that you didn't live up to my expectations."

What he was saying to me was cruel. If I were at all the woman I used to think I was, I would have stood up to him and defended myself, but I had no defense, because he was right. Luke was only reinforcing some of the very thoughts I've had for over a year.

"You do love Lucas, though," he continued after a moment of staring at his General Tso's. "You're a good mother, I will give you that."

I nodded as a thank you, but said nothing.

He looked at me for what seemed like an eternity. I was staring at a wall across the room, but I could feel his eyes on me.

"Anyway," he sighed, and finally looked away. "I have to put the past behind me, for Lucas's sake. I want to be part of his life. I just started my own firm, so I'm not really in a position to do too much traveling right now. I don't know anything about your situation," he paused before hesitantly asking the next question. "Do you have your job to get back to in Philly...or anyone...waiting?"

My eyes widened and I shook my head. "I haven't been in Philly since January. My family packed up the house and sold it."

"You loved that house."

I shrugged. "Whatever sentiment I had attached to that house was obliterated."

He looked like he wanted to ask about it, but didn't. "You say your family packed up - where were you?"

"The French countryside."

"Is that where you live?"

"Oh, no. I've been stateside since a month before Lucas was born. I'm not really tied down anywhere."

"No boyfriends or anything?"

"If you're wondering about Kyle Sterling, I haven't seen him since I left Philly."

"I was curious, but it wasn't just about him."

"I'm completely single," I said darkly.

"I've been thinking about this most of the day."

"Thinking about what?"

"I want you and Lucas to move in with me."

I shifted uncomfortably. I wasn't expecting any suggestions like this. I wasn't sure what to expect really, but I never imagined this. We only just reunited - if you want to call it a reunion - just this morning. He was still unapologetically bitter, hurt, and angry. How was this going to play out?

Sensing my discomfort, Luke tried to argue his point. "It will be good for Lucas to have his parents raising him together, at least at first. It gives him the best of both worlds, and just developmentally speaking, he will do well to have us both there at once. We'll both be able to participate in the everyday little things that parents get to experience with a child. I don't want to miss anything," he said with emphasis, balling his hands into fists and looking at me with a small amount of pleading.

"What if you start seeing someone?" I didn't include myself, because I didn't see it happening. Single, white female. Forever.

"I'm not seeing anyone, not really. That's a bridge we'll have to cross when we get to it."

I hated that analogy. Who came up with it and why the hell can't you go around or under the bridge instead? Or turn and go back the way you came?

"You won't have to worry about anything," he continued. "I'll take care of the bills, buying the diapers and whatever either of you need."

"That won't be an issue. I can take care of me and Lucas."

"Then take care of yourself if you insist, but I want to take care of my son."

I sighed. Things would be awkward for a while, and there was no predicting how we were going to interact. It wouldn't be worth it to raise a child in a hostile household, but I felt no negativity towards Luke, and he said that he was going to put the past behind him. Moving in with him was probably the least I could do.

"How big is your apartment?" I asked. "Lucas needs a crib, and some other things."

"It's only a one bedroom, but you and Lucas can have my room. I'll take the couch. We can look for a bigger place later. Does this mean you'll do it?"

I nodded slowly.

Luke breathed a sigh of relief and actually smiled at me. I tried to smile back, but couldn't quite pull it off, so I kept my face stoic.

***

We went on our first "family" shopping trip the following day, in search of a crib, a pack and play, toys, and more. Luke stayed up half the night before finding the safest equipment and the best rated toys and the cutest clothes. I couldn't meet his enthusiasm, though, and I really did try.

Luke wanted to go visit his family for dinner so they could meet Lucas, but I didn't want to go. I was terrified of the reactions I would get for keeping something so sacred from them. I didn't say it out loud, but Luke must have read it in my face.

"They're going to be fine," he insisted. "No one is going to be nasty. They're not like that."

Because I'd lost the will to fight for myself a long time ago, I didn't object any further. As it turned out, Luke was right anyway. Dinner was at Lorraine's, with the whole family in attendance, ten kids between the three siblings, two spouses, both of Luke's parents, me and the family dog.

Even though I was greeted as a member of the family, and Lena picked up talking to me as if no time had lapsed between us, and no one excluded me (except maybe Luke) from conversations, I still felt like an outsider, a traitor. Lucas was passed from one person to another, each person ecstatic to hold him and in some cases even tearful. He laughed in only a way a baby can laugh, inciting smiles and excitement. I felt like a tool for not only keeping this good family from my son, but for not letting him get to know them from day one.

I was so overwhelmed by the treatment I was receiving and for basically being rewarded for my own despicable behavior, half way through dinner I excused myself and locked myself in the bathroom inside Lorraine and Chuck's bedroom. I sat on the edge of the tub and folded over until my head was between my knees. I don't know how long I stayed like that before there was a knock on the door and Lena called my name.

"Just a minute," I said, trying to find the motivation to get up.

The door swung open, and Lena leaned against the frame.

"You okay?"

"How do you know I wasn't on the toilet?" I asked.

"So what if you were? Honey, we've had our private parts spread wide open for the world to see while trying to push out miniature human beings, and at the same time, emptying our bladders and colon. Seeing you on the toilet would have been nothing."

I felt my mouth hanging open. "No wonder my mother likes you so much. You have some strong similarities."

"Are you having a moment?"

"If I were, you've just taken it from me."

"You look upset."

"I might be."

"Why? Everything is going so nicely."

"Maybe I feel like I..." I almost spilled my guts to Lena, which maybe wasn't a bad thing in ordinary times, but this wasn't an ordinary time.

"Emmy, what's done is done. No one is punishing you for it, and you can't punish yourself. Come on," she held out her hand and waved me on. "Mom made apple pie specifically for you."

I looked at her hand. "The same apple pie she made before?" I asked.

"The same."

"I could have eaten that whole pie by myself." I stood up and took her hand and followed her back downstairs.

***

Luke told me to make myself at home. I felt more at home at Lena's than I did in the apartment I was now sharing with my baby's daddy. Unless Lucas was directly involved, Luke steered clear of me, and I steered clear of him. He left for work around eight every morning and was back by six most nights. Sometimes he would come home long enough to eat dinner and spend time with Lucas, but once the baby was in bed, he would return to the office.

We moved through the apartment in silence when Lucas was asleep, not because we didn't want to wake him, but because Luke was still struggling not to live by my past deeds. As for me, I felt like I was intruding on his life, even when Lucas was at the center of attention. I slunk around with my head and ears down, and my tail between my legs, trying to stay out of his way, trying to go unnoticed until me or my breast milk were needed.

I made myself useful, cooking dinner every night, keeping up the housework and doing laundry. Luke always thanked me as if I were the help.

One day I was sick with a cold and didn't get around to cooking. Lucas and I were knocked out on the couch when Luke came in. I was startled awake when Luke took Lucas from my arms to put him to bed. When he came out, I was up and groggily picking up the living room.

"I'm sorry I didn't cook dinner tonight," I said.

"It's okay. Don't worry about it."

He loosened his tie and sat down on the couch.

"I can make you something."

"I'm fine, thank you."

After I finished picking up, I offered once more to make him dinner.

"I said no!" He snapped. "My god, it's not like you're my wife, Emmy."

I stood in front of the bedroom door frozen for a moment. I knew he was right, but it was harshly said.

"Okay then," I said softly and left him alone.

***

As Chicago announced the beginning of January with wind and snow and short days and long nights, there was little improvement between Luke and me. I was on the verge of screaming or crying or eating a whole apple pie every day. To make matters worse, Lucas was calling Luke "Dah-Dah" and had not even tried "Ma."

"He doesn't even know what he's saying," Luke had argued one afternoon.

"He looks right at you when he says it."

"Dah-Dah," Lucas agreed, looking right at his Dah-Dah.

One day in early December, Luke came home from the office, swooped Lucas into his arms and actually came into the kitchen where I was cooking.

"I need a huge favor," he said.

I looked at him expectantly.

"My office is a mess. It's so disorganized and we're incredibly busy. My receptionist...well, she's just a receptionist. I need someone to come in and get us organized and on track."

"You're asking me?" I said, not hiding my surprise.

"Yes, I am. You're a very good office manager. I wish I had thought to ask you sooner."

I didn't know anything about Luke's firm except that he and three other attorneys worked there. I had never even set foot in the place. And he never talked to me about work, because he never talked to me.

"I can try." I shrugged and refocused on the stove. "When?"

"Tomorrow."

"What am I supposed to do with Lucas?"

"Lena will take him."

This was it. The time has come where I have to part with my child for hours a day while I worked, except I didn't expect it to come so soon. I was financially stable, didn't need to earn a living, and would have been able to stay at home with Lucas until he was ready for school. But Luke's success had a direct impact on Lucas, so I would have to bite the bullet.

"I'll do it," I said.

"Thank you so much," he gushed. "I know you will be a big, big help."

"I hope so."

"You will be. I know it. Hey, at least this gets you out of the house for a little while. Maybe this will be good for you. You haven't been yourself." He tried to sound casual when he said it, but there was more lying under his tone.

"I haven't been myself in two years," I said, keeping my eyes on the task at hand.

"Look, I know I haven't made things any easier. I guess I didn't realize how bad things are here until Lena brought it to my attention."

I looked at him for clarification. I never discussed Luke unless Lucas was involved. I was curious to know what Lena said.

"She said it was like a tomb in here, that unless we're talking to or about Lucas we don't talk at all. She said that even when we're at family functions, I barely acknowledge you."

He answered Lucas's babble for a minute, and then stood there quietly for another minute until I spoke.

"What else did Lena say?"

"She said that she thinks you're depressed and that you think you deserve how I treat you, and that you're still beating yourself up. I guess I didn't stop to think about it before today, or I just looked the other way, but I suppose she's right, on all accounts. I argued with her at first, but she got really pushy, as only a big sister can do."

I said nothing. I turned the stove off and started to clean up some of the mess while I waited for the white wine sauce I made to thicken up.

"I'm really looking at you for the first time since the day I met Lucas. Em, you just seem...hollow. Like everything that makes you who you are is missing."

"Who am I really?" I asked, scrubbing a pan. "The woman who steals another woman's man? Am I the woman who cheats a good man out of everything he deserves? Or am I the woman who lets herself be used and abused? Maybe I'm the woman who keeps a child from his loving father. That's who I am, Luke. You're not missing anything great."

Luke stood there staring at me with his mouth hanging open, oblivious to Lucas's slobbery hands on his face.

"Don't look so surprised," I said, taking plates and silverware out. "You said yourself that you were wrong about who I am."

He tried to argue, sputtered out words and half sentences for a full minute before giving up. I took Lucas from his arms.

"I'll put him down for bed," I said. "Enjoy your dinner."

The following morning, our discussion from the previous night was temporarily forgotten. There was a lot of rushing around before piling Lucas, his stuff, and ourselves into Luke's car. He wanted to get into the office early, so I didn't have a lot of time to say goodbye to Lucas. I had to suck it up and make it quick and leave.

In the car, Luke gave me some information about his firm. There were four attorneys, one receptionist and one paralegal. They had sixteen open cases, and had to turn away a few people because they didn't have enough lawyers, and they weren't organized enough either. There were boxes of papers that needed to be filed, equipment that still had not been set up and the office looked a little trashy. I also found out my brother Emmet was strongly considering moving to Chicago to join the firm. I wasn't sure how I felt hearing it from Luke opposed to hearing it from Emmet.

Nothing Luke said could prepare me for the mess that was Kessler and Keane, Attorneys at Law. I stood in the center of the main room where there should have been desks and filing cabinets and office equipment, turning in slow circles, looking at the disaster.

"I tried to warn you," Luke said.

Steven, the Keane of the business, stood on the other side of me with a cup of Starbucks coffee, looking bored.

"Luke said you can fix this shit," he yawned.

"How much money can you spare?" I asked. "You need more people here."

"Money is a little tight right now," Luke answered, running his fingers through his hair. "We have a few big ticket cases, but only one is close to settling and the others are still tied up in paperwork. We're basically working for nothing."

"This place looks terrible. It's a wonder you have even sixteen clients."

Luke suppressed a smile. "Please, tell us how you really feel."

I narrowed my eyes at him and then at Steve. Luke bowed his head, Steve shrugged. The door opened and a young woman in her early twenties with blue and green streaks in her black, large, Amy Winehouse hairdo, greeted us with the enthusiasm of a rock before taking her seat at what I assumed was the reception desk. Her makeup was too loud and bright for her current line of work and her outfit was wickedly tight, and severely cheap, and looked out of place. She sat at the desk, chomping on gum and texting.

I heard the door open again, but I was already approaching the girl and didn't want another distraction. I stood over her desk, which was very messy, I noted.

"What is your name?" I asked her.

"Kacey," she answered in a bored tone.

"Kacey, spit out your gum."

"Excuse me?" She looked up at me, surprised by my tone.

"Spit out your gum. No client wants to look at the wad of gum and spit in your mouth while you're talking. And you have a week to fix your hair or buy a wig, or do whatever it is you need to do. It's unprofessional. This isn't a club, so don't come in here dressed for one, and that includes your make up. Tone it down, and your attitude needs improvement."

"Who the hell are you and who the fuck do you think you're talking to?" She stood up, angry and ready to pounce, but I didn't back down.

"Listen, Kacey, this is a professional office, or at least it's supposed to be. I have nothing personal against your style, but it does not fit into this office - or many others for that matter. You are going to be the first person a client sees when they walk in here, and the first one they speak to on the phone. You need to look and behave professionally. If you don't want to conform to our standards, I can hire someone who does. It's your choice."

She looked behind me at her bosses, and realized that they were with me on this and eased herself back into her chair.

"I don't want to lose my individuality," she looked panicked at the idea.

"You can go work somewhere else if you want," I shrugged.

After a moment of thoughtful silence, she quietly said "I'll stay."

"Good," I said and turned away. "Spit your gum out."

"I'm in love," a third man said, standing between Luke and Steven. All three looked at me in awe.

"This is Jordan, another attorney," Luke said, unable to take his eyes off of me.

Jordan stood there with a dumb smile on his face.

"Why are you three looking at me like that?" I asked.

"We can just tell that you're going to be awesome," Steven said. "I've been trying to get my niece to fix her hair for two years."

We all looked over at Kacey, Steven's niece apparently. She was texting again, but when she saw us watching her, she quickly put her phone away and got busy trying to make sense of her desk.

Our little huddle soon dissipated. The men went to their respected offices and I began what felt like an impossible task of getting the office in order. I started with hooking up all of the equipment - printers, fax machines, and computers. By lunch time, I had a whole back section of the office set up, and a small area up front to receive clients.

"This looks great," Luke grinned, looking around.

"We still have a very long way to go, and your files are a mess. I have Kacey fixing some of it, but it's going to take a while."

"I have to be in court in a little while. I'll be back to get you around five."

"No," I waved him off. "Just get Lucas and go home. I will be fine getting back."

He started to say something, but the door opened and two people hauling files walked in, bickering. Luke interrupted them for introductions. They were the fourth lawyer, Lanna and a paralegal named Craig.

Lanna looked like she was fresh out of law school, and Craig looked like he was fresh out of high school. They were both pleasant when introduced and complimented me on the work I did so far. After some small talk, Lanna closed herself into her office and Craig plopped down at a desk near Kacey.

"Don't work too late," Luke said and smiled at me before walking out the door.

I stood there for a minute. He had smiled at me more than once today. After weeks and weeks of barely acknowledging me, this should have been refreshing, but instead it was unnerving. I didn't allow myself to think about it much longer though. I still had a ton of work to do.

When I got back to Luke's that night, dinner was on the table (last night's meal that apparently went uneaten) and Lucas was bathed and ready for bed. I eagerly took him from his father and bathed him in kisses. I had never been away from him for such a long period of time.

"Mommy missed you so much!" I cooed at him. He smiled and laughed, showing off his three teeth. "Aww, your breath smells like string beans!"

"My mom made you another apple pie," Luke said, hovering nearby. "She said it's a gift for returning to work."

"If I didn't know any better, I'd say that your mother wants me to stay fat." I still had a few extra pounds of baby weight that refused to go away.

"You're not fat, but if you don't want the pie, I will gladly take it off of your hands."

"Touch my pie and I'll break your fingers. Lucas, say night-night to daddy,"

"Dah dah dah dah dah!" Lucas squealed at Luke, scrunching up his face.

After getting Lucas to sleep, I peeled out of my work clothes, took a quick shower, and then put on some warm pajamas. Luke had just reheated dinner again and was bringing it back to the table. We almost never ate together. I almost didn't sit down.

"Are you ready to quit yet?" he asked after sitting down.

"I was ready to quit when I walked in the door."

"Sorry. There just hasn't been time to set up."

"Kacey and Craig both could have been helping with that."

"Maybe so, but in Craig's defense, he's one paralegal working for four attorneys."

"Fair enough. I think Kacey worked more today than the total time she's been with you."

"I guess Steve and I should have handled her better. I think she thought this would be a free ride because Steve's her uncle."

"You can't afford free loaders. I think she will work out though. I need to ask you if it's okay that I hire a cleaning company to come in and clean three nights a week."

"I can't afford it."

"I can. I'll pay for it."

"No, I can't let you do that."

"And I want to hire a few more people. You need at least one more paralegal."

Luke looked at me funny. "There's no money for that."

"There's my money."

"No. I won't do that."

"Let's be frank," I said, between bites of food. "If your firm doesn't get its shit together, you're going to drown. Chicago is full of other small firms that already have their shit together and that's where the clients will go. I can even help you bring in upscale clientele, but you have to have your shit together first."

"I know your family is well off, but do you personally have that kind of money? I doubt it."

"You don't know that. We've never discussed my finances before."

"So, let's discuss them."

I looked at my wrist. I was wearing only a small fraction of the assets I actually had.

"I am a trust fund baby," I started. "I've been getting an 'allowance' dumped into an account every four months since I was eighteen. My parents paid for my education, my car, and all of my needs until I got out of college. I've always worked and saved most of what I earned. My family doesn't flaunt their wealth, and unless you looked a little deeper, you probably didn't know that we not only have our one 'plantation' in Louisiana, but several spread out in other states. Your cotton undershirt probably originated on one of my family's farms. My father is highly invested in oil and a couple of other resources. The bar I love so much? It's mine. I own it, and it does well.

"When Donya was modeling, she paid me to handle her finances. Then other models paid me to handle their finances.

"When I first started working at Sterling, I bought stock as soon as I could. I sold it soon after I left, and they were doing extremely well."

I paused before divulging the next bit of information. I wasn't sure how Luke would feel about it.

"I also left with...with compensation."

"Like a severance package?" he asked, unable to hide his shocked expression from all that I told him.

"Something like that. Walter Sterling paid me out of his own pocket to go away."

"Are you fucking serious? You took a bribe?" He looked shocked that even I could be so stupid.

"Yep. I was going to return it, but after...after what happened before I left Jersey, I decided to keep it. I haven't touched any of it."

"What happened?" He leaned forward.

I wasn't ready to go there with him, so I gently shook my head.

"I don't want to talk about that," I said. "My point is, I want to help you and I'm perfectly capable of helping you. You should let me."

We sat in silence for a long time. Luke stared at his empty plate, tapping it with his fork. Every now and then he would look at me with the same thoughtful expression.

"A loan," he said finally. "Everything you spend, I pay back, with interest."

"No interest."

"With interest," he said firmly.

"One percent."

"Eight percent."

"Two and a half," I countered.

"Seven and a half."

"Four."

"Six and three quarters."

"Five percent is the highest I'll allow," I said firmly. "You're being ridiculous."

"You're being too generous," he argued.

"I feel like I owe you something."

"You gave me a kid, Em. You don't owe me anything."

"What if he grows up and turns out to be a loser?"

"Then I may insist on some compensation. Until then, you don't owe me anything. So, I'll accept a capped loan, with five and a half percent interest."

"Capped? I don't know how much I'll have to spend in your crappy office."

"Then I suggest you set a budget, Miss Grayne."

"Fine," I said. I took our plates into the kitchen and loaded them in the dishwasher. Luke leaned against the counter, drinking a beer.

"You agreed to that too fast."

"No, a budget is fine." I wiped down the counters and stove and then got myself a beer.

"So, what kind of budget did you have in mind?" Luke asked cautiously.

"Oh, I don't know. Not much."

"I don't believe you. How much is not much?"

"Well...you need more staff, more equipment and furniture, advertising, and money just to function for your clients."

"How much, Em?"

I shrugged. "I guess...one and a half million."

Luke choked on his beer for a few seconds. "One and a half million dollars!"

"I can do two or three," I said, knowing he wanted me to go lower and not higher. I was amused by his reaction.

"I thought maybe a hundred grand, at most two fifty. Not over a million!"

"I said I can do two or three!"

"You're crazy. Two fifty, and no more."

"What's wrong with one mil?"

"Did you ever consider the possibility that I won't be able to pay that back?"

"You will," I insisted.

"You're insane."

I sighed. "I really want to do this, Luke."

"It's a lot of money, Emmy," he said, shaking his head.

I shrugged. We stood on opposite ends of the kitchen staring each other down. Luke looked away first.

"Okay," he said grudgingly.

"Okay," I said.

"Can we have pie now?" he asked with a pout that I reluctantly found rather cute.

Chapter Thirty-Five

As the weeks strolled on, Kessler and Keane's office transformed from a second rate office into a high class office meant to bring in high class clientele. I replaced all of the cheap furniture with good, well-made furniture. I rearranged the entire office so that it not only looked good, but so that work could be done more efficiently. I moved the reception area directly in front of the doors, where the newly professional Kacey greeted anyone who stepped through the door.

I created a waiting area that featured a huge Keurig with every variety of coffee, tea and hot chocolate. I used mugs, not paper cups, and also had other beverages in a small refrigerator with a glass door. There were cookies and cakes and crackers and Danishes and donuts. I even arranged for the little kitchenette in the back to be remodeled.

In addition to working on the cosmetic aspects of the business, I also had to hire and train new employees. This move took a huge load off of the lawyers and they were able to better focus on their clients and take on more.

I worked day and night, even when my parents flew in to visit. I made sure I was home to see Lucas before he went to bed and I stayed home with him every Sunday but worked every Saturday.

My relationship with Luke had improved so much, I could say with a certainty that we were friends again. I was still struggling with the horridness I felt inside, but at least I was able to forget about it sometimes. Honestly, I was starting to feel more like the person I was before Kyle, but not enough.

My brother Emmet moved his family to Chicago and started working for Luke. I never had a very close relationship with any of my siblings, but I took advantage of the situation to spend more time with him, his wife Casey and their son Owen. We had them over for dinners and folded them into Luke's family.

By early May the firm was fully functional and generating actual revenue. The clients paid very well and there were a lot of perks that Luke and Steve always passed on to the staff. One client owned a four star hotel in the city and offered five suites to the firm. Another client owned a very popular restaurant and they provided us with free food on many occasions.

Just before Lucas's first birthday, I decided I wanted to spend more time with him, and less time in the office. I cut myself down to three days a week, and no weekends. I went in at ten instead of eight-thirty, and left at four. Twice a week, if Luke didn't have court or wasn't too busy, he would leave work by two or three so he could also spend more time with Lucas.

We celebrated Lucas's birthday at Lorraine's. Her house was the biggest, and able to handle the volume of people that were invited: all of the Chicago family, a large portion of the Louisiana family, a very pregnant Donya, Mayson and my cousin Tabitha, and to my utter surprise, Leo.

We acknowledged one another, but I knew without asking that Tabitha was unaware of our last encounter. My relationship with my cousin was already fickle, and I didn't want to make it any worse by informing her that I made out with her boyfriend and tried my hardest to get into his pants - again. I thanked her for coming, was surprised that she came at all, but she kindly informed me that it was convenient due to the fact that she had a book signing nearby that weekend. Whatever. I took it as a kind gesture anyway and moved on.

I wasn't as happy as I should have been on this occasion. Not that my son wasn't a big deal, but I didn't recall any other kid in my family getting such big attention on their first birthday. I shared that thought with Luke, in what I thought was a quiet corner, but my mom appeared out of nowhere.

"Well, nobody thought either of you would ever have any children or settle down," she said. "That's why this is a big deal." She left us alone in our corner.

"I guess that's true," Luke rubbed his neck and sighed. "My mom and sisters thought that about me at some point."

"I didn't know that. You seem very much like the settling down type."

He let out an uncomfortable chuckle. I looked at him with strong curiosity. He looked at me as if he didn't want to tell me, but then relented when I pinched him.

"I played the field...a lot. I had a different girl on my arm every other month."

"I didn't hear anything like that back in Philly. You had two steady girlfriends over the years."

"Correction. I had three steady girlfriends over the years." He gave me a knowing look. "The first two were always on and off, not as steady as you think, and there were more before and between."

"Oh," was all I could say, because what else could I say? I was number three and I broke his heart.

"The second woman, Vicky, she was basically just a distraction."

"From what?"

"From number three who didn't yet know she was going to be number three." He walked away, leaving me standing there looking dumbfounded.

After that, I was able to enjoy the festivities. I had not felt that content in over two years. I found myself smiling a lot, and was surprised to hear my own laughter in my ears several times. At dinner, my appetite returned full force. I used to love food as much as I loved tequila, but the details of my life in the past had made it un-enjoyable. Every time someone spoke to me, my mouth was crammed with food. It was a great day, the best I had in a long time.

And that day was also a turning point.

Throughout the day, regardless of where I was or what I was doing, my eyes would often fall on Luke. I liked watching him talk to my mom, because he had a way of handling her with kid gloves, and making her feel that she was heard, even if what she was saying was ludicrous. I liked the relationship he had with Donya and Mayson, joking with them, making them laugh, or talking to them as if he had known them forever. Luke got along well with everyone; someone was always vying for his attention, including all of the kids, because he was able to go down to their level without being patronizing. Watching him laugh made me smile. Watching him with our son made me all warm and gooey inside.

When I went to bed that night, I assumed that I would be back to normal by the time I woke up, that it was just the excitement of the day that had me feeling a little off kilter. I went about my Sunday morning as usual. I rolled out of bed to find Lucas missing from his crib, but could hear Luke talking to him in the living room. I used the bathroom and brushed my teeth before going into the living room.

Lucas was tottering around the room carrying his favorite toy, the stuffed whale Luke gave him the first day they met. Luke sat on the couch with the Sunday paper spread out on the coffee table, and Sesame Street was on the television. I stared at Luke's chiseled bicep peeking out from under his tee-shirt. Not a good sign. When he looked up and flashed me a smile and said "Good morning, number three," my heart hammered in my chest.

I stuttered out a greeting and quickly exited the room to the kitchen. I was silently kicking myself as I poured myself a cup of coffee. Lucas came into the kitchen with his dad on his heels.

"Cup?" Lucas asked, looking up at me questioningly.

"You want your cup?"

"Ya. Cup." He patted the whale's head and waited patiently while Luke got him a sippy cup of juice. He padded back into the living room and shouted "Emmo!"

"Elmo," Luke and I said together.

"You want some breakfast?" I asked him.

"Sure. I could use some food. I tried Lucas's cereal, but it wasn't for me." He made a disgusted face that made me laugh. "Oh, my god it's that sound again!"

I knew he was talking about my laughter, but I played dumb.

"What sound?" I asked, trying to reach a box of Bisquick. "Why do you put things way up on the third shelf where I can't reach?"

"Because it's funny watching you reach for it." He stood almost directly behind me, reached over my head and grabbed the box. I could feel his chest muscles against my back.

"Thanks," I said and snatched it from him. I kept my back to him to hopefully hide the redness that had seeped into my cheeks due to his close proximity to me.

"I'm going into the office after breakfast. I have to be in court first thing tomorrow morning and I want to make sure I am well prepared."

"Okay," I said, moving around him to get out eggs and milk.

"You had a good day yesterday," he said, poking his head out of the doorway to check on Lucas.

"Yes, I did," I agreed. "My mom only irritated me a little bit."

"About what?"

"What do you think?"

"I don't know." His forehead wrinkled as he thought about it, which I realized I found attractive. "It can't be your hair or your clothes. You looked amazing yesterday."

Damn it. I could feel my face glowing.

"Thanks," I said.

"Hmm. Oh," he said knowingly. "Your sex life."

"Bingo. She really feels that it's one of those use it or lose it things, which made me wonder about her and my dad and that's when I decided to have a drink."

"Yeah, no one wants to think of their parents getting it on."

"Oh, stop! Please!" I covered my ears while he shouted out sexual innuendos about my parents.

"Okay, okay, I'm done," he chuckled.

"My god, that was horrible."

"Now I'm curious."

"About what?" My eyes widened. "My parents? Gross!"

"No, dummy," he shook his head. "About you."

"What about me?" I asked, hoping he wasn't really asking what I thought he was asking.

"Are you, you know, on the verge of 'losing it' from not using it?"

I tried to look indignant at such a question, but instead my expression only gave him his answer.

"I don't have time!" I said.

"There's always time."

"I am either with Lucas or at the office," I argued. "Like you have so much time on your hands for sex."

He checked on Lucas again and then leaned in the doorway and crossed his arms. His arms and abs looked yummy.

"I have made time," he said.

"When?"

Now he looked uncomfortable. "It doesn't matter when."

"Why not?"

"We don't need to discuss it anymore." He turned to leave, but I threw a big spoon at the back of his head.

"Luke, that's not fair! You started this conversation!"

"I know, but now I don't want to talk about it."

"Why not?"

"Because. My answers will make me look...dishonest."

I looked at him in confusion for a few seconds before it hit me. I pointed my spatula at him.

"Some of your late nights at the office were booty calls!"

"Some, but not all," he answered, looking at the floor.

"Oh my god!" I laughed because it helped dissolve the lump in my throat. "And when was the last time you got some?"

"If I answer, you have to answer the same question," he insisted.

I looked away, flipped some pancakes. I didn't want to play twenty questions anymore. I said "don't answer" at the same time he answered with "two weeks ago."

I stared down at the pancakes, feeling a pressure building in my chest. Luke had been sleeping with at least one woman, and while it shouldn't have bothered me in the least and was even something I had expectations of at one time, things had changed and this revelation was hurtful.

"Now, your turn," he said from the doorway.

I put some pancakes on a plate and added more mix to the griddle while he patiently waited for my answer.

"Almost a year and a half," I said quietly.

"You're kidding me."

"Nope."

Lucas yelled for Luke, who reluctantly left the kitchen. I let out a big breath and chastised myself for giving him that information, making myself look ridiculous and hopeless.

I put Luke's breakfast on the dining room table and started out of the room.

"Aren't you eating?"

"I want to take a shower before you leave," I called over my shoulder and shut the bedroom door behind me.

I took forever in the shower, unable to focus on the simple task of shaving my legs and nicked myself a few times. Washing my long hair always took a while, but I would wake up from a daze with my hands unmoving in my soapy head. By the time I stepped into the bedroom in a towel, Luke was dressed and tying his sneakers on the bed.

"Lucas crashed," he said. "Hopefully he'll sleep this afternoon, too."

"Okay," I said. I started rooting around in drawers for something to wear.

"I'm sorry," Luke said from the doorway.

"For what?"

"I was really insensitive a little while ago."

"It's fine," I shrugged.

"No, it's not fine, Emmy. I was an ass, and I'm sorry."

"Okay. Forgiven."

"Okay. I'll be back in a few hours, maybe around three."

"Take your time."

He walked out of the room but returned seconds later.

"I'm really going to the office to work, nothing shiesty will be going on. I promise."

"Luke, you don't owe me any explanations."

"I do, and I'll just be honest about it next time. So, there will be no question about it in your head."

"I don't want to know," I said. I meant to sound firm, but instead I sounded like I was pleading, and I guess I really was. I didn't want to know every time he was going to go fuck some girl.

He stood there staring at me, his mouth open. "I'm sorry."

"Dude, stop apologizing and go to work already," I forced a chuckle. "It's fine - I'm fine. Really."

"Okay. I'll be home as soon as I'm done."

"Okay, okay." I waved him away, but he stood rooted to the floor. "What now?"

"I don't want you to think that you're not...attractive or desirable."

"Oh my god, Luke! Can you just go!" I buried my face in a shirt.

"Because you are. You're probably hotter than ever before, but we just have so much...shit between us and we're not really on the same page and..."

"You know what?" I asked, uncovering my face. "If it will make you feel better, I will go get laid tonight. I'm sure I can find a date. Then you won't feel so...weird, and you are being really, really weird."

His face fell. "Sorry. I'm leaving." And with that, he finally left.

Chapter Thirty-Six

Weeks passed, but not without some small changes. For example, one morning when Luke was leaving for work, he kissed Lucas on the head as he always did. Without any hesitation, he kissed my cheek before going out the door. He did the same when he got home from work that day. After that day, the kisses to the cheek became commonplace, even in the mornings as a greeting.

Then there was the hand holding. This started in the park one day. Luke carried Lucas, because Lucas was tired, cranky, and didn't want to walk anymore. With his free hand, he took mine, in the middle of a conversation, so I didn't comment on it. Then I thought it would be rude to do so, so I didn't. That, too became commonplace, not just in the park, but wherever we went together.

Luke stopped working late in the office, opting to bring home his work instead. I don't know if he just wanted to be home with Lucas, or if he was trying to prove to me he wasn't sleeping around, but then I didn't think it mattered what I thought. We weren't a couple. I dismissed that line of reasoning and just assumed it was about Lucas and the creature comforts of home.

"We need to move," he said one night, trying to find room at the table for his papers. "We're outgrowing this apartment. We need a house, where Lucas can play outside."

"Oh," I said. I never thought this far ahead. I never imagined leaving this apartment, but he was right. It was getting tight.

"I'll call an agent tomorrow," he said, frustration laced throughout his voice.

"Can I get you something before I go to bed?"

"No, I'm fine. If I need anything, I can get it. Thanks."

I turned to go into the bedroom when a thought occurred to me, and I instantly felt guilty for not considering it sooner.

"Luke, why don't you sleep in the bed tonight? You've been working your ass off and sleeping on a blow-up bed. It hardly seems fair."

"Are you trying to seduce me, Miss Grayne?"

I snickered. "I'm pretty sure my girly parts have withered up and turned to dust by now. I'm serious, though. Just come to bed when you're ready. I can come out here."

"I'll think about it," he nodded slowly. "Goodnight." He took a few steps and kissed my cheek.

"Lata." I gave him the peace sign and disappeared into the bedroom.

I don't know what time it was when I felt Luke climb into bed next to me. I mumbled something about taking the couch, but his hand on my hip restrained me.

"Does it bother you to sleep in the same bed as me?" he asked.

I looked over my shoulder at him. There was just enough moonlight seeping through the windows to highlight his facial features. The view was stunning, so stunning I forgot what he asked.

"What did you say again?"

"Does it bother you to sleep in the same bed as me?" he repeated patiently.

"No. I thought it bothered you."

"Maybe in the beginning, but not for the reasons you would think."

I rolled my head back to my pillow. "I didn't put much thought into it."

For a little while, it was quiet. Only Lucas's soft snoring could be heard. Luke's hand stayed on my hip, unnerving me a little.

"I want to ask you something, and I want you to be straight with me."

I rolled over onto my back so I could look at him. He readjusted his hand so that it rested on my belly and propped up his head with his other hand.

"What is it?" I asked.

"Did Kyle hit you?"

I held my breath for a moment, tried not to look as startled as I felt. "Why are you asking me that?"

"You alluded to it months ago. You said something about being used and abused, and then when I asked you about your last day in Philly, you said you didn't want to talk about it."

"That doesn't mean anything," I said as panic settled in.

"Yeah, I knew you would react this way, so I talked to your mom and Mayson."

"What the fuck," I muttered. I rolled away from him and out of bed. He followed me into the living room, talking.

"Mayson said you came back from a trip to Miami with a broken wrist, and the day after the cast was off you were walking around with that fancy bracelet. You told her you fell while you were drunk, but she didn't believe you, and she especially didn't believe you after you started wearing the bracelet. She thought it was some kind of compensation from Kyle, probably for breaking your wrist."

"Mayson is a crazy bitch. You can't believe anything she says," I snarled.

"That's cruel and wrong and you know it," he said firmly.

I kept walking away from him, but he kept following me.

"Your mom said she didn't even know about the broken wrist until I asked her today. You gave her a different story about the bracelet. She also said you called her a little after midnight New Years and told her you were going to be there later in the day. You got there a day late, claiming you were in a car accident to explain away the fresh bruises on your face, on your arms, and even on your back."

I stared at him in horror. Every day I had to work on eradicating those memories from my head. I kept only enough as a reminder of the things that can happen to me when I fuck other people over.

"He really fucked up your head, didn't he?" Luke asked. "You feel like you deserved everything he did to you."

I didn't have anything to say. I just stood there staring at the floor, and he stood there watching me watch the floor.

He sighed, shuffled around a little.

"I'm sorry. I shouldn't press you like that. When you're ready to talk about it, I will always be ready to listen." A lingering kiss on my cheek and he was gone.

I looked at the clock on the oven. It was three-thirty in the morning, and I knew sleep was going to elude me the rest of the night. I shuffled into the living room and planted myself on the couch. I sat there until the sun came up, trying hard not to let the bad shit from the past take over my emotions. I was able to get a grip by the time Lucas woke up.

I bathed him, dressed and fed him all before Luke rolled out of bed. He looked as bad as I felt, tired, worried, drained.

"I'm not going in today," I said, packing up Lucas's diaper bag. "Can you drop him off at Lena's?"

"I'm not going in either," he yawned. "I'll drop him off anyway."

Okay, so I was being unreasonable, I realized. I had never spoken to anyone about the things Kyle did to me. Speaking about it aloud was distressing. I didn't want people to know how weak I was, how stupid I was, and did I think I deserved it? I felt that karma was a bitch, and karma got me good.

What happened to me was humiliating and made me feel ashamed. I knew everyone would look at me differently, and even though I was definitely different in countless ways, I didn't want to be pitied. I'm sure Luke didn't want to extend me his pity. Honestly, I wasn't sure what Luke's intentions were. His behavior over the past several weeks were confusing. I didn't know where it all was going.

I was exhausted. I picked myself up off of the couch and dragged my tired ass to bed. I wanted to occupy my mind for a while, with someone else's life. I picked up my kindle and started to read. Luke came in a little while later.

"I have such a crazy headache," he grumbled as he kicked off his shoes. "I feel like my head is going to explode."

Forever ago, when Luke was my boyfriend, when he had a headache, he would lay his head in my lap and I would run my fingers through his hair, letting them gently graze his head. As if no time had passed since the last time we did this, he got into bed and put his head in my lap. Hesitantly, I put my free hand in his hair and began the old ritual.

I went back to reading while my hand was lost in his soft hair, pretending that this wasn't an unusual event, pretending that it wasn't giving me butterflies big enough to make me want to hurl. I read the same sentences over and over again before I understood the words, taking forever to get through a few short paragraphs.

Luke was silent and I heard his breathing slow down. I looked down at his sleeping form, amazed. What the fuck was happening here?

Chapter Thirty-Seven

Eventually, I was able to fall asleep after readjusting myself under Luke so that his head rested on my stomach instead of my lap. When I woke up a couple of hours later, he was sitting up, remote control in hand, lazily changing the channels.

"You hungry?" he asked, when I sat up.

"I could eat."

"I'll order some pizza and wings."

"Sure," I said and got up to go pee. "How's your head?"

"Perfectly fine thanks to your magic fingers."

"Cool."

When I came out of the bathroom, Luke had his laptop open on the bed.

"I ordered our food."

I sat down next to him and looked at the screen. He was on a real estate site, scrolling through pictures of houses.

"Where do you want to move to?" I asked.

"Maybe closer to Lena? What do you think?"

"It doesn't matter to me. As long as it's pretty safe. You want to get away from the city?" We currently lived almost in the heart of Chicago, not far from downtown and all of the tourist areas.

"I think so, but I don't want a two hour commute to work either. Maybe somewhere close to public transportation."

I nodded in agreement. "How big of a place are you thinking of?"

"Four bedrooms and a space for an office."

I nodded again, counting who was going in what bedrooms in my mind. "So, we'll have one room left over for a guest room. What are we going to do if, you know, you get married or something? I mean, it's something to think about if we're buying a house together."

He looked at me funny, like I just said the dumbest thing.

"What happens if you get married?" he asked.

I almost laughed. A stupid chuckle left my mouth instead. "I think my current state is as good as it's gonna get for me. I'm so not on the market."

"Why would you even say that?" he said, irritated.

"No one buys broken items," I sighed, and reached over him and scrolled through the houses.

"People buy broken cars and fix them up all of the time."

"I'm not a broken hot rod. I'm more like...a shattered vase. No one buys those."

"Why are we talking about you like you're an inanimate object?" he growled.

"What about this house?" I clicked on a four bedroom house, but Luke pushed my hand away and slammed the laptop shut.

"This is driving me crazy," he said, jumping to his feet. "Sometimes I see that woman I knew so well, but as soon as she starts to come out, you push her back down into the dark."

"That's poetic," I smirked, also getting to my feet. I needed something to do instead of sitting there. I started folding some clean laundry sitting in a basket.

"Why?" he asked. "Why are you so afraid to be her?"

"Maybe you've forgotten, but that woman you knew so well screwed you over and broke your heart."

"You know what? Honestly?" He said, snatching the clothes away from me. "More often than you think, I do forget, and really, I may never forget entirely, but I have forgiven you. I forgive you entirely, no more animosity, but you can't forgive yourself."

"Luke, really!" I snapped. "Why are you bombarding me with all of this serious shit lately?"

"Because in order for us to move forward, we need to deal with that shit, Em. You need to deal with what Kyle did to you and you need to deal with your feelings about yourself."

"I am dealing with it!"

"Hiding behind your kid and your job will only hold up for so long."

I rolled my eyes and exhaled loudly and walked out of the room. Luke was hot on my heels.

"Great idea! Run away! That's a great way of dealing with your problems."

I paced the living room, while Luke stood off to the side.

"So, you've made some mistakes," he said, with a little less aggression. "We have all made some mistakes."

"Yeah, your mistake was, how did you put it? Oh yeah. You had this inflated idea of who I was and it's not my fault that I didn't live up to your expectations." I stood in the middle of the room, staring at the floor, breathing heavily. Saying it out loud really made me understand how badly it had hurt me when he said it.

"I was hurting pretty bad," he said softly. "I wanted you to feel my pain. I apologize, I didn't really mean it. Had I known then how deeply damaged you really were, I would have behaved differently, and I should have anyway. I didn't treat you the way I should treat the mother of my child. I've really been trying to make it up to you and be a better man."

I didn't know what to say to that. I was a little surprised.

"Em, I know you're broken, okay?" he said with a sense of urgency. "But I need to know what broke you so I can fix you."

I stared at him for a dumbfounded moment before returning my attention back to the floor. "Why would you want to bother? Is it making me a bad mom?"

"You're an excellent mother. I want to because I love you, and it kills me to see you like this."

"Oh."

I didn't have to respond any further, because the buzzer sounded. Luke grabbed his wallet and went down to meet the pizza guy. I sat down on the couch, feeling anxious and confused. Luke had not told me he loved me in a very long time. Did he love me love me? Or just love me as his baby mama?

When he returned with the food, I expected him to pick up where we left off, but he didn't. We sat on the couch for the rest of the afternoon nibbling on pizza and wings and watching television. He sat close to me and always had an arm behind me across the back of the couch. My anxiety grew until I thought I would burst, but just before reaching that point, Luke got up and left to get Lucas.

We slept in the bed together again that night, but this time my rest wasn't disrupted by intruding questions about my past. We crashed on opposite sides of the bed, much to my relief. In the morning, I woke up to find Luke and Lucas at the dining room table having a meaningful conversation about Elmo. I could only understand a few words, but Luke nodded and spoke at what seemed like the appropriate times.

"Are you playing hooky again?" I asked Luke after kissing the baby good morning.

"Impossible. I am co-owner of the firm. I can do whatever I want."

"Humble."

"I want to take Lucas to the zoo today and tonight you and I are having a date night."

"Date night?" I asked doubtfully.

"Yep. I already asked Diane to babysit."

Diane was Luke's nineteen year old cousin. She was cute and perky and all of the Kessler kids loved her.

"I know I'm not Brad Pit, but I think I make a pretty good date," Luke said when I didn't answer.

I couldn't hide my small smile. "I guess."

"Oh my god, Lucas! Did you see that?"

"Smartass," I muttered and went into the kitchen.

The boys went to the zoo, but I stayed home to clean and do laundry. Luke wasn't letting me off of the hook for date night, explaining that I needed to get out. Maybe he was right, because unless it was a family function, I didn't do anything or go anywhere. While he and Lucas were gone, I convinced myself that this was a good thing, that it didn't necessarily signify anything romantic.

Diane arrived at four-thirty and Luke and I were out the door a few minutes later.

"Where are we going?" I asked as we stomped down the sidewalk.

"Let's just see where our feet take us," he said, taking my hand.

"You mean you didn't plan anything?"

"Nope."

"You suck a little at this dating thing," I said.

"Was that a joke?"

"Nope."

An hour later we found ourselves at a Barnes and Noble, standing a few feet apart, quietly sifting through books.

"This is a hot date," I said.

"I know you think so. The only thing missing are your sexy pink rubber gloves."

"Maybe we should go buy some, I mean if that's what rocks your boat."

"Only if you promise to wear the gloves and nothing else."

I snickered. "Yeah, because my body is so rockin' after having a baby."

"I think your body is even more rockin' than before you had a baby."

I threw a sideways glance at him. "I haven't lost any weight since the day Lucas was born."

"You're hot, I'm telling you," he tried to reassure me.

"You think so now. You haven't seen the stretch marks on my belly."

"I don't care about your stretch marks," he said, putting his book back on the shelf.

I felt the conversation was going in a direction I wasn't ready to go in, so I changed the topic.

"Are you flying to Jersey with me and Lucas for Labor Day?"

Donya's baby was a couple of weeks old and I was anxious to see her in person. She named her Rosa, after her husband's deceased mother.

"Do you want me to?" He looked at me.

"Yeah. Sure."

"Don't be so excited about it," he frowned. I think I actually hurt his feelings.

"I don't get excited about anything these days. Don't take it personally."

He looked at me doubtfully.

"I would love for you to come," I said with as much excitement as I could muster.

"Right here in the book store?" He feigned shock. "I knew my bad ass girl was in there somewhere. I haven't done it in a public place since that one time in the bathroom at the diner."

"Walking away now," I said and left him in the aisle with the two older women who had just witnessed our whole conversation.

We went to dinner after the book store. The first thing Luke did was order us some hardcore drinks. I eyeballed my drink with apprehension. I haven't had a hard drink since before I found out I was pregnant with Lucas.

"Drink up," Luke insisted after devouring his.

"This is going to hit me like a pile of rocks."

"It will loosen you up a little."

I narrowed my eyes at him. "Are you calling me uptight?"

He pressed his lips together and we had a staring contest, but I quickly lost, because he was right. Every day I felt tightly wound, knotted even. Sometimes it was hard to breathe, because everything inside of me felt squeezed tightly, as if there was a boa constrictor slithering around inside of me, squeezing and squeezing, suffocating me.

"Hey, are you okay?" Luke reached across the table and took my hand. And the snake squeezed a little tighter.

Why does Luke make my condition worse? So stupid.

I picked up the drink and took a deep breath. I wasn't going to sip it like a little bitch. I was a master at drinking in my past life. I was going to make this tall, hard ass drink my bitch. I downed it faster than Luke had downed his.

He looked at me with a crooked smile while I made a face. Well, I couldn't allow that drink to make me make a face. I called the waitress over.

"Two more please, and some shots of Hennessey."

By the time our main course was served, I was lit. The snake was still there, but he had loosened up a little, or I was just numb and would feel it again during sobriety. I didn't have even half the drinks I would have had in the past, but all of those months without liquor made me feel like a drinking virgin.

Luke drank some, but he wasn't feeling it like me. He had a perpetual grin on his face watching me and listening to me ramble on about nonsense. When we got up to leave, I forgot that I had on strappy sandals that Carrie Bradshaw would die for and almost fell on my face, but Luke caught me and kept a steady arm around my waist. I wrapped both arms around him.

"You're sooooo good to me," I cooed as we waited on the sidewalk for a cab.

He kissed the top of my forehead in response and waved down a cab. He helped me inside, leaned forward to tell the driver where to go and then settled back with his arm around me.

"What's with all of the fucking little kisses lately?" I asked. "I don't know if you're kissing me like I'm a pet or like a friend or like a lover. They're really conflicting kisses!"

He laughed and looked at me with something like adoration and said "I'm sorry. Let me clear that up for you." He put his hand under my chin and gently tilted my head and kissed me.

Fireworks went off in my head. Heat exploded from my mouth where his tongue caressed mine. Electric currents sizzled from where his hand was under my chin and spread throughout my body, right down to the tips of my toes. Oblivious to the cab driver up front, I locked my hands around his neck and without taking my lips from his, slithered on to him and straddled him. I could feel him hard against me and I wanted it super bad. I didn't realize I was grinding against him until I felt his hands on my hips.

"Hey," the cabbie called from the front, breaking our kiss and grinding session. "Why don't you pay me and take your sexcapades to your bedroom?"

I opened the door, grabbed my pocketbook and stumbled off of Luke and onto the sidewalk outside our apartment building. I didn't wait for him, and rushed inside, not acknowledging the doorman or the guy that does security at night. As I rode the elevator to the sixth floor, I felt my boa constrictor again, squeezing me. Like a taught rubber band, things were snapping back into place. I was still fairly drunk though, but not enough to soothe the alarm that was beginning inside.

I let myself into the apartment, forced a smile at Diane who was sitting on the couch with a Vogue magazine.

"How was your night out?"

"Great," I forced a smile.

"Wow, you're drunk as hell," she giggled. She got up, picked up her backpack. "Where's Lukester?"

"On his way up. How was Lucas?"

"Perfect. He told me he 'wuvved' me."

I smiled, because I thought I was supposed to.

The door opened behind me, but I didn't turn to look at Luke.

"Are you sober enough to drive me home?" Diane asked. She lived a good half hour away, longer when using public transportation as she did earlier, but I think we all would feel better if Luke took her home at this late hour.

"Yeah, I'm good. I didn't have that much."

"Thanks, Di," I said, giving her a hug goodbye.

Luke touched my arm and I jumped.

"I'll be back in an hour."

"Drive carefully," I said, because I thought I was supposed to.

They left and I collapsed onto the couch.

While Luke was gone, I took a long shower, drank a bottle of Gatorade, and ate a baked potato. I was lying in bed in a tee shirt and shorts, staring at the dark ceiling when he came home. I heard him drop his keys on the table by the door, kick off his shoes knowing I would probably pick them up myself later, and then I heard clicks as the lights in the living room went out. Once in the bedroom, I heard the jingle of his belt as he slid out of his jeans, and then I felt the bed shift as he climbed in beside me. He cuddled up close to me and draped his arm over me.

"Too much too soon?" he whispered.

"No. Maybe. I don't know," I said.

"Tell me what you're thinking."

I sighed. Now was as good a time as any.

I told him about the snake, the suffocating, and how he sometimes made it worse. This was the most candid and open I had been with anyone in a very long time. I didn't exactly bare my soul, but I put enough out there to make me nervous; to feel vulnerable.

"I didn't realize I make you feel worse," Luke said and started to pull away, but I grasped his arm and held it where it was.

"It would probably be a good feeling if my past wasn't my past," I said quickly.

"I only know some of it," he said carefully. "I know my part in it."

"I know, but I'm not ready to talk about that. One thing at a time. It was hard enough telling you what I just told you." I sighed wearily.

"Do you feel any better after getting it off your chest?"

"No. It made it worse," I admitted.

"Let me help you release some of that tension," he whispered and then began nuzzling my neck. His hand worked its way down to my inner thigh, but stopped there. "I won't continue unless you want me to."

My body's natural reactions were winning. When I didn't answer him, Luke asked "Do you want me to continue?"

After a brief hesitation, I answered, my voice barely heard above the pounding in my chest. "Yes."

The word was barely out of my mouth before he was kissing me and sliding his hand up my shorts and quickly finding a spot that automatically made me quiver. For the first time ever, I understood and felt what the song "Like a Virgin" was all about.

At first, I felt apprehensive about getting it on with my kid asleep in his little toddler bed a few feet away, but I quickly got over it.

Luke remembered everything that turned me on, seemed familiar with every part of my body, inside and out. His hands and lips and tongue were everywhere. When he entered me, I had an instant orgasm, one of many that I had already had. He started out slow, but deep, but the animal inside of him took over and my head was soon slamming into the headboard and he had to keep a hand over my mouth so that my cries of ecstasy wouldn't wake our child. As we climaxed together, I clung tightly to him, wrapped my arms and legs around his body. It took several minutes afterward for me to slowly release him.

"How do you feel now?" he whispered before we drifted off to sleep.

"Much, much better," I sighed and instantly fell into a solid sleep.

Chapter Thirty-Eight

I woke up in bed alone and naked. Lucas was missing from his bed, and I didn't hear anything from the living room. I pushed myself up and out of bed and shuffled into the master bathroom for a shower.

Standing under the hot water, I tried to sort through my feelings. I was feeling so many things at once; I couldn't decide which emotion was bigger than the others. I was embarrassed, elated, angry, sad, giddy yet depressed, and definitely, definitely horny. I laughed one big "Ha" out loud.

After getting dressed, I stepped into the empty living room just as Luke walked into the apartment, toting a bag from Panera Bread.

"Where's Lucas?" I asked, feeling panic rising.

"With Casey and Emmet. They're taking Owen and Lucas to the zoo."

"Oh," I sighed with relief. "That's nice. Lucas loves No-nen," I smiled at the name my son gave my nephew because he couldn't say Owen.

"I brought breakfast," Luke held up the Panera bag.

"Cranberry orange muffin?" I asked with a hopeful expression about my new favorite muffin.

"Of course."

I almost kissed him, but caught myself. I awkwardly patted his arm while he handed me the bag. Then I felt stupid for just patting his arm and cursed under my breath.

"That was an impressive pat on my arm," Luke teased.

"I know. I worked hard on it."

"I can tell. You could teach a class on awkward arm pats."

"You're jealous that your arm pats aren't as great as mine," I said as I walked into the kitchen to make a cup of coffee.

"I have something for you," Luke said behind me.

"If it's another muffin, I may have to pat both of your arms."

"Damn. I don't have another muffin."

"I'm sad."

"I'm sad, too. I really could have used a double arm pat. All I have is this stupid piece of paper." His hand appeared in front of me, holding a check written out to me for two hundred and fifty thousand dollars.

"What is this?" I asked, reaching out for it. I turned around to give Luke my full attention.

"It's some of the money I owe you," he said.

"I don't want it." I tried to hand it back, but he took a step back. "Luke, you can't afford to give this back to me yet."

"Yes, I can. We've done extremely well, just had a big settlement."

"Yes, you've done well, but..." I sighed and again held the check out to him. "Listen, I strongly suggest you talk to a financial advisor and hire an accountant full time. It may seem like you're good now, but shit happens."

He sighed and reluctantly took the check from me. "I felt really good about paying you back."

"Aww. Do you want me to pat your arm?"

"Maybe later. I want to talk," he said seriously.

"Oh boy. Can I at least have my coffee first?"

"Are you incapable of talking with a cup of coffee?"

"The damn stuff dribbles out of my mouth every time I try."

"Maybe it's best to swallow rather than spit," he grinned.

"Are we still talking about coffee?"

"You're successfully avoiding an inevitable conversation."

"You got me," I admitted. "I'm so not ready for that conversation."

"I'm not going to let this one go."

"I know," I said, and bit my bottom lip. "Maybe we can just postpone it."

"I would need a damn good reason to postpone it."

Without any longing looks or hesitation, he grabbed my ass with both hands, pressed my body to his and kissed me. His tongue felt so good in my mouth, I kissed back hungrily, trying to taste every ounce of him. He unbuttoned my capris and slipped his hand into my panties and slid a finger into me. I moaned into his mouth, and it didn't take long for me to reach an orgasm.

Fired up and ready to go, Luke yanked my shorts and panties down and pulled my shirt off. He was out of his pants and boxers in a matter of seconds and before I could brace myself, he had lifted me up and slid into me. It reminded me of another time that I got dirty in a kitchen, but I quickly pushed the thought away.

We ended up on the kitchen floor, ignoring the cold tiles. Luke slowed his rhythm down as he ran his thumb gently over a scar in my hairline. He kept his eyes locked with mine.

"I really love you," he said, slightly out of breath. "Do you love me?"

"Always," I panted and then groaned when he pressed deeper inside of me.

"Really?" he whispered, unconvinced.

I knew he needed to hear it. I dug my nails into his back during another deep thrust.

"I love you," I said.

He kissed me and slammed into me so hard I slid backward. He held me close and slammed it home again, groaning and digging his fingers into my skin. He slowed down again after a moment.

"You love me, but you don't want me," he said with such sadness, I burst into tears.

While crying, I had the biggest orgasm of my life as Luke held me tighter than ever and rocked into me and climaxed with me. He wiped at my tears.

"I didn't mean to make you cry," he said.

I covered my face, unable to stop the gushing tears. I had not cried since the day Lucas was born, and even then, it was because my vagina felt like it was being torn to pieces. Every painful memory and emotion I had stored up decided this was a good time to be released.

Luke helped me off of the floor and tried to soothe me, but I was inconsolable.

His phone rang in his pants on the floor. He ignored it, even after it went off a second time, choosing to hold me instead, but when my own phone rang in the bedroom, he released me.

"Maybe Lucas is sick or something," he said.

I wiped my face with a couple of paper towels and tried to get a grip. I could hear Luke talking in the other room, but I couldn't hear what he was saying. When he returned, his expression was dark.

"My mom was just rushed to the hospital."

Out of sheer panic, I stopped sobbing. We scrambled around the kitchen to get our clothes on. Luke made a quick trip to the bathroom and then we were out the door.

Chapter Thirty-Nine

Grace Kessler had fallen down the stairs of her home. She broke her left arm and hit her head, requiring ten stitches and a twenty-four hour stay in the hospital for observation.

While the siblings argued about whether or not she should be permitted to live alone, or whether or not she needed to move into a safer environment, I stood by myself on the other side of the waiting room, looking out of a window. My mother was on her way to Chicago, summoned by Lena. I was trying to mentally prepare myself for that, but just couldn't do it. I almost didn't care. I had bigger things on my mind. Like Luke.

Eventually, the conversation would arise, and I had to have straight forward answers. That wasn't easy considering I didn't really have any. All I knew for sure was that when I was confronted with any opportunity to love and be loved, I had the intense reaction to run the other way.

"Are you okay?" Luke asked.

I didn't know how long I had been standing at the window, but Lena and Lorraine were gone.

"You've barely said two words since we left the apartment," he said.

"I'm sorry," I said, turning to face him. "Are you okay? How are you holding up?"

"I'm okay. I'm having a hard time accepting the fact that my mom is getting so old."

"It's funny. Your mom falls down the stairs accidentally, and I want to shove my mom down the stairs on purpose all of the time."

He attempted a smile, but it quickly faltered and ended in a sigh.

"I said I would wait until you were ready," he said quietly. "But..."

"You want to know what is ultimately keeping us apart," I filled in.

"You are ultimately keeping us apart," he said patiently. "But I need to know why."

He reached out and pushed my hair out of my face. His fingers on my cheek were deeply comforting. I pressed my hand against his, savoring his touch before he could withdraw it. I wrapped my arms around him and kissed him. Enormous butterflies fluttered in my belly and migrated throughout my body. The tingling down my spine made me weak.

We kissed in front of the window, slow and easy, oblivious to the sights, sounds, and smells of the hospital. It wasn't until someone cleared their throat about three times before we broke apart and looked for the intruder.

Lorraine stood just inside the doorway, grinning ear to ear.

"Sorry to disturb you," she said. "But the doctor wants to talk to all of us."

"Oh, that's embarrassing," I whispered as we followed her out of the room.

As it turned out, Grace had a mini stroke, which was probably the main contributor to her fall. She was going to be in the hospital longer than originally anticipated.

Luke, Lena, and I left a couple of hours later. Lena was going to pick my mom up from the airport, a task I was thankful wasn't asked of me. Luke and I went to meet Emmet, Casey and the kids for dinner and all of us traveled back across town for dessert at Lena's with my mother.

"You look...different," she said, eyeing me carefully after a hug.

"I look the same," I insisted, but I knew she could tell I've been getting some.

"Hmm," she said doubtfully. "At any rate, you always look beautiful." She started to turn away but turned back and said "Except when you wear red lipstick. It makes you look like a whore."

I cringed, but said nothing. Luke looked at me with sympathy and then gave me a double arm pat.

"Can I double pat her face with my fists?" I whispered to him.

"No, but you can put on some red lipstick when we get home."

We politely hung around a little while longer before using the excuse that it was well past Lucas's bedtime and quickly bowed out. Lucas was asleep long before we got home, so putting him to bed was effortless. An hour and some change after leaving Lena's, I was stark naked in the living room, riding Luke as if my life depended on it.

"Maybe we should stop having sex," he said afterward. "I'm being a girl about it. My feelings just grow stronger every time."

"Mine do, too," I argued.

"Not enough."

"You don't know that."

"If it were enough, we wouldn't be having this conversation."

We were quiet for a minute or two. My head was in his lap and he absent mindedly stroked my hair, staring at the floor, deep in thought.

"I feel really fucked up inside," I said, breaking the silence. "I feel scarred and dysfunctional."

"Everyone is dysfunctional sometimes."

"No," I objected. "I feel dysfunctional all of the time. It's something that stays with me all day and all night, no matter what I'm doing or how else I feel. I always feel fucked up, and I feel like I can't be fixed. You want to fix me, but I feel like I'm a lost cause, and I don't want you to even bother trying."

"What did Kyle do to you to make you feel so lowly about yourself?"

I sighed loudly, and pushed myself to my feet. I was so frustrated.

"Luke, stop blaming Kyle. I did this to myself. I mean...he did a lot to contribute to it, but he didn't force me into anything. I made my own decisions. If this was all of Kyle's fault, it would be easy to just throw all of the blame where it belongs and move on, but it's not all his fault."

"You're not a lost cause," Luke said, also on his feet now. "Yes, you made bad decisions, but you're not doomed. I love you, Emmy, scars and all."

"Look...I'm afraid I'm going to fuck up again. I'm afraid that I won't be able to ever give you what you deserve."

He started to object, but my cell rang in the dining room. I walked away, to escape the conversation, and to answer the call. It was Mayson.

"What's up?" I asked.

"You have a problem," she said carefully.

"What is it?"

"Uhh...your bar."

"What about it?"

"It's on fire."

Chapter Forty

Change of plans. Instead of flying to the east coast in a couple of weeks, I was packed and at the airport with Lucas in my arms by noon the following day.

My bar, according to Mayson, had burned to the ground. There was probably nothing left to salvage. No one was hurt, even though it was a full house. The fire marshal thinks the fire started in the kitchen with faulty wiring to the stove.

"I'll be out there in a couple of weeks, if my schedule permits," Luke said to me.

"Okay."

"I'll miss you guys."

He took Lucas from me and talked to him about the "air ane" and how much he'll miss him. He kissed his head and handed him back. My kiss was a little more elaborate.

"I love you, buddy," Luke ruffled Lucas's hair. "I love you," he said to me.

I hesitated before repeating it back to him, which was clearly a mistake judging by the expression on his face.

"I'm sorry," I rushed. "I didn't mean..."

"Don't worry about it. Have a safe trip." He walked away without a backward glance.

When we landed in Philly, I was able to forget what an ass I was to Luke. I was excited to be back to the tri-state area I called home. My exit from said area was a memory I pushed out of my mind. I didn't want to focus on that.

Mayson waited for us at the airport. After some discussion, we packed into her car and drove the few seconds away to a rental car agency. She left me there and took Lucas with her to do whatever she had to do. Before I left the parking lot of the rental company, I texted Luke to let him know we landed safely.

There was always traffic in Philly, whether it was a Sunday or Doomsday, traffic never ceased. I easily fell back into bad driving habits and yelling at other drivers. The traffic slowed a little when I crossed the bridge into Jersey, but not by much. The air quality changed a little, too. I loved the smell of factories and refineries on a hot summer day. Mmm mmm!

I had mentally prepared myself for the disaster I would see when I got to what was left of my bar. I just had not prepared myself enough.

What was left of the building was blackened by the fire and smoke. Rubble and unidentifiable items were melted together. It looked like a bombed out building you see in war movies.

I got out of the car, and stifled a scream. I walked toward the site in a daze, stupefied by what I was seeing. Just outside, I found a half a bottle of vodka, intact, just lying there. I picked it up, studied it for a minute and then opened it and took a big gulp. After a couple more big sips, I felt ready to venture inside the disaster.

"I wouldn't go in there if I were you," a familiar voice said behind me. I was so startled that I dropped the bottle as I turned around, shattering it and spilling the rest of the alcohol.

"Shit. You scared the shit out of me and perfectly good vodka has been spilled."

"Sorry. I thought you saw me."

"No," I shook my head and nodded across the lot. "Didn't even notice your car until now."

We looked back at what used to be the bar.

"I don't think it's safe for you to be in there, hence the yellow tape."

"The tape is a formality. How else am I supposed to assess the damage?"

"That's what your insurance guy is for, and he left a few minutes before you got here."

I sighed loudly and kicked at a burnt piece of wood. We stood there in silence for a while, just staring at the charred mess. I decided to take some pictures so I could send them to Luke and my mom.

"So, how long are you in the area?"

I shrugged. "I don't know. A couple of weeks, I guess. Depends."

"On what?"

"What I'm going to do with this mess, for one, and I don't know. I may get homesick or something."

"You don't miss Jersey?"

"Are you kidding me? Every day of my life! I miss the people, the food - my god I could go for a real Philly cheesesteak right now. And some water ice. Real water ice. It's hot as hell out here."

"Where are you staying?"

"Probably in Mount Laurel in a hotel. I guess I should take care of that now," I said. "What are you doing here anyway?"

"I heard about the bar, wanted to see it for myself."

"Did you think I would come?"

"No, I didn't. I was surprised to see you."

"Oh."

"Well, look, I don't want to hold you up. Why don't you text me later? I know I'm going out on a limb here, but maybe we can have lunch or something before you go."

"Maybe," I said, not committing to anything. "Is your number the same?"

"Yeah. If you don't contact me, I will understand."

I nodded an okay.

"Be careful - and stay out of there."

A moment later Kyle Sterling drove out of the parking lot and I felt myself breathe again.

Chapter Forty-One

Early the next morning, I found myself standing in the lot of my destroyed bar again. I didn't know what to do with the mess. Rebuilding meant more time in Jersey - a lot more time, and as much as I had missed it, I wasn't sure if that was a good idea.

For hours after Lucas fell asleep, I had to talk myself out of calling Kyle. I would dial the number, but never initiate the call. I must have a hundred drafts of text messages that will never be sent. I don't know what I hoped to accomplish. The only reason I didn't finally call was because I fell asleep. No will power.

"Less go!" Lucas shouted in the car behind me. I was only standing about two feet from the car.

"Okay, let's go," I answered and got back into the car.

We went to visit Donya and her new baby for a little while. I was pissed off that she had already lost her baby fat and again looked like the runway model she was.

We only stayed a couple of hours, because she had a doctor's appointment and Lucas was restless. I took him to the zoo for a couple of hours and then we ate an early dinner in the city. By six, we were back in the hotel. Lucas fell asleep around seven-thirty, and I was bored. If the rest of my trip was going to be this way, I was going to cut it short. Everyone I knew was busy with their lives and couldn't spare more than a few minutes. Donya was busy with her new expanded family, Mayson had a boyfriend, and Tabitha wasn't exactly on the welcoming committee. My old co-workers were busy with work or had also moved away. At least in Chicago I had family and a few friends, and a job, and Luke.

I knew one person who would be available as much as I wanted him to. I dialed, held my breath, and pressed the send key. It started to ring at the very moment someone knocked on my hotel door. Surprised, I sat there staring dumbly at the door with the phone ringing in my ear.

"Hello?" Kyle said.

"God. I'm sorry. I know I just called but someone is knocking on my door," I said as I ran to the door. I looked through the peephole.

"Em?" Kyle's voice lit up.

"Tabitha," I said when I opened the door.

"Tabitha?" Kyle asked, confused.

"I'm sorry," I said into the phone. "My cousin Tabitha just showed up. I'll call you back." I ended the call.

"Can I come in?" Tabitha asked.

"Yeah, of course." I stepped aside and let her in.

"Where's Lucas?" She asked, standing in the middle of the room letting her eyes wander.

"He crashed a while ago. Probably out of boredom. Have a seat. You want something? A soda or water?" I started toward the kitchenette, but she stopped me.

"No, I'm fine," she said and sat down on the couch.

I sat down in a chair across from her. I felt nervous, probably because this was out of character for Tabitha, to just show up at any door I may be behind. The funny thing is that when we were kids, we were cool. We were close even. Somewhere around fifteen or sixteen, it suddenly became what it is now, awkward and tense.

"Who was on the phone?" she asked.

"Umm, Kyle."

"Sterling?"

"Yeah."

"Met him a few times. Kind of got a bad vibe from him, like he was a dick," she said staring into some point in the past, but then she caught herself and straightened up. "Sorry. I shouldn't have said that. I don't know for sure if he's a dick. You're the one that worked for him."

"It's okay, and yeah, he had dick-like tendencies."

"What about now?"

"I wouldn't know," I said quietly.

She looked at me curiously, but didn't mention Kyle again. "Mayson told me your room number. I hope you don't mind."

"I don't mind, but..."

"You want to know why I suddenly care to make a social call."

I nodded.

She looked away, silently thinking of how she was going to start.

"Let's talk," she said, and we did.

Tabitha stayed for nearly three hours. When she left, I felt better about our relationship. I was glad that I hopefully fixed something while I was in Jersey. After she was gone for a good ten minutes, I picked up my phone and called Kyle.

"Are you going to hang up on me again?" he yawned.

"Maybe."

"What are you doing?"

"Nothing."

"Can I come see you?"

"Absolutely not," I huffed.

We were silent for a moment. And then "I like your hair."

"What?"

"Your hair," he said patiently. "I like it. Still smells good."

"How could you smell my hair through the smell of smoke and burned dreams?"

"I don't know the science of how. I just know that I did."

"Huh," I said, because I didn't know what else to say.

"So," he started. "I think we have a lot to talk about."

"No," I said quickly. "We don't need to talk about any...any of that. I don't want to."

"Em, I don't even know what happened. I know I...hit you, but I don't remember. I want you to tell me."

"No, I don't want to talk about it. Please," I said with a hint of begging. "It's just that...it was painful and I'm trying to move away from any kind of negativity."

He was silent for a moment and then I heard him sigh. "Okay. Then what do you want to talk about?"

"I don't know," I sighed. "Maybe I shouldn't have called."

"I still love you." There. He put it out there. Now what was I supposed to do with it? "If you still loved me after everything, especially that last night, I would be surprised."

"I said I didn't want to talk about that!"

"Sorry."

Another bout of silence.

"You looked really good yesterday. Did I mention I like your hair? It's so long."

I sighed, thinking maybe I made a mistake calling him.

"Emmy, I want to see you."

"When?" I asked, instantly forgetting my folly in calling him in the first place.

"How about now?"

"I already said no."

"Well, say yes."

"I can't."

"Are you...are you and Luke together?"

It took a moment for me to answer. "Not officially. He wants to be with me, though."

"And you?"

"I am undecided. I don't want to talk about that either."

"I'm coming over."

"You can't! My son..." I realized this was the first time Lucas was brought up.

"Right, your son, which is why I should come there. Tell me where you are. I'll bring you diner food and a diner shake. Jersey food, Em. Mmm yum."

Okay, so who could resist some good diner food? I caved.

"I come bearing gifts," Kyle said when I opened the door forty minutes later.

I snatched the food from him and let him in.

"Can't get good diner food in Chicago," I said, stuffing a chili cheese fry with bacon into my mouth. "I mean Chicago has its good food, but not good diner food. Mmm this is so fucking good."

"Nice to see your appetite hasn't gone anywhere," he looked at me with fake disgust as I stuffed more food into my mouth and followed it up with some chocolate shake.

"What's in the brown bag?" I stopped chewing and pointed to the bag he was holding.

"I replaced your spilled vodka."

"I'm not going to drink that," I said after swallowing my food.

"Why? It's your favorite vodka - cotton candy flavor."

"You and me with alcohol makes matters...gray."

"Gray matter isn't all bad all of the time."

I looked at his chest muscles bulging against his black tee shirt and his biceps stretching the fabric.

"I can't drink right now," I said, tearing my eyes away with a loud sigh.

He put the bag down on the coffee table and sat down on the couch.

"Maybe you'll change your mind."

"Don't count on it," I said from the kitchenette where I got paper plates and plastic forks.

I sat down in the chair instead of the couch, ignoring Kyle's looks of disappointment. We ate in silence for a while. My eyes kept roaming from the vodka to Kyle. To the vodka, back to Kyle. Vodka, Kyle. Kyle, vodka. I wasn't sure which one I wanted most. It had been a good long time since I really enjoyed vodka. It had been only a little less time since I really enjoyed Kyle.

Shit.

"I can almost see the gears turning in your head," Kyle said. "You're thinking about how much you want some vodka." He took the vodka out of the bag and held it on display. "You're also thinking about how much you want some Kyle. You can't decide which one you want more."

"Fuck off, dick," I growled.

He grinned. "I miss your potty mouth. Besides hookers, I don't know any other woman who uses such colorful language."

"How many hookers do you know?" I asked, raising an eyebrow.

"One or two."

"Ew."

He gave me a disgusted look as he opened the vodka. "Not like that. I don't have any trouble getting a woman."

"No, the trouble comes when you have one too many," I said dryly.

"I deserve that."

"And more."

"And more," he nodded before taking a sip of vodka.

"Still drink like a girl," I muttered.

"Why don't you show me how it's done?" He offered me the bottle.

"I don't drink like that anymore. In fact Friday was the first time that I was drunk since before I knew I was preggers with Lucas."

"Slacker."

I shrugged. "Motherhood. Who woulda thought it would make me a responsible person?"

"Having a drink won't make you irresponsible. Driving drunk would make you irresponsible, but since you're in for the night..." He again offered me the bottle.

"No," I said firmly.

"Your loss." He put the bottle down. "So can I see pictures of your little boy or what?" He was asking to be polite and probably with a little curiosity, but I knew it might hurt him. He had wanted to be a dad to Lucas, even if he wasn't the father.

I hesitated, chewing on my cheek for a moment before I pulled out my phone and tapped the icon for pictures. I handed him the phone. His expression was hard to read from where I was sitting, but when he glanced up with a big smile, I could see some pain behind it.

"He's a cute kid. You look really happy in these pictures," he said softly. "You look like a really loving mother."

"I am a really loving mother. Lucas makes me feel...worth something."

He looked at me with a seriously sad expression. "I always thought you were worth something."

I looked away, afraid of being completely taken in by his imploring eyes.

"Who are these people? Luke's family?" he asked, flashing me the phone.

I moved over to the couch so I could point out who was who in many of the pictures, or give him a story about some of the pictures, like the one of Tabitha and Leo at Lucas's party. When we reached the end of the pictures, he handed me my phone, but I didn't immediately get up. He smelled so good, I wanted to inhale him completely.

"How's work?" I asked, trying to appear relaxed by sitting back and crossing one leg over another.

"Busy. My department has grown. The office is ridiculously crowded now, but you taught Eliza well. She's almost as good at office management as you are."

"Give her some credit. She learned some basic stuff from me, but she probably really does just know what she's doing. Are you any nicer to your employees?" I asked with a raised eyebrow.

"Yes, I am. Probably too nice sometimes."

"I'm impressed."

We sat staring at each other for half a minute. I knew him well enough to know that he was about to do something he shouldn't. My hand caught him, just as he was moving forward.

"Don't kiss me," I whispered.

"I really want to," he whispered back. "We're both single, right? So who could we hurt?"

"Each other."

The answer caught him off guard. He looked like I had just slapped him. He backed off, moved over a foot, and looked down at the floor.

"I guess I should go," he said and then stood up.

I didn't make any move to stop him, even though I really wanted to not only stop him, but let him kiss me. I walked him to the door, and allowed a brief embrace before the door closed after him. I stood there a minute, looking at the door. If I were going to stop him, I only had about a half of a minute to do it, but then a question pressed into my brain. Why would I want to stop him? What would I accomplish by doing that, and would the end result really be one that I wanted?

Chapter Forty-Two

Lucas was up at the crack of dawn. I didn't know what to do with him, or my time in Jersey. After chasing him through the suite for an hour, I made a decision. A half hour later, Lucas and I were checking out of the hotel. I made another stop at my personal disaster area.

I had hoped that if I looked at it hard and long enough, an idea would form in my head, but I had no such luck. Before I could leave the lot, my phone rang.

"Hey," Luke said. He sounded like he was walking and I could hear morning Chicago traffic in the background.

"Hi," I said and smiled.

"How are you guys?"

"We're great. We're getting ready to go to the shore for a few days."

"Oh, Lucas's first beach trip. I'm jealous I'm not there."

"Sorry. Are you still going to come out here?"

"I don't know. Depends on your plans. You got there a week earlier than expected because of the bar, but are you still staying until after Labor Day?"

I sighed. "I don't know. Depends on what I'm going to do with the rubble that used to be my bar."

"Well, things are pretty busy here. I'm in court all week this week. You let me know what your plans are and I will let you know if I can come."

"Okay. You want to talk to Lucas?"

"Of course."

I put the phone on speaker and supervised the cute father and son conversation, sometimes translating what Lucas said. When Lucas lost interest in the conversation, I put the phone back to my ear.

"So, what else is up?" Luke asked. It was a general question, not directed at anything in particular, but I instantly felt guilty.

I hesitated, and stumbled over my words until I got my words straight. I told him about running into Kyle at the bar, a little about my initial phone call and my time with Tabitha, and then I told him about Kyle's visit. I didn't leave anything out, including the attempted kiss.

There was a stretch of silence from the other line, and I would have believed the call had disconnected if not for the traffic noises.

"Hello?" I said.

"I'm here. I don't know what to say. I guess I'm fucking blown away."

"Nothing happened. I told you every detail."

"I don't doubt your honesty, Emmy. I doubt your decision making."

What could I say to that? So did I.

"Look," he said after another stretch of silence. "You made it pretty clear where we stand, so you do whatever you want, but you keep that asshole away from my son."

The line went dead, and I think part of me did, too.

I bit my lip to keep from crying, but the tears came anyway. Up until last week, I hadn't cried in forever, and now I was crying again.

"Go, mommy! Go, mommy!" Lucas was impatient now, tired of looking at my trashed bar.

"Okay, baby. We're going."

I drove away, trying to dry my eyes, with the awful feeling that I had ruined everything once again.

Chapter Forty-Three

I rented a small room a block from the beach. Lucas was instantly in love with the sand and water. Watching him laugh and splash in the shallow water made me temporarily forget that I pissed off his dad.

We played in the sand, built lopsided castles, collected sea shells and chased seagulls. We stuffed ourselves on boardwalk fries and pizza, cotton candy, funnel cake, and salt water taffy. We shopped in the little shops, buying crap we didn't need, like a couple of hermit crabs.

At night, I watched bad cable television, ate junk food, drank the vodka Kyle bought me, and ignored his phone calls and texts. I texted Luke and even tried calling him, but he would only say he was busy and only accepted a phone call if he knew he was only going to speak to Lucas.

After three nights in Ocean City, Lucas and I headed up the coast to Belmar. Leo had a house there, and he and Tabitha invited us to stay with them for a while. Donya and Jerry and Mayson and her boyfriend Fred were also invited, but Jerry was still in the regular baseball season and would only be able to pop in here and there.

"So, are you guys like...together?" I asked Leo later that morning. We were making lunch. Tabitha was at a nearby playground with Lucas and the others were expected to arrive shortly.

"I guess," he shrugged. "I know she loves me and that she wants to be with me, but..." He sighed. "It's complicated."

"I hope it works out. I think you make a nice couple."

"Thanks. So, what's up with you and Luke?"

I made an exasperated sound.

"That good?"

"It could be better," I admitted.

When I didn't elaborate, he changed the topic, although it was parallel.

"What happened when you left my house that night?"

He was referring to the night I tried to ride him like a stallion, while drunk, while Kyle waited for me back in our hotel room, seething and feeding his anger.

"What have you heard?" I asked carefully.

"I heard that you had an accident," he said, but I could hear in his tone that he didn't believe it. "But I couldn't comment on it either way. No one knows that I saw you again after dinner that night, for obvious reasons."

Obvious reasons being my cousin Tabitha who I just made up with.

"So what really happened?"

I bit my lip, contemplating whether or not that was information he needed to know. I trusted Leo, though. He's kept more than a few of my secrets in the past.

"Long story short," I started. "We argued and things got a little physical. He accidentally broke my wrist."

"Accidentally."

"Yes, it was an accident."

"Why didn't you come back? I woulda accidentally broke his face." He was holding a knife, and he looked pissed. I believe he really would have broken Kyle's face.

"Don't tell anyone, Leo. Mayson is suspicious, but she doesn't know for sure."

"My lips are sealed, but if I see that guy on the street..."

The front door opened and I heard a baby screaming and knew Donya had arrived. We dropped the subject and went to greet the others.

***

I thought sharing a few days with my closest friends would be a distraction from my own head, and I thought I would have a great time, but after one day, I realized I was the odd man out. Donya had Jerry when he wasn't at a game, Mayson had Fred, and Tabitha had Leo. I had Lucas, but that wasn't quite the same.

In addition, since my exit from the state nearly two years before, Donya and Mayson had grown close, and it seemed that more recently, Tabitha made the duo into a trio. They talked about things I didn't know about and had inside jokes. I felt so left out.

I called Luke a few days before Labor Day to ask him if he was coming. Without an explanation, he simply said no. When there was only the sound of his fingers clicking on his keyboard, I lost my head for a moment.

"If you're going to be like this again, I may as well not come back. Lucas and I can settle down somewhere else."

"I can't come out there, Emmy! I'm busy! Don't you understand that?"

"The only thing I am understanding is your bad attitude."

I ended the call, shut my phone off and left it on my bed. The other girls were waiting for me on the deck for a girls-only dinner. The kids were in bed and the guys went out to do whatever it is guys do when they get away from their women for a night.

For the first part of dinner, I didn't say much. I listened to everyone else talk about their sex lives and their men. I just kept pouring myself wine until I got bored with that and started making drinks out of liquor I found at the bar inside. I didn't have much to contribute to the conversation since my sex life only picked up recently, and I didn't really have a man, per se. By the time conversation got over to me, I was pretty well lit.

"So," Donya said, looking at me over a fork full of chocolate cake. "I was looking in your purse for some gum today and I found that gorgeous bracelet Kyle gave you."

I couldn't even be mad at her. I go through D's personal things like they're my own, especially her closet.

"Who gave you a bracelet?" Tabitha asked, knowing the least about my life before Lucas.

"Kyle Sterling gave her a bracelet, about two years ago. Em said it was for her job performance."

Tabitha shrugged. "So? Lots of employers give their employees gifts. I knew a guy who even got a new car as a bonus."

"Emmy is middle management, Tabitha," Donya pointed out. "If the bracelet was worth a few hundred bucks - hell, even a couple grand, that would be one thing. That would be believable. Emmy, tell your cousin how much your bracelet is worth."

"At the time it was bought or its current value?" I asked before taking another long sip of one of my concoctions.

"If I bought that bracelet from Tiffany's two years ago, how much would I have paid for it?"

"About seventy grand."

Tabitha's jaw dropped. "Shut up!"

"Exactly," Donya said to her.

"So what's your point?" I asked, feeling a little annoyed.

"What is the real reason the bracelet was bestowed upon you? May and I have some theories, but only you can tell us for sure."

"Why are you asking me now?" I asked. "Why didn't you ask me before?"

"You seemed a little...unstable," Mayson said. "Now you seem to be more like yourself...which is still...rather unstable."

"Just answer the question," Donya said. "It's us, not your wacky mother or your stuck up sisters."

"I'm so lost," Tabitha said, looking at me with big eyes. All three of them were looking at me with big eyes.

I guzzled the rest of my drink and with a drunken smile said "Kyle bought me the bracelet as an apology for breaking my wrist."

"I knew it!" Mayson slammed a hand against the table, making dishes and glasses rattle.

"That mother fucker broke your wrist?" Donya asked, incredulously.

"Yessss," I rolled my eyes. "That's what I said."

"On purpose?" Tabitha asked and before I could answer, shook her head and waved her arms. "Wait! You were screwing Kyle Sterling? The dick?"

"Yes, I was, Tabs and no he didn't do it on purpose."

"Were you screwing him while you were with Luke?"

"Yes, Tabitha!" Donya said, irritated that my poor cousin wasn't catching on fast enough. "How did it happen, Emmy? I can't see you taking that shit."

"We had dinner with Leo while we were in Miami, and during dinner Leo and I eluded to the fact that we fucked around when we were kids and -"

"Whoa!" Tabitha slapped the table now. "You had sex with Leo? When?"

I waved a hand. "A long time ago, when he and Leslie were broken up."

"Which time?" Tabitha spat out, sarcastically. She didn't really expect an answer, but I was drunk.

"I don't know." I shrugged. "Two, maybe three times. Maybe four. I don't remember…"

Her jaw again hung open, but now she looked pissed off instead of surprised and quizzical.

"Interesting how he's never mentioned that to me."

"It was a long time ago, Tabitha! Damn." Donya snapped before turning back to me. "So, Kyle got pissed off and broke your damn arm?"

"No. Back at the hotel, we started arguing about it and I got pissed off and left. I went back to Leo's, drank a lot of alcohol, and things got a little heavy."

"You fucked him again?" Tabitha yelled.

"No," I said bitterly. "He didn't want to take advantage of me apparently, because I was drunk."

"What the fuck," Tabitha grumbled.

"Then what happened?" Mayson pressed, and then "Wait! Did you sleep with any of my boyfriends?"

"No, I promise."

"Okay, good," she said, relieved.

"I just made out with one."

"You see?" Tabitha said. "She's a whorebag."

"Cum bucket," Mayson nodded in agreement.

"You guys," Donya made a disgusted sound. "Can we save the name calling for later? I want to hear the hoe's story."

I told them the rest of the story, all the way up to the night the bracelet was presented to me.

"Okay, Mayson wins that bet," Donya said, digging into her purse. She handed Mayson a few bills. "I thought it was like a promise gift, you know?"

"Now you have to spill the beans about New Years, Emmy," Mayson said seriously.

"What happened on New Year's?" Tabitha asked. "Did you try to hump Leo again?"

"Okay, you need to deal with that another time," Donya said. "Leo didn't do anything to you. Nobody knew you would end up with him."

Tabitha slumped in her chair and mumbled "He knew."

"New Years," Mayson pressed.

"I've never spoken about the New Year's incident," I said quietly.

"Speak about it now," Donya insisted. Even Tabitha looked interested underneath her anger.

I had to pour myself another drink before I started.

Chapter Forty-Four

It's funny how I can omit certain, crucial details and have you believe one thing, when in fact circumstances were completely different. I'll bet the average onlooker thought Kyle was squeaky clean and was only a dick by nature. Maybe he was a dick by nature, but crystal meth had a way of turning a dick into a monster. My broken wrist in Miami was the result of jealousy and a little bit of meth up a nostril. Up until New Years, there was nothing worse than some shoving and aggressive yelling and empty promises of getting off of the drug, along with promises of ending his relationship with Jessyca.

I was smarter than my actions proved. I knew that I should have broken up with Kyle months before Luke left, and especially afterward. I knew that when he started taking hits of meth for "therapeutic reasons" that I should have bowed out, but I guess my addiction to Kyle was just as bad as being addicted to any drug. The results were the same: on the surface it felt really good, but the damage to one's body and mind was irreversible, deadly.

In the early hours of the New Year, our addictions consumed us. Kyle had struck me, and even as I sat there on the floor in confusion, thinking it had to have been a mistake, he was already lost to me. When he took a handful of hair and tried to force me to my feet, I clawed at his hand. The blood seeping from the gouges I created did nothing to deter him before he slammed my head into the mirror over my vanity. As the glass shattered to the floor, all I could think about in that moment was about the destruction of the last gift my grandmother had given to me before passing away when I was only nine years old.

While Kyle roared like a beast and destroyed other mementos in my room, I crawled through the glass to the side of my bed and pulled myself to my feet. I watched with an open mouth as he overturned a tall dresser, still full of clothes and other miscellaneous items. When his eyes turned on me, I didn't see Kyle. I saw madness, and it took my breath away. As he yelled at me, cursed at me, and threatened my life, I understood that there would be no reasoning with him, and there would be no escape.

I would like to tell you that I defended myself, that I fought back, and I kicked his ass, but then I would be lying. The meth made Kyle's level of strength inhuman. I was a mere mortal, with no stupid drug in my blood. Nothing short of a miracle was going to turn me into Wonder Woman or some other awesome female super hero. This wasn't one of those happy ending hour long prime time shows where the heroine stands up to her attacker and overcomes him with wits and luck. If I further provoked Kyle by fighting back, he was going to kill me.

I avoided his blows as much as possible, but my primary goal was to protect my unborn child. Instead of holding up a defensive arm, I covered my belly and took whatever he was delivering. When I was shoved to the floor, I had enough sense to put my hands out so that I wouldn't fall, literally right on top of my child. As soon as I was able, I ran into my bathroom and locked the door just as he reached it. Kyle screamed from the other side of the door, kicking and punching at the door, demanding that I open it. I was afraid that he would eventually kick it down, but when it seemed that the door would hold, I slid to the floor with my back against the tub. I stared at the door in horror, bleeding all over my white rug, every part of my body throbbing in pain.

I didn't cry. Crying wasn't going to help my situation. There was nothing to help my situation - my phone was lost in the chaos that was my bedroom and my neighbors were a little too far away to have heard my screams and Kyle's yelling. I had to wait for him to either leave or pass out, and eventually he did pass out, but so did I.

When I woke up, sunlight was pouring through the bathroom window onto my face. I was stiff and sore and it took me a few minutes to get to my feet. I looked at myself in the mirror and shrunk back at what I saw. My head was covered in dry blood, cuts and bruises. My lip was busted, my eyes blackened, and there were bruises forming on my arms. I lifted up my shirt and forced myself not to cry when I saw the light bruises on my chest and belly. I felt Lucas moving around as he always did first thing in the morning, and I took some comfort from that.

I looked away from the mirror and plucked glass from my hands before putting my ear to the door. I listened hard until I heard the unmistakable sound of Kyle's light snoring. Carefully, I opened the door a crack and peeked out. Kyle was asleep on the floor right outside the bathroom, his head leaning up against the door frame and his legs across the length of the door. As quietly as possible, I stepped over him and tip toed through the carnage and out of my room. I went into the kitchen, picked up the phone and slumped into a chair.

I didn't know who to call. It would have been wise to call the police, but I had relatives on the police force and no matter what secrecy they were sworn to, this would get back to my parents, and then my dad would shoot Kyle, only after my mother cut off his nut sack with a rusty knife. I didn't want to see my parents go to prison for my mistakes, so I didn't call the police, and I didn't call my mom and dad. I could call Donya, but the result would be the same - prison for dismemberment and murder. I wish I could tell you that I was exaggerating.

After a few more minutes of thought, I decided who to call and punched in the number. Walter Sterling answered on the second ring. He sounded tired and hung over. He probably had a hell of a night at the party, and the after party he no doubt went to at the gentleman's club.

"Your son is unconscious in my bedroom," I said into the phone. My voice sounded terrible, like I had screamed all night. Oh wait. I had.

"Sounds like a personal problem," Walter said.

"It's going to become your personal problem if you don't come get him right now."

"I don't think you're in a position to make demands, Miss Grayne."

"Oh, but I jest, Walter. Kyle had a cocktail of meth, alcohol, and god knows what else last night. He destroyed my bedroom and beat the shit out of me. So, you have a choice. You can come get him and you and I can have a little talk, or I can call the police to come and get him and you can have a talk with them. Please choose quickly, because my patience is non-existent right now."

There was a moment of stunned silence, and then "Fuck."

Twenty-five minutes later, Walter Sterling and three big goons were standing in my foyer. The goons showed no emotion, but Walter looked at me with regret - not regret that I was hurt, or that his son was a derelict, but regret that his pockets ran deep and that I was about to dip into them.

"Take Kyle to the guest house on the estate," Walter told the goons. "Keep him there, don't let him leave. I'll be in touch."

They nodded and went upstairs. Walter followed me into the kitchen. I took a long sip from my third bottle of water since escaping the bedroom while he poured himself a glass of Tequila that had been sitting on my counter for months, untouched, except to clean under it. Okay, I didn't clean under it.

A couple of minutes later, we heard incoherent mumbling from Kyle coming down the stairs. The door opened and a blast of cold air blew through the house before the door slammed shut and all was silent.

"He may need a doctor," I said.

"I'll take care of it. What do you want, Emmy?" He looked tired, worn out, and old. I almost felt sorry for him. Almost, but not really.

"I need to see a doctor, someone who won't ask too many questions or report what he sees."

He pulled out his cell phone and dialed a number. There was a short conversation with very little information exchanged and then the call ended. He wrote down on a napkin the name and address of a Doctor Larkin.

"He's expecting you and he will be discreet. What else do you want?"

"I need someone to come clean up the mess Kyle created when he hulked out. The bedroom is trashed and there's blood in the carpet."

"I will send someone before the morning is out. Surely, that isn't the end of your demands."

I was not in need of anything. I had more than enough money for myself and the baby. I didn't need extravagant things, a house on the Mediterranean or a fancy car, but I wanted to hurt the Sterlings, and the way to hurt the Sterlings was through their pockets.

"I know you're not straight with your business dealings, Walter. Pillow talk, you know. So, why don't you anti-up and I'll pretend to be completely ignorant of your fraudulent behaviors?" I sounded so bad ass, but I was really weak, tired, and pretty much shattered inside. If he gave me a hard time, I was going to jump across the table and try to kill him with my water bottle.

Walter Sterling studied me carefully. "A year ago, I would have never taken you for an adversary. You were such a good girl."

"Yeah, well. Shit changes. Are you going to pay me or is Jessyca going to dip into her allowance again?"

A half hour later, arrangements were made for my money, and Walter promised to have Kyle in rehab by the following morning. I figured by the time he was out, I wouldn't be easy for him to find. The cleaning crew arrived as I was on my way out the door to go see the doctor. Doctor Larkin only asked me questions about my age and my pregnancy. He didn't seem surprised by my injuries, as if he did this kind of thing all of the time. I imagined him pulling bullets out of members of the mafia or stitching up hookers that were beaten by politicians. By the time I returned home, the cleaning crew was gone, and so was the mess, blood included. I packed my things, again, and this time took more time to collect special items that held some kind of sentiment. I packed it all inside of my car and by the early evening, I was ready to go.

As I pulled out of the driveway, away from the home I spent most of my life in, I allowed myself a moment for tears. I loved that house and I had loved the life I had in it, even with my mother. Leaving it behind was probably inevitable, but not under these circumstances. If I stayed, Kyle would come back, and this ugly cycle would never end, and next time my baby could be hurt. I had to go.

I drove south, newly homeless, heartbroken, and forever fragmented.

***

The girls all stared at me with their jaws practically on the table. I sighed, feeling tiny pin pricks of pain in my chest at the memory and from reciting it aloud. It was most likely the most painful twenty-four hours of my life and I was unlikely to experience anything like it again, especially since I wouldn't allow myself to ever be put in a position like that again.

Mayson went to speak, sputtered a few words, and then burst into tears. Tabitha poured four glasses of tequila and passed them out with shaking hands and Donya sat there staring at me, stunned into silence. May downed her tequila and poured another.

Donya abruptly stood up, knocking her chair over in the process. She looked around as if she had lost something, before marching into the house. We looked into the house with curiosity until we heard the familiar jingle of keys. I jumped up and ran after her, catching her before she could make it out of the front door.

"What are you doing? Where are you going?" I asked, alarmed by her sudden departure.

"I'm going to go kill that mother fucker," she said.

"No, no," I shook my head adamantly. I knew she was serious, too. If she got into her car, she wasn't going to stop until she reached Kyle's house, where she would attempt to kill him.

"He needs to be dead," she argued.

"No, Donya, you can't go kill him. You have a baby here."

"You can take care of the baby."

"I can't! Listen, calm down. Come on back to the back yard." I tugged on her arm, but she was like a brick wall.

"No, Emmy. He hurt you - he put his hands on you!"

"D, I know, but he doesn't even remember it. Come on, you can't go to prison. Your baby needs you."

"You can take care of her," she insisted. This was madness. This was a true example of temporary insanity.

"I can't."

"Why not?" She demanded.

"Umm...I don't ...like..." I couldn't say diapers. I had my own baby! "I don't like...black...babies..."

She stared at me as if I had just grown a second nose and a third eye. I stared back at her with a stern expression, as if to really impress that I didn't like black babies. The corner of her mouth twitched for a moment, and then she let out a bark of laughter, but quickly covered her mouth.

"Oh, my god…" she said from under her hand. "This isn't even funny."

"No, but if I didn't make you laugh, I would have had to hit you with something to make you stop."

She wrapped her thin arms around my neck in a fierce hug. In all of the years I've known Donya, I had only seen her cry three times. The first time was when her dad died, the second time was when her mom died, and the third time was now. You would think it would be reversed, that I would be crying on her shoulder, but I understood. She and Mayson, and even Tabitha, felt that they had somehow let me down. They felt that they were deficient in their friendship and love for me for not knowing and for not being there for me after that day. They watched me transform into an entirely different person with no solid reasons as to why. They watched me detach myself from those I loved and the life I had once enjoyed. They were clueless as to how to pull me out of the hole I had dug for myself. It hurt them that I had suffered in silence. In a matter of seconds, I was being embraced by three sets of arms, and I didn't push them away.

***

"I want to hear more about Luke," Tabitha said awhile later, after I was sure Donya wasn't going to go murder Kyle.

I had insisted that we not discuss that night with Kyle again. I had asked them to never bring it up, pretend that they didn't know. This didn't go over well, and turned into a big argument, but it was Mayson who convinced the other two. Unfortunately, they jumped from talking about one man to talking about the other.

"What about him?" I sighed.

"Is there anything going on there?"

"I had no idea you were such a nosey person, Tabitha."

"Give me a break, Em. You and I have been out of touch for a long time and I don't know what everyone else already knows. I don't know if you and Luke are sliding around between the sheets or at each other's throats."

Thankfully, the candlelight wasn't enough light for them to see my face burn when she mentioned sliding around between the sheets.

"How is his mom?" Donya asked.

"She's better," I said, pouring a glass of wine. "She wants to move into an assisted living home, but the siblings are fighting her on it. They should let her go if she wants to, if it's a decent place, because it isn't like any of us can take her in. Lorraine and Lena don't have the space or the time to care for her, and Luke and I don't have the space either. Even after we buy a house, I'm not sure if that's a responsibility we want to undergo."

"Wait a minute," Mayson said, waving her hand to stop me from continuing. "You guys are buying a house together?"

"Yeah, actually we are," I said it as if it should be obvious. "We're living in a one bedroom apartment with a growing child."

"One bedroom?" Tabitha asked. "Who sleeps where?"

They all stared at me with big eyes again. I quickly drank my glass of wine.

"Lucas, obviously, has his own bed in the bedroom, and I sleep in Luke's bed."

"With Luke?" Mayson asked. She was only joking, but I hesitated long enough for her to jump to the correct conclusions. "You're sleeping with Luke!"

"You are?" Donya gasped.

"Oh boy," I said and drank directly from the bottle this time.

I told them everything, from the day I told Luke about Lucas to present. By the time I finished, between the questions and answers and objections of "Oh shit!" and "No fucking way!" and "Shut up!" my alcoholic high had worn off, and a headache was forming at the front of my skull.

"So…"Donya said, her hands clasped together in front of her. I could tell by her tone that she was about to lay into me about something. "Let me get this straight, Emmy."

"Are you going to lecture me?" I sighed, rubbing my head.

"Maybe you need a lecture!"

"Maybe I need you to stop yelling."

"Emmy, I don't know if you know this about yourself, but you are obnoxious."

"Thanks."

"And you drink too much, and you have a seedy past what with your drugging and screwing other women's men."

"I only did that…like…twice…"

"Whatever. You have a lot of shit attached to you is what I am saying, and for some ungodly reason, Luke Kessler wants you again."

"And may I point out that the man is smokin' hot?" Mayson said and fanned herself with her hand. "Woo!"

"He is hot," Tabitha said with a stupid grin. "Your boyfriend is definitely sexy."

"Your boyfriend is sexy as hell," Donya agreed. "If he wasn't your boyfriend, and if I weren't married, I would definitely want to roll around in bed with him."

"And in a few other places," Tabitha giggled.

My three closest friends proceeded to talk about all of the ways they would have Luke if the opportunity were ever to be a reality. The giggling and obnoxious comments were getting under my skin a little bit, but I sat patiently, waiting for them to get their shit together.

"Sorry," Mayson said a few minutes later. "We shouldn't talk about your boyfriend like that."

"He's not my boyfriend," I objected.

"Well, he should be," Donya said.

"You already live together," Tabitha pointed out. "And you have a child together. What's one more step?"

"His family and our family get along so well, too," Mayson said. "Especially Sam. Sam and Luke's family are more like family than you and Sam. They talk to her like she's the matriarch of their family."

"Thanks for reminding me of how much I don't fit in," I said dryly. Mayson hit a raw nerve.

"I didn't mean it the way it sounded," she tried to back track, but I cut her off.

"My mother finds out all of the family news before I do and I see these people almost daily. When Lena thought she had cancer again, I heard it from my mom first. If something news worthy happens in Louisiana, I hear it from Lena or Lorraine first."

"I thought you all got along really well," Donya said.

"We do, but...Luke's sisters are the kind of daughters my mom wants. They're a lot like my sisters in the sense that they're very family oriented and traditional. They got married young, then had children, and they don't drink or cheat or give their kids mohawks."

"Lucas's mohawk is so cute," Tabitha said.

"Well, whatever. They don't do that stuff. And my mom doesn't nag them about everything they do wrong, because they never do anything wrong.

"Luke's family is good to me, don't get me wrong, but sometimes I feel like I'm just Lucas's mom. I'm not Emmy, with my own needs and desires. I'm just the woman who gave birth to Lucas."

The liquor had really opened me up. The girls were quiet for a few beats, but then Donya broke the silence.

"If the rest of his family were the Manson family, it shouldn't matter. If that man loves you and wants you, that's all that matters. As long as he's not the Charlie of the family."

I don't want to hurt him again," I admitted out loud.

"Then try your damnest not to," Mayson said.

"I don't want him to hurt me either."

"It's going to be a different kind of pain if you don't give it a shot and he ends up with someone else entirely," Donya said.

I let that thought resonate in my head for the rest of the night, and throughout the following day. While I played in the sand with Lucas, I imagined what it would be like if I had to share him with not just Luke, but with another woman. I couldn't think about it without my chest tightening, but I realized that couldn't be the only reason to go into a relationship. It was time for me to be honest with myself about my feelings for Luke, but I had one problem. I couldn't stop thinking about Kyle.

<u>Chapter Forty-Five</u>

I entrusted Lucas with Donya and my cousins and headed to South Jersey Thursday evening. Traffic was a bitch, but it left me plenty of time to reconsider what I was doing. My brain ping ponged back and forth, back and forth, as I considered the ramifications of what I was about to do, but by the time I reached Cherry Hill, my decision was made and there was no going back.

I checked my hair and makeup in my car before taking a deep breath and throwing myself out into the lukewarm September night air. In the elevator, I stupidly wondered if I should ring the bell or use my key. I was still asking myself that question when I got to the door.

"Stupid," I muttered and hit the doorbell.

The door opened almost immediately, as if he were waiting just on the other side of the door.

He smiled down at me.

"Why didn't you use your key?" Kyle asked, as he stepped aside to let me in. "Or do you not have it anymore?"

I held up my spare key. "Right here. I wasn't sure if I should use it or not."

I looked around. There were boxes everywhere, some full, some in the process of being filled. Other packing supplies were visible.

"Are you moving?"

"Yeah," he said, standing beside me surveying the room. "Going back over the bridge. I bought a really great apartment not far from work. It has three bedrooms, two and a half baths, and a lot of space."

"Why do you need so much space?"

He shrugged and then looked at me. "Maybe someday I won't be by myself."

I looked away, feeling slightly flustered.

"Are you hungry?" he asked. "I can order something, or we can go out. I have stuff we can make."

Just do what you came here to do and leave.

"We can cook," I said, tossing my tote bag on the couch.

"That's a big ass bag," he said as I followed him into the kitchen.

"Yeah, I am usually carrying diapers and sippy cups and little annoying toys in it. I just didn't feel like changing over to a smaller bag."

He stood at the open refrigerator. "I have steaks, I have fish, hotdogs, chicken and some other unidentifiable items."

I slid in close to him and also looked at the contents of the fridge.

"Do you have ingredients for chicken parm?" I looked up at him and his eyes were on me.

"I think so," he said in a distracted tone. "Your hair..."

"You have a hair fetish," I said. "You may need to seek professional help for your addiction."

"It's not everyone's hair that I have a thing for, it's yours and yours only."

"Would you like me to give you a lock of it?"

I looked away from him and started taking items from the fridge and freezer. Together we prepared dinner, talking about minor things while we worked, nothing too heavy. Despite the rift between us, it felt comfortable moving about the kitchen with Kyle, felt like old times, maybe better than that. When he touched me, it didn't nearly incapacitate me like it used to, but it did feel warm and tingly.

When dinner was put on the table, Kyle poised a bottle of wine over my glass and looked at me for permission. I nodded my consent.

"Are you sure?" He asked in a teasing tone. "I know you feel vulnerable with me when you drink."

"Pour," I demanded.

When dinner was finished, we carried our glasses and our second bottle of wine to the living room. After small talk, I asked the question I had been wanting to ask.

"Kyle, what happened with you and Jessyca? I've heard bits and pieces, rumors mostly, but I haven't been able to confirm anything."

He sighed and sat back.

"It got ugly," he nodded. "Long story short, I broke up with her about a month after...after you left. Jess had some dirt on my dad's personal life and some of his illegal business practices, and she had been holding me down with it for a long time, but I just didn't care anymore. I had already lost the most important thing in my life," he brushed the back of his hand against my cheek, making me shiver.

"Jess's dirt definitely ruined the connection Sterling Corp had with her father's business, and we lost a lot of perspective clients. My dad went on a rampage, fired me, cut me off financially, and banned me from all things Sterling, but then he had no choice but to resign. I was hired back into the company by my more honest family members and other board members, and my parents got a divorce. Since my mom took practically everything, he's now the one banned, and on house arrest for a little while."

"Wow," I said, because I felt that I had to say something. I readjusted myself so that my face wasn't so visible, because I was feeling...slighted. Kyle kept me hanging by a thin thread for a long time because of Jessyca's dirt on his dad. While I understood the desire to protect one's family, I thought he should have immediately let me go, or immediately accepted the fallout from such dirt being dished. His decision to try to have both nearly ruined me, and maybe him, too.

"I looked for you after everything went down," he said softly. "I looked all over for you. Your family wouldn't tell me anything, Donya wouldn't tell me anything - except to fuck off. I hired someone to find you, but your trail ended in London. I didn't hear anything again until after you settled in Chicago. I figured you were with Luke, so I let you go. Again."

I gave a short nod, acknowledging I heard him, but didn't trust myself to speak.

"You hate me for what I've done to you," Kyle said.

"I hate myself more for not having enough of...whatever it is I needed to resist you in the first place," I said in a shaky voice. I stood up to get away from him. "I wish you never found me in the bar."

I stood in front of the window with a distant city view, trying to get myself together. I could sense him standing behind me, and then I felt his breath on my neck and his hands on my hips.

"If it wasn't there, it would have been somewhere else," he whispered in my ear.

For a moment, I froze, and for a moment, I was vulnerable. If he kissed my neck, I would surrender. If his hands moved to the front of my body and touched me in sensitive places, I would have given in. If he even wrapped his arms around me, I would have willingly been his slave. But it was only for a moment that I felt so impressionable. The window of opportunity closed, my vision cleared, and the fog in my brain dissipated. I realized my near folly and hastily stepped away from Kyle.

"I should go," I said and made a beeline for my giant bag.

"Emmy," Kyle was on my heels, and stopped me at the door. "I can't deal with losing you again. What do you want me to do?"

"I don't think..." I shook my head and stared at him.

"Nothing I can do? We just had a really nice night. I know you don't really mean that. You had a good time."

"I did, but...it's not enough."

"Kiss me."

"No," I said and started to move away, but he grabbed a hold of my shoulders. "Kiss me, and then if you still want to walk out of the door, I will let you."

"I can't," I whispered.

"Because you know how it will make you feel," he said and pressed me against the door. "You want to kiss me, though. Don't you?"

His lips drew so close to mine, I could feel his warm breath going into my mouth. It had a taste, a familiar taste, the taste of Kyle's mouth. I was centimeters away from tasting him again. I closed my mouth tight. His tongue flicked across my lips, but my lips were sealed.

"Open," he whispered and pressed his tongue on my lips, trying to pry them open. "Open your fucking mouth. You want to kiss me. Open."

He again tried to force his tongue through my two lips, but failed. I started to feel a little triumphant until his hand went up my skirt faster than I could react, and his fingers made contact with my sweet spot. I gasped and in that moment, his tongue was in my mouth. I wanted to ride his hand and suck on his tongue, but I forced his hand out of my skirt, and broke free of the kiss.

"You want me," he whispered in my ear.

I bit my lip to the point of pain, and with an extreme amount of effort, pushed him away from me.

"I didn't come here for this!" I cried out.

"Then what did you come here for?" He barked back. "Did you think that we could just pretend that nothing ever happened between us?" He closed the distance between us again. "I know you love me, Emmy."

He reached out to touch me, and I almost let him, but I shoved him away. I couldn't control how my body temperature rose in his presence, or how moist it made me when he touched me, but I could control almost everything else.

"You hurt me!" I screamed. "You put your hands on me and you hurt me."

"I was fucked up on drugs, Emmy. I'm sorry. I don't even remember it."

"It's not just the drugs and the abuse, Kyle. You weren't strong enough to stand up to your dad and to Jessyca."

"But I eventually did!"

"Eventually was not soon enough, Kyle," I said bitterly. I reached into my bag and produced the bracelet. I held it out to him, but he stepped back.

"That was a gift. I don't want it back."

"You need to take it back," I said. "This is why I'm here. I've been holding onto it, in essence holding on to you. I have to let you go."

"You don't have to," he said, and I could see the hope in his face.

"What do you expect me to do, Kyle? Tear my son away from his father and move into your shiny new apartment with you? Tear him away from his family and everything he knows? Is that what you want? It probably is, Kyle, because you don't give two shits about the aftermath when you get what you want. You smooth talk your way into getting things your way and then when it gets too fucking hard you duck out or shove some meth up your nose. You beat me and you could have killed me and Lucas. That broke me. I will never be with you again." I shook the bracelet at him and shrieked "Take the fucking bracelet!"

In a stunned silence, Kyle reached out and gingerly took the bracelet.

"Thank you," I breathed.

I opened the door and stepped onto the landing.

"I am very sorry," Kyle said to my back.

I had nothing left to say and let the door close behind me, cutting myself off from Kyle forever.

Chapter Forty-Six

"So what's up? What do you have to tell me?" my mom asked.

We were sitting out by the lake at the family house in Louisiana. Lucas and I drove in the Friday after Labor Day for a short visit before returning home to Chicago. My mom had helped Grace get settled into her new place before returning back to Louisiana.

I took a deep breath and told her about what happened with Kyle. I wanted to come clean with her. I had a strange sense of obligation, like I'm supposed to tell her because she's my mom. I no longer needed her to kiss my boo boo and make it feel better and give me a cookie, but I needed her to know because it was a secret too deep to keep from your mom, I guess.

Her face didn't change during the entire story. I wondered if she was really hearing me. When I was done, we sat in silence for a full minute, staring at one another.

Abruptly she stood up.

"What are you doing?" I stood up with her.

"I gotta go," she said distractedly.

"Go where?"

"Kill that son of a bitch Kyle Sterling."

"No, no killing."

"He needs to be dead!"

"What is up with you and Donya and the death thing?"

She burst into tears and I again become the one to provide comfort. It took me awhile to convince her that she shouldn't go cut off Kyle's nut sac, and awhile longer to convince her not to tell my dad.

"I need a drink," she said. "You want a drink?"

"No, I don't want a drink."

She was walking back toward the house but stopped and looked at me with her hands on her hips.

"Whaddya mean you don't want a drink? What's wrong with you? Are you in AA?"

"No, I'm not in AA. I have to stay alert for Lucas."

"Oh. Right."

I watched my mom drink until she mellowed out and then I went to check on Lucas. He was in the yard with my dad playing catch. It made me think of Luke and a house. If we had a house with a yard, Luke could play catch with his son. Lucas still couldn't catch the ball, but he could throw like a pro.

I slipped away, back to the chairs by the lake and called Luke at work.

"We need a house, with a yard, so you can play catch with Lucas," I said when he answered.

"That's random."

"Sometimes I'm random."

"Sometimes?"

This was our first real conversation since I yelled at him when I was still in Belmar. We had spoken briefly when I told him that we were driving to Louisiana, and of course he spoke to Lucas daily.

"Are we still fighting?"

"Depends. Do I have to fight anyone for you?"

"You would fight for me?"

"To the death."

I smiled, even though in a roundabout way, Luke was also associating death with Kyle. Disturbing.

"I'm sorry I was being an ass," he said.

"I'm sorry for giving you a reason to be an ass."

"You don't have to apologize, Emmy. I've been trying to get you to open up to me for months and I blew it the first time that you said something I didn't like."

"Well, I didn't exactly make you feel secure in our relationship."

"If I'm insecure, it's my own fault. I trust you, one hundred percent. Listen, I have to go. I have a client waiting for me. I'll call you tonight."

"Okay. I love you," I said and held my breath.

"I love you, too, babe."

My heart flopped around happily in my chest.

Later that night, after Lucas was already in bed, Luke called. I told him about the bar, how I had the remains leveled and then cleaned up and put the property up for sale.

"You did all of that in a week?"

"The right amount of money can almost move mountains in a week."

"What's the rush? I thought you were going to think about it for a while."

"I had to let it go in order to move forward. My life isn't in Jersey anymore. My life is in Chicago."

"You sound sad about it."

"It's a little sad," I admitted. "But I don't fit there anymore, not even with my friends and my family. I felt like an outsider in Belmar. Truth be told, I feel like an outsider almost anywhere." I didn't mean to get so deep, the words just tumbled out, and now I had a lump in my throat. Sometimes I can be so lame.

"You're crazy. Everyone loves you. My mom loves you like a daughter and my sisters love you like a sister. Your own family..." He hesitated, because he knew he couldn't begin to fudge that one. Emmet and I had grown close since his move to Chicago, but my other siblings remained emotionally and personally distant. Even my relationship with my father wasn't like it was when I was a kid. I don't even need to elaborate on my mother.

"I have you and I have Lucas," I said. "But...I don't know. It's not that you two aren't enough..."

"We're not, but I understand. You need to talk to your mom. Talk to her, not at her. Speak, don't yell."

"Blah," I said.

The next morning I pulled my mom outside again. I was so calm and cool when I told her about Kyle, but when I started telling her about how I felt about her and our relationship, I felt my blood boiling beneath my layers of skin. When I was done with my spiel (after many interruptions), she sighed and slumped back in her seat.

"You're my favorite, you know," she said.

"Let's not tell lies, mother."

"I'm not lying. You're everything I wished I could have been when I was young."

"A weak, cheating, man-stealing, heart-breaking, under achieving, single mom?"

"No. A strong, independent, beautiful, resourceful, successful, wonderful mother."

"What are you talking about, mom? You got everything you've ever wanted, right? A husband, children, a nice home, and a great figure."

"Those are all very nice things," she said with a small shrug. "But I sometimes wish that I would have waited a little while before doing all of that. Long before Lucas was even a thought, you had traveled the world, climbed mountains, swam in distant seas, had a successful career, and experienced love and sex in ways a woman who gets married at nineteen will never experience."

Yuck!

"I thought you were happy," I said, suddenly concerned she was going to go through a mid-life crisis twenty years too late and divorce my dad and date someone a little older than Lucas.

"I am happy. I'm very happy, but that doesn't mean I don't have my regrets."

"If I'm everything you wish you were, then why do you hassle me so much? I have daydreams about shoving you off of cliffs or drowning you in gelatin."

Her eyes turned to the lake. The slight wrinkle in her forehead told me she was trying to find the right words to use. At least she was thinking before speaking.

"Sometimes I think you're not being the best you can be," she started, turning her attention back to me. "Sometimes it seems like you want to blend in with everyone else and be ordinary, but you're not ordinary. You stand out in a crowd, you always have. It's not that you don't fit, honey. You're just too dumb sometimes to see that you're the center piece, and the rest of us are trying to fit around you.

"So, maybe I do hassle you sometimes. Some of it is typical mom stuff, you'll understand when Lucas is older, but sometimes I know you are better than the things you sometimes do. And I'm just a little crazy, so I suppose I'll always annoy the hell outta ya."

Chapter Forty-Seven

"Guess what, Lucas?" I cooed, as we walked down the hallway to our apartment. "We're home!"

I slipped the key in and opened the door. Lucas ran in ahead of me while I struggled with our luggage.

"Daddy!" I heard him screech.

"Hey, buddy! I'm so surprised to see you!" Luke exclaimed and I heard the "Muah" of a kiss being planted somewhere on our son. A second later, Luke appeared in the hallway, carrying Lucas. They were both grinning ear to ear.

"Surprise," I said, trying to drag in a suitcase.

"I am surprised. I wasn't expecting you guys for a few more days." He stepped over a couple of bags to give me a quick kiss on the lips.

"We were homesick, weren't we Lucas?"

"Homethicks," he agreed.

Lucas and I piled into the rental we had picked up in Jersey, and started back to Chicago a few days after my talk with my mom. I really was homesick, missing the sounds and sights of Chicago, the craziness of Lorraine's house during family functions, and of course Grace's apple pie.

And I missed Luke. Since our "make-up" phone call, I felt like a teenager again, sending love notes during the work day, but spending hours on the phone at night. I had a perpetual smile on my face and when we weren't talking, I often found myself recalling our latest conversations and reawakening the butterflies in my stomach.

Unlike being a teenager, there was nothing stopping me from rejoining Luke in Chicago. No interference from parents or jealous friends and money wasn't an issue. So, one night after another long, heart palpitating phone call, I packed up the rental and we left the next morning.

"I'm really glad you're home," Luke said later that night after Lucas was in bed.

We were in the living room, trying to organize the mess I brought from the east coast and the gulf, but after a half hour we gave up and collapsed on the couch.

"I'm glad to be home," I smiled at him.

"Did you ever talk to your mom?"

"Yes, and it went surprisingly well."

I told him about the conversation, including the drowning her in gelatin part.

"Why gelatin?" Luke asked.

"Why not gelatin?"

"Gelatin is tasty."

"Gelatin is scary."

"What? You don't like gelatin?" He looked at me as if I had grown a third eye.

"Not even when it has vodka in it."

"Oh. My. God. I'm in love with a gelatin hater. Not even strawberry gelatin?"

"Nope," I smiled at his words.

"Grape?"

"No."

"Cherry?"

"Are you deaf? I don't like the stuff."

"I'm insulted," he said, shaking his head. "I can't marry you now. I can't marry someone who doesn't share my love of gelatin."

"Damn. I guess I'll have to marry Tom Cruise instead."

"He's crazy. He won't let you take an aspirin if you get a headache, and he's married to Joey from Dawson's Creek."

"She has a real name. It's not Joey Potter."

"Whatever. You can't marry Tom Cruise."

"I think this is simultaneously the most ridiculous and most serious conversation we've ever had," I said. "I don't like Jell-O and you wear stripes, and I think that is far more offensive, but I'll still marry you despite the stripes."

I pushed myself off of the couch and went to bed. As I lay there, listening to Luke moving around the kitchen, I had to cover my mouth to keep from giggling. We just had a conversation about marriage using stripes and gelatin as a cover up for the fact that we were talking about marriage. Luke proposed through Jell-O and I accepted through stripes. The idiocy of it all had me shaking with excited, silent laughter.

When the bedroom door opened, I covered my head with a pillow to hide the stupid grin on my face and took deep breaths to quell my laughter. After a moment, the pillow was ripped away from me and I could see Luke's face over mine clearly thanks to moonlight shining through the spaces in the blinds.

"What's so funny?" He whispered.

"We are," I said and then pulled him into a kiss.

Again, I felt young, as we made love with giggling, laughter, and absolute delight. And when it was over and Luke was nearly asleep, I whispered a secret into his ear that I had been holding onto for days.

Epilogue

A year has passed, and life is good, most of the time. My father had a heart attack, but is recovering well. My mom spends most of her time in Louisiana now, happily caring for the love of her life. She still invokes my most violent tendencies when I have the pleasure of her company, or when I'm stupid enough to answer her phone calls.

Lucas is giving us the true meaning of Terrible Twos, with tantrums, disobedient behavior and his inability to sit still for even two minutes. I never knew that I had so much patience. My mother tells me that I was horrible at Lucas's age, and on a really crazy day, I can almost forgive her for being the person she is today. Almost.

We bought a house in a Chicago suburb, a few weeks after I returned. It has five bedrooms, two and a half baths, a family room, a formal dining room, a huge back yard, and all of the other normal parts of a house. The travel time to the firm isn't horrible and we're near Lorraine, Lena, Emmet, and Grace. Now our home is used just as much as Lorraine's. It's often full of family and friends, children and good food and drink.

I've made new friends, and though none of them can replace my old friends, they are good, reliable, and fun women. Donya, Mayson, and Tabitha keep in touch regularly with the occasional visit, and I've accepted that they're all able to be good friends without me.

After three months on the market, the property my bar was on was sold. Kyle bought it. He didn't contact me directly, but contacted Luke. Apparently, he ran into my old barmaid, Lilly. After several conversations, they decided to go into business together and open a sports bar.

By the time Kyle called, Luke had already known about what had happened that New Year's night. I imagine that it took an unfathomable amount of self-control for Luke to remain professional and civilized. He dealt with his anger alone, because I wasn't made aware about any of their meetings until the deal was about to close. The way Luke handled the situation made me love him that much more.

Even Kyle's actions were admirable. He apologized to Luke for his treatment of me and insisted on keeping their meetings quiet so not to add any unnecessary stress on me.

I was curious about a lot of things, like if Kyle was going to quit Sterling Corp, if he was still clean, and especially if he and Lilly were dating. Maybe later, I'll make a phone call and find out. Then again, maybe not. In the grand scheme of things, it doesn't really matter.

For the record, the money that I took from Jessbitch and Walter Sterling was donated to shelters across the country that catered to women and children that are victims of domestic violence. Luke said the money was dirty, and using it for our own personal needs and entertainment would be equally dirty. I, personally, have no problem getting dirty. I feel that I deserve the money, but I really didn't need it, and I didn't want to fight about it.

Only less than two weeks after the gelatin and stripes proposal, the proposal became real, with a diamond ring. Of course I said yes. We were married four months later, in front of all of our family and friends. We skipped a honeymoon for the time being. Luke was very busy at the firm and we were still trying to get settled into our new home.

The secret I had whispered into Luke's ear that long ago night bloomed into a beautiful baby girl named Kaitlyn. She, too looks exactly like Luke. Lucas is in love with his baby sister, calling her Kaywen, the best he could do for a two year old. He watched her sleep, he watched her eat, but he ran away screaming whenever there was a poopy diaper.

Like I said, life is good, most of the time. I argue with my husband, and I am daily tempted to tie my two year old boy to a chair. My house gets out of control with toys and baby items, and I sometimes realize I haven't showered in a couple of days. Sleep eludes me and tequila is out of the question with a breast feeding baby, but I am finally completely happy. My life makes sense and my many mistakes have been left in the past. God knows I'll make a thousand more before I die at an old, ripe age.

261

Every day I am thankful for Luke, the real love of my life, my Prince Charming, my rescuer. He saved me from my biggest enemy: myself. Parts of me are still broken and cracked, but my children and Luke keep me grounded, and heal me with their constant love and affection.

And let's face it. I am my mother's daughter. I supposed I will always be a bit cracked...

The End

Made in the USA
Charleston, SC
31 March 2014